Finding Hope

A Horses and Hearts Inspirational Romance

ALSO BY PAMELA GOSSIAUX

Praise for Mrs. Chartwell and the Cat Burglar

A runner-up in the 2018 New York Book Festival

"Mrs. Chartwell and the Cat Burglar is a highly suspenseful, self-described romantic mystery that tugs at your heart and satisfies your intellect.

— John J. Kelly, *Detroit Free Press*

"Mrs. Chartwell and the Cat Burglar is a lovely story and I highly recommend it! It has everything you could wish for: mystery, suspense, romance and a great adventure. I just couldn't put it down!"

— Susan Keefe, *Midwest Book Review*

"Pamela Gossiaux is fast becoming a major player in the realm of writing. She deserves the wards and attention that are bound to come her way!"

— Grady Harp, *Top 100 Amazon* Hall of Fame Reviewer

"The story is well thought out, well written and well worth your time to read."
    – William D. Curnutt, *Amazon Vine Voice*

"What a fun read! If you like the feel of movies on TMC you'll like this book. It's a good story spun with great lines and interesting characters."
    – Diana Lesire Brandmeyer, *award-winning Christian author*

"It's a cozy, uplifting read for anyone looking for a good story to curl up with. Optional accessories: a cup of something warm and a cat in their lap."
    – Xanthe Muller, *Goodreads Reviewer*

"This is a mystery, perhaps a Cozy, but really much more, and is marked by constant cliff hangers and a great ending (that I won't give away)."
    – Greg Jolley, author of the *Danser* novels

Finding Hope

A Horses and Hearts Inspirational Romance

PAMELA GOSSIAUX

Tri-Cat Publishing

This book is a work of fiction. Names, characters, businesses, places, events, and incidents are either the products of the author's imagination or used in a fictitious manner. Any resemblance to actual persons, living or dead, or actual events is purely coincidental.

Scripture quotations are taken from The Holy Bible, New International Version, copyright 1973, 1978, 1984 by International Bible Society.

Visit the author's website at: PamelaGossiaux.com

First Printing, May 2020
Library of Congress Control Number: 2020907098

ISBN: 978-1-7348968-0-0 (paperback)
ISBN: 978-1-7348968-1-7 (ebook)

Cover Design: llewellen Designs
Formatter: Dallas Hodge, Everything But the Book
Editor: Rachel Song, Songbird Editing
Author Photo: Vera Davis Photography

Published in the United States by Tri-Cat Publishing.
Chelsea, MI

Tri-Cat Publishing

"For I know the plans I have for you," declares the Lord, *"plans to prosper you and not harm you, plans to give you hope and a future."* Jeremiah 29:11

Chapter One

"I don't understand," said Victoria Jones. "*Who* is this guy?"

She adjusted the Bluetooth speaker in her ear so she could hear her friend Emma better. They were talking about tonight's dinner in New York, and she could have sworn Emma just set her up.

"Relax, Tori," said Emma. "He's just my husband's co-worker."

Tori flipped open the carry-on suitcase that was on her bed and tossed in a few pairs of socks. She was packing light since the trip was short. She'd arrive this evening, Friday, and return on Sunday morning. She was flying to New York to promote her new book on horse training and give a live performance at an indoor arena.

"I've set up some fun things for us to do," said Emma.

"I'm only there for one full day," said Tori. "And I have to work all day on Saturday."

"I know," said Emma, "but you'll be here early evening tomorrow, which is why we're going out for dinner."

"With the *co-worker*," said Tori, hoping the dread came across in her voice. "What's his name?"

"Colton."

"Sounds stuffy."

Emma laughed. "Colton Rausch, and he's a banker, like my hubby." Then she sighed. "Tori, it has been *four years*."

"I know," Tori said quietly. She opened her drawer to look at her t-shirts.

"Oh, and wear something nice. For dinner with Colton and for earlier tonight. I found something fun to keep us busy until the men are off work."

Emma was Tori's best friend. They had bonded during freshman year of high school when they were partnered together to dissect a frog, and Emma had thrown up on Tori's textbook. Then, after graduation, they had shared an apartment briefly before Tori married Tim. Emma was more like a sister to her than best friend.

"You mean, like a *dress?*" Tori moaned.

"Just something *nice*. Then on Sunday you can come to church with us and we'll go out for brunch before you catch your plane"

"Okay. Look, I need to go pack. I'll see you tonight. You're picking me up at the airport, right?"

"I'll be there!"

Tori hung up the phone and turned back to her suitcase. Simon, her orange cat, had crawled inside and was already asleep.

"Oh *no*," Tori said, but she stroked his head. He cracked open an eye to peek at her. "So, since you're in the middle of this, what do *you* think I should wear this weekend?" She walked over and pulled open another drawer. "Blue jeans? Or...blue jeans?"

Simon answered with a yawn.

Packing was usually easy. She didn't need to be stylish for horse seminars. As a professional horse trainer and nationally known author, she was well respected and well known in her field. She used to train horses for shows, but her techniques were so well received that people started asking her to give demonstrations. The seminars paid better, beat the everyday back-breaking work of training show horses, and gave her a chance to see the country. She had seminars booked for the next year and a half, plus her fourth book at a publishing house ready to be put into hardcover.

"Meow." Simon climbed out of the suitcase and walked across the bed to demand petting. She obliged, scratching him behind the ears. Then she tossed two pairs of jeans, three fresh t-shirts, and some underwear into her suitcase. She threw in an aqua colored sundress that would accentuate her hazel eyes, and a pair of white, strappy sandals with low heels. She grabbed her bag of toiletries that she always kept filled and ready, threw in the book she was reading, and zipped up the suitcase.

She was wearing a soft blue cotton dress that hung just past her knees, and decided to pair her western boots with it, because she'd need them for the horse-training seminar anyway. It was easier to wear them on the plane then pack them. She'd maybe change into the sandals later, depending on Emma's choice of restaurant.

She ran the brush through her brunette hair. It framed her fair complexion, hanging about halfway down her back. She'd leave it lose today.

"I guess I'm ready," she said to Simon. He curled around her leg, pressing up against her in a cat hug. "I'll miss you too, boy."

She had a few minutes left, and she had already said goodbye to the horses and given the housekeeper and the barn assistant directions. So, she opened her bedroom window and climbed out onto the roof.

Hopeful Farm—*her* farm—stood on the shores of Lake Michigan, just north of Ludington, about mid-way up the mitten state. It overlooked the Great Lake and its swelling waves that rolled in just beneath the sand dunes on top of which her house, now a popular bed and breakfast, sat.

She stood on the widow's walk, which offered an incredible view of the mighty lake. The small walkway, about three-feet wide, ran the length of the roof along of her two-story house. The piece of architecture got its name from history; the wives of sea captains stood on it to watch for the safe return of their lovers. The tall mast of a ship, which could be spotted at a great distance, was a sign of rejoicing and welcome. Its absence could mean many things. That was how the widow's walk got its name.

She came here often to reflect and to gaze out over the vast acreage of shoreline she owned. The wind caught her hair, blowing it out behind her. She wrapped her hands around the weathered railing and breathed in the fresh lake-tinged air, much as other women had done over the years. Many of the older homes that faced the Great Lakes had similar widow's walks.

"Tori, you're going to be late!" a voice called to her. Tori turned to see her housekeeper and cook, Phyllis, peeking her graying head out of the window. "Let's go!"

Tori nodded and climbed back through her window, grabbed her suitcase and followed Phyllis out to their car. A few of their guests waved at her as she passed. As usual, they had all five guest rooms filled this weekend.

She saw Hope, her horse, grazing in the front pasture.

"Bye, Hope!" she called, waving her hand in the air. The mare lifted her head and gave a joyous whinny.

"She thinks you're bringing carrots," Phyllis said.

"She's going to be disappointed," said Tori. She climbed in the passenger side of the car and watched Hope until they turned off the driveway onto the dirt road, where large beech trees blocked her view. Then she turned to face ahead. She believed in always looking forward. New York and a fun time with Emma (minus the date she was going to try to get out of) awaited her.

Emma rushed forward, squealing, to embrace Tori. She hugged her so hard that Tori nearly lost her balance.

"I missed you too!" Tori said, laughing. They hadn't seen each other in over six months, when Emma came to the farm to stay a long weekend last winter. But they talked several times a week on the phone. They knew every detail of each other's lives. Or, almost every detail.

"This is going to be such a fun weekend!" said Emma. "Oh, and I made reservations tonight at the Opal."

"About that," said Tori.

"But *first*," said Emma, "I have found something for us to do that you will *love*."

Emma was always so energetic. Sometimes it was draining. What Tori loved was curling up with a good book someplace quiet.

"What?" Tori asked. "Please tell me before I die of anticipation."

"An art show," said Emma.

Now *that* was different. They had attended author events (they read books together), plays, and movies, yes… but an *art show?* They had never done that before.

"Yay!" said Tori, trying to sound more excited than she felt. She thought longingly of her book.

"Don't get all poo-pooey on me," said Emma. "You'll *love* this. He's a *horse* artist. He paints pictures of horses, and he has this very popular series of paintings which I heard advertised on the radio. I guess he's really famous. I've never heard of him, but I figured if it had horses it *had* to be good. Right?"

A horse artist. Well at least it wasn't nudes or abstract. "What's his name?"

"The artist? Let me see." Emma rifled through her purse as they walked out of the airport toward the parking lot. "I have a brochure in here somewhere…" After a moment, she gave up. "I have no idea. Let's just go. They have champagne and cheese and a showing, then we can go out to dinner and meet Brian and Colton. I made reservations for that as well."

"So you said. At the Opal."

"They serve seafood."

The showing started at 4 p.m. and it was nearly 6 p.m. "It only lasts until eight, so we need to go straight there," said Emma, clicking away on her high heels. "We can just throw your things in the trunk." She turned to Tori. "And you look *adorable!*" She grabbed Tori's hands and squeezed them, then used her keys to pop the trunk of her car.

The art gallery was about twenty miles away from the airport, and it took them over forty-five minutes in traffic to get there. Emma found a parking place on the street, grabbing a spot as an older gentlemen pulled out. She looked at her watch. "We still have over an hour before they close. Let's go!"

They were in the meat packing district of Manhattan, not far from where Emma lived with her banker husband. Emma didn't work at a paying job. Instead, she filled her hours doing charity events in Manhattan and hosting dinner parties for Brian's work. She loved every minute of it.

The art gallery looked like it was a former warehouse but had been warmed up with drywall and fancy lighting. They walked through the front doors and were greeted with servers in black aprons carrying trays.

"Champagne?" offered the first server they saw.

"Um, I could use some water," said Tori. The plane had been dry. She was thirsty.

"Water?" Emma whispered, grabbing a champagne flute. "*Really?* Oh, hon I never thought to offer you a bottle in the car. I'm such a dunce! Oh, look!" Emma pointed. There was a poster on a wall in front of them. It read, *Matt Cheval. Presenting 'The Woman and the Horse series.'*

"Look! There's a picture of him!" said Emma. "Oh, he's *cute!*"

But Tori wasn't looking. She was enthralled by a painting of a black Arabian stallion that was nearly as tall as her and sitting on an easel to her left. She walked over to see the painting closer.

Tori hadn't had much interest in dating since her husband had died four years ago. Emma had let her grieve for two years, then started gently prodding her to get back out. Tori was trying to at least *look* at men. Emma reminded her regularly that she wanted kids and she was already twenty-nine. Her clock was ticking.

They walked around the wall to see the display room. Several paintings hung from panels coated in black cloth. These didn't seem to be a part of the series. There was a landscape. A painting of one of the Great Lakes that Tori found soothing. But no horses other than the stallion out front.

"Let's get to the good stuff first," said Emma, grabbing her hand. A sign pointed back deeper into the gallery, and she pulled Tori around another wall. They came to a different room, and here apparently, was the series "The Woman and the Horse."

The room was filled with people, so it was hard to see the paintings. Tori counted nearly a dozen paintings, at least. Most were big canvases, about 3 x 5 feet. There were a few smaller 8 x 10s. They hung on panels much like the ones in the previous room, only these panels had royal blue clothes on them. Each painting had its own light shining down on it. It was all very fancy.

"Here," said Emma, and pulled her in between a middle-age couple and a group of women in business attire. They found themselves facing a painting of a field of lavender flowers, with a tree line in the background. Sitting on a tree stump in the field was a woman, her back to them, her head tilted slightly so you could just see her cheek. Her long, dark hair trailed down her back from under a wide-brimmed straw hat.

"That looks like a hat you own," mused Emma, quietly, almost to herself.

But Tori was looking at the horse. The white mare was standing near the woman, her head down, her muzzle near the woman's shoulder. The mare's long white mane hung down her neckline, but it didn't conceal the marking on her shoulder. The red, distinctive marking that Tori had memorized, had traced with her fingers over the smooth hair so many times.

"That's Hope," Tori said.

"What?" Emma turned her eyes to the horse. "*Hope?* But how…?" Emma stared. "That can't be right. It must be a coincidence."

Emma grabbed her hand. They pushed their way through the crowd to the next painting. This one had the backdrop of a shoreline. It looked like Lake Michigan with its characteristic dunes and grass. On the beach, the same mare walked quietly behind a woman. The only disturbance in the picture was the wind, whipping the mare's white mane and tail behind her, and the woman's long, dark hair. The woman was barefoot, wearing a flowing white dress, her shoulders bare. In her hand, she carried the wide-brimmed straw hat.

The horse had a distinctive marking on its shoulder. Almost like blood. But exactly like Hope's.

"Emma," Tori said, and reached for her friend's hand.

"Come on," said Emma.

She pulled her to the next painting. Same horse. Same woman. The woman's face was never shown. Only her dark hair, and often just a glimpse of her cheek or her nose.

But the horse. The horse was Hope.

Emma turned to look at Tori. Tori's heart pounded. This was creepy. More than creepy. She had books out about the horse, yes. So, Hope wasn't unknown. But these paintings were so...personal. The white dress was one that she owned. The hat was at home hanging on the hook by her back door. The hair...that was *her* hair.

"Where is this creep?" Tori said, probably a little too loudly.

They went to the next painting. It was quieter, calmer than the ones with the wind, a painting of the same woman standing at a stall door, the barnwood weathered gray. Her back was to them, her hair down. There was no hat in sight, and she was wearing jeans and a faded yellow t-shirt. Tori noticed, absurdly, the incredible lighting in the folds of the material.

The mare had her head over the stall door, her neck arched around the woman, and the woman's hand was on the horse's neck. The picture was one full of emotion, and the love between the woman and the mare was evident.

The stall door was low enough to reveal the marking on the mare's shoulder. It was Hope. And there was no mistaking, that was Hope's stall door.

"*Where is he?*" Tori said louder. She was clenching her teeth, a habit it had taken her years to break after Tim's death.

"Ma'am? Can I help you?" said a short woman wearing a tight suit and skirt combo.

"Yes, I need to see..." Tori cast her eyes around for the man's name but couldn't see the sign at they had passed at the entrance or read it on his paintings. "The artist. *Now.*"

"Can I tell him your name?"

"Oh, he *knows* me," Tori said. She glared down at the woman, and her anger must have shown through, because the woman said, "Just a moment. He's just coming back from an early dinner," and hustled off.

"Oh my gosh," said Emma. "Tori. What on earth...? I mean...?" Emma was, for once, speechless.

A moment later a man entered the room.

"That's him," whispered Emma. "He's wearing the same shirt as in the photo. Tacky."

He wore sunglasses, faded blue jeans, cowboy boots, and a black Stetson hat.

He followed the woman further into the room to where Tori and Emma were standing, and the crowded parted for them, people eyeing him reverently.

He had a smile for the cameras, for the people, but when he saw Tori, he stopped so suddenly that a waiter bumped into him and spilled some champagne on the dark burgundy carpet.

He kept his sunglasses on, but his face seemed familiar. Where had she seen it before? She cast her mind about to the many events she attended over the years. She could have met him anywhere.

"*What is this?*" she said. The room had grown quiet. "What are these paintings? Why have you painted my horse?"

"And Tori," said Emma. "Why have you painted Tori? That's just…creepy."

"Way to give him my name, Em," Tori hissed.

The man looked at a loss for words. Tori wasn't sure if she wanted to hit him or run from him. She had a million questions going through her head.

The man gathered his composure and turned to the woman in the pants suit. "Allison, please bring these two women to my office. I'd love to speak with them."

"I'd love to speak to you *right here*," said Tori, keeping her voice low.

"I think we should have some privacy," he said. He glanced around. Tori followed his eyes. People had started to take their phones out and were snapping photos of her. Because no photos were allowed in the gallery, security started ushering people out and threatening to take phones.

"Is it *her?*" someone said.

"I think it is. It's the woman in the paintings! Look at her hair!"

Voices went from whispers to murmurs. Tori felt her anger turning a little bit to fear. This whole problem was getting worse.

"Okay," she said. "Let's go talk."

She looked at Emma for support. Her friend nodded and put on her "tough face." Emma's "tough face" consisted of a frown that didn't do much to make her slightly round five-foot-three-inch frame look stronger. Her blond bob swung as she turned. Tori followed. She had to know why *her* horse—and *her* clothes—were on canvases for the entire world to see.

Chapter Two

Matt's mind was spinning as he entered the office at the back of the room, followed by the three women. The room was small, used by the owner of the gallery for her bookkeeping. She had offered it to Matt as a place to make his phone calls and escape from the crowd over the three days that he was in town with his showing.

He sat in the dark blue swivel chair on the other side of the desk. He took a deep breath and tried to look relaxed.

The women, Tori and her friend, filed into the small room, followed by Allison. Allison came to stand next to him and leaned down to whisper in his ear, "Who are these women?"

Matt ignored Allison's question. "Please have a seat," he said, motioning to the two chairs opposite him. Victoria Jones had her arms tightly crossed against her chest, her eyes showing a mixture of fear and anger. He'd never forgotten her. Not her face. Not her name. Not her horse.

"I'd prefer to stand," said Tori, frowning. He knew she preferred Tori over Victoria. The woman next to her was smaller, shorter, and looked quite angry.

"You have *Painted. My. Horse*," Tori said, biting off each word.

"And her clothes," said the short woman. "I gave her that white dress for her twenty-second birthday."

Tori nudged the woman in the side with her elbow.

"This must look a little weird," Matt said. He was stalling for time. He'd always known that there was a chance he'd run into her someday. The odds of her finding his work, especially with how popular he had become, were pretty high. But he had always thought it would be different. He'd go to her

11

farm, talk to her, explain. He never thought she'd just show up at a gallery.

He unscrewed the cap of his water bottle and took a sip so he'd have time to think. "You want one?" he offered. She shook her head.

"That's my horse in your paintings," she said again.

"Yes," he said slowly, "that's your horse."

"That's a *real horse?*" Allison asked quietly. "I mean, a horse…that is *real?* I thought it was the stuff of legend. Something you made up."

"Who *is* this woman?" spat Tori.

"This is Allison Hunt. She's my publicist," said Matt.

"And who are *you?*" asked the short blond woman with Tori. She was glaring at him.

"I'm Matt Cheval."

"That can't be your real name," Emma said. "*Cheval?* Are you kidding me?"

"How do you know *me?*" asked Tori. But she was squinting at him, her eyes narrowing, as if she recognized him. His hair was longer than when she had seen him four years ago. And he had a beard now, one of those almost-shaved looks that was so popular. Phyllis said it made him look rugged. He still had his sunglasses on. Maybe he could hide behind them until she left.

"I think we should call the police," said the blond woman.

"Who is *she?*" Matt asked.

"Emma is my friend," Tori asked. "You don't want to mess with her."

"I know half the people in New York City," said Emma, lifting her chin.

Matt raised an eyebrow, but who was he to judge.

"There's no need to call the police," said Allison. "We can get this all sorted out." She leaned down to Matt. "No police. That would be terrible publicity."

"I thought all publicity was good publicity," said Emma.

Allison frowned at Emma.

"What *are* you, *Matt Cheval?*" Tori said. "Some kind of *stalker?*" Her arms were still crossed protectively in front of her.

"I'm *not* a stalker," said Matt.

"He's definitely a stalker," said Emma.

"Please, just wait," said Allison. "Matt can explain."

All three women turned toward him.

He swallowed. He had practiced this speech a million times to himself. It was just supposed to be for Tori. He never thought he'd have an audience.

"I was at your bed and breakfast four years ago," he said. "You showed me around the farm one day and showed me your horse. I love horses, as you can tell from my art, and I was never able to get her out of my head. She's incredible. And I was taken up with the story you told me, about the marking on her shoulder. So, I started painting her."

Tori's frowned deepened. "You had no right."

"And what about *Tori?*" Emma asked. "You painted *her* too! Could you not get your mind off *her* as well?

Matt felt the blood rush to his cheeks. To hide his embarrassment, he took another long swig of water.

"It's not like that," he said. "She's just…"

He glanced at her. Her brunette hair fell around her shoulders in waves, and she still had the few freckles across her nose that he remembered. Her incredible hazel eyes peered out from under dark lashes. She had very little makeup on. Maybe some on her lips. She didn't need it.

And she was standing there in a pretty blue dress with cowboy boots on. She was as beautiful as he remembered. And just seeing her again brought all his feelings to the surface.

"It's just creepy, don't you think?" Tori said, her eyes flashing. She had gone all defensive. "And you're making *money* off of me!"

"I'm not making money off of you," he said, suddenly offended. "I *painted* those pictures!"

"But they're pictures of *me* and my *horse!*" Tori said. "I'm calling a lawyer."

Matt stared at her for a moment. "Maybe your influential friend here knows one."

That flustered Tori, and he was instantly sorry he had made her mad. Who was he to poke at her, when he should be trying to smooth out her ruffled feathers before she sued him?

Suddenly, he wanted to comfort her. He wanted to put his arms around her and tell her it was going to be okay. But, right now, she looked like she was about to kill him.

"Your horse is so beautiful," he said. "She's famous, too. She's in all of your books."

"You've read my books?"

"Of course he has," Emma said. "That's what stalkers do. He probably sits at the end of your street and watches you go about your business, too."

Tori glanced at Emma then back at Matt.

"Is that true?"

"What? No! I am *not a stalker!* I'm an artist, and I saw something beautiful, and I painted it."

"*Two* beautiful somethings," Emma said.

"You claim you were at my bed and breakfast. I don't remember you," Tori said.

Just as well. He glanced at her ring finger, but the wedding band was missing.

"My hair was longer then," he said. "And I didn't have a beard."

"Take your sunglasses off," Tori demanded.

He hesitated. Would she remember him? He wasn't sure he wanted her to. He suddenly wished he could call up a taxi and leave.

All three women were watching him. There was no escaping this now. He reached up and slowly removed the cowboy hat from his head and ran his hand over his hair to smooth it down. Then, he removed his sunglasses. Tori's eyes widened and she turned pale, then red.

She remembered him all right.

"Do...do you *know* this woman?" Allison said, seeing Tori's expression.

"Tor?" Emma was looking at her friend.

"Um. Maybe I *do* remember you. Sort of," Tori said. "He looks a *little* familiar. I'm not sure."

But the flush in her cheeks said otherwise.

The room was silent. Matt and Tori were starting at each other. Then Tori cleared her throat and looked away just as the gallery manager poked his head in the door.

"Matt, it's time for you to do your thing," he said. "I've got the crowd waiting."

Matt tore his eyes away from Tori and stood. He put his hat back on. "I've got to go," he said. "You can wait here. I'll be done in about twenty minutes. I have to give a brief talk about the paintings."

"I'd *love* to hear it," Tori said, her voice sarcastic. She had recovered.

"I think it would be best if you wait here," Allison said.

"I disagree," said Tori and turned and walked out. Emma gave Matt one more glare, then followed her.

Allison turned to Matt after both of the women were gone. "Who *is* that?"

"Never mind," Matt said. "I need to go. We can talk about it later." But he had no intention of talking about it, with Allison or anyone.

There were close to a hundred people gathered near the front of the gallery, holding flutes of wine or goblets of water in their hands. Matt saw that Tori had taken a spot near the back, and Emma was standing beside her. Tori looked frightened, upset, or angry; he couldn't tell which. Or maybe a mix of all three. A few people were glancing at her, but nobody was taking photos.

He let the gallery manager clip the wireless mic to the lapel of his button-down blue shirt. "Good evening, and thank you for coming," Matt said.

He had the talk memorized after doing it so many times over the past several months of his tour. "My publicist thinks it's a good idea for me to talk about these paintings since they mean so much to me," he said, avoiding Tori's eyes. "Obviously, you are all wondering about the horse."

He was standing in front of the largest painting, which showed a full side-view of the mare. It was one of his best paintings using light. The horse was standing up to her knees in a field of lavender, the morning sun shining on her coat and creating a splash of light across the entire canvas. He was proud of that work. The rippling muscles in the animal, the sparkles of dew on the lavender flowers, and the grass all added color and texture to the work. The horse's head was

15

raised, her nostril's flaring, as if she smelled something. A breeze was blowing her long, white mane back, revealing the marking on her shoulder.

"That marking is rare and is only found on the Arabian breed of horse," said Matt. "Horses with these markings are known as bloody-shouldered Arabians and are considered to bring luck to their owners."

He swallowed, and smiled at the crowd, still avoiding looking in Tori's direction.

"The blood-stained marking has been prized by Arabian horsemen throughout the Middle East for hundreds of years," he said. "The legend goes something like this, although there are variations:

"There was a powerful sheik who ruled over a warlike tribe. One day he went for a ride in the desert on his favorite mare, a pure white horse. Arabian horsemen prized their horses above all else and considered them family. The bond between rider and horse was very strong, because they spent so many hours together. They were ridden for countless hours every day, and the horses often slept in their master's tent at night as well.

"To be called the favorite horse of the sheik, the mare must have been a really special horse. She would have had to be incredibly beautiful, fitting for a man of his power and position, and she also would have had to be a brave war horse, proving herself in battle as worthy of her warrior master.

"On their ride across the desert this fine day, as bad luck would have it, they encountered a band of horsemen, led by a rival sheik. The two sheiks began to battle with their swords, and all knew it was a fight to the death. Both were excellent swordsmen and both avid horsemen, so it was a long, hard battle. The clashing of swords echoed across the desert for a long while, and each opponent was cut deeply several times. Finally, the sheik on the pure white mare drove his sword through the warring sheik, killing him. The other party wrapped their dead leader in a blanket and laid him across his horse, to carry him home.

"The sheik on the pure white mare was badly injured and swaying in his saddle. He was bleeding heavily, especially from

16

a deep gash in his chest and shoulder, and blood dripped down the front of him onto his horse and the sand below. He felt darkness rushing in.

"The little mare began to walk home slowly and carefully, so as not to topple her master from her back. She traveled for a day and a night, as her master, slumped forward in his saddle, lay across her, dying and soaking her in his blood as his life ebbed away.

"She finally arrived home, back to their camp, and delivered her precious master to his people. But it was too late, and his wounds were too severe. Upon arrival, he was dead.

"The entire camp was grieving. The mare slowly made her way off to be by herself, and that night, gave birth to a colt, just a little way away from the camp. The next morning, the others were surprised to find that her colt had chestnut markings on his shoulder that exactly matched the bloodstained markings on the mare.

"Legend says that the dead sheik arranged with the gods to commend the dedication of his mare, so that from then on, any descendant of hers who was possessed of outstanding courage or ability would bear the bloodstains as a mark of honor."

Matt paused here for effect. Most eyes in the crowd, as usual, were on the horse in the painting.

"This painting is of a real horse," he said. He had never admitted that before. He had always kept it a mystery, and smiled when people asked that question. "I saw her on a trip I took once. She was beautiful, and when her owner told me the legend…" He smiled at his audience. "Well, I'm a painter, so my muse took over from there! I hope you enjoy looking at them as much as I've enjoyed painting them!"

The audience clapped. Matt stole a glance at Tori, but she was gone. He saw her and Emma slipping out the door.

"What about the woman?" someone asked. There were always a few in the crowd.

He smiled. "The woman?" he said. "Well, every man has a dream woman. I guess she's mine."

There was a small chuckle in the crowd, but one woman persisted. "Is she based on someone you know? What about that woman who was in here earlier claiming that this is her horse? I saw her back there." She turned to point, but Tori was gone.

"That's all folks," said Allison. "Matt needs to come back with me and sign some papers. Thank you! Enjoy!" Allison grabbed him by the arm and steered him clear of the crowd.

Matt was glad for the interruption. He had *no idea* who Tori was to him. Not now. Not then. And probably not ever.

Chapter Three

Tori was glad to be in the car, away from the gallery. She buckled herself in and took a mint out of her purse and put it in her mouth. The cool taste calmed her, and she closed her eyes and took a few deep breaths, trying to slow her racing heart.

"That was super, super creepy," Emma said. "I think we should call the police." Emma was trying to navigate through the heavy traffic of Manhattan. "I have no idea why we drove," she said. Emma did that, jumped from subject to subject. "It would have been much easier to take a cab."

"Because we didn't want to lug my suitcase around," said Tori, her eyes still closed.

"About that," Emma said. Tori could tell by the change in direction of her voice that Emma turned to look at her. "You look super cute, but do you want to change your footwear?"

Tori opened her eyes and looked at her friend. "What's wrong with what I'm wearing?"

"Weeeelllllll," Emma said, putting on her blinker to turn left. The guy behind her wouldn't let her over. She honked her horn at him, then pulled in behind him. "Idiots." She didn't say more until she made her turn. Her navigation system told her she had four more blocks to go and then to turn right.

"We're going to a pretty fancy restaurant," she said. "Did you bring some pumps or some sandals?"

Tori thought about the white, strappy sandals in her suitcase.

"I want to wear these," she said, clicking her cowboy boots together. She was feeling antsy now, and defensive after her encounter with Matt. *Matt.* She had thought she'd never see him again. She didn't want to change her footwear.

"You'll be meeting Colton."

"Yeah, about *that*," Tori said, glad that Emma was distracted from the subject of the artist and his paintings.

"Colton is cute and lonely. Thirty-two. Never been married. Super nice."

"Why's he lonely? If he's cute and thirty-two, there's a reason he isn't taken." Tori closed her eyes again and wiggled her toes in her leather boots worn soft with use. She wished she was back on her farm. Or that Emma had planned a girls' night, just the two of them. After the stress of seeing Matt and those paintings, she wasn't sure she could take a blind date.

"You'll like him. And it's not a date. My hubby made sure to tell him we were just hanging out with a friend."

"It's a date," Tori said.

"Speaking of which...." Emma's voice took on a conspiratorial tone. "Do you *know* that artist?"

Tori was hoping to avoid this topic. She usually told Emma everything, but tonight she just wanted to leave it alone. And she had never told her about Matt.

"No."

"Yes you do. You definitely know him. Your face went all weird when he took his sunglasses off."

Tori thought about it. It must have been...what? Four years ago? Just before Tim died.

"The bed and breakfast had a theme weekend for painters," said Tori. "Maybe about four years ago. I think he was one of the painters."

"You *think?*"

"Yep."

"Hmmm. Well, if it was four years ago, no *wonder* you can't remember. That was a really bad time for you."

The traffic was heavy, and Emma had to concentrate. She was quiet for a few minutes. Tori thought about this Colton guy that Emma had fixed her up with. She knew Emma only had her best interests in mind, and that this guy must be a catch or she would never had suggested dinner with him. But she hadn't really given Tori the option.

"I think you should call the police," said Emma again.

"I will," Tori said. "I just need to process this for a while." She wasn't sure the police were the right people to call in this situation. She wasn't exactly being *stalked*. At least not physically. Then again, did she even *know* if he was following her? Had she been paying attention? Did one see a stalker when one wasn't aware they were being stalked? Maybe she had read Matt wrong all those years ago.

After all, she had read Tim wrong.

"I'm tired," Tori said. "And this night has been too much. Can we just go home?" She was staying with Emma and her husband for the weekend.

Emma looked over at her, and when she spoke, her voice was gentle. "I know this isn't your thing, and your evening has been a bit frightening, but let's go. Home is too far away with the traffic for me to drop you off and return, and I think it will be good for you, tonight especially, to get out and get your mind off of what just happened. Let's enjoy ourselves and then afterwards we'll both be thinking more clearly about what you need to do regarding the artist."

"Matt," said Tori. "I think the artist's name is Matt." She really wasn't sure what his real name was though. When she had tried to search for him on the internet a few years ago, she couldn't find him. He didn't exist. He had obviously signed into her bed and breakfast under a false name. She wasn't ready to tell Emma that.

The restaurant was nice, with cloth napkins, soft lighting, and a view overlooking the Hudson Yards. Emma and Brian had money. They loved to treat Tori whenever she came to town.

The men had a window seat near the back. They both stood when they saw the ladies. Brian hadn't changed in the six months since Tori had seen him. Colton was of average height, with brown eyes, dark hair, and a nice smile. He was dressed in a well-cut, navy blue suit, and he pulled out her chair for her. Tori was suddenly uncomfortably aware of her cowboy boots. She sat down next to Colton's place, across from Brian, and Emma sat next to her husband.

Emma did introductions.

"Nice to meet you," Colton said. On first impression, he seemed like a normal guy.

A waiter brought them water and menus. Tori opened hers and noticed a large seafood selection. She *loved* seafood, and she knew Emma must have picked out this restaurant with her in mind. Brian was allergic to shellfish. Poor guy.

"They do have pasta," she said apologetically, looking over at Brian.

He smiled. "We know who Emma loves best."

Tori laughed. It was good to be with them. She felt her shoulders starting to relax, despite the fact that she was on a blind date. What was she nervous about, anyway? She didn't have to talk to Colton. Or even *like* him. She would relax, enjoy her evening, and worry about the paintings later.

They ordered, and Colton asked her about herself. She told him about the horses and her books.

"And that's why I'm in town," she said. "To give a training seminar tomorrow at Dixie Briar Farm just west of here. They have this beautiful indoor arena and are bringing in an unbroken horse. A wild mustang."

"Tori will be riding that horse before the day is over," said Emma proudly

"Really?" Brian said. "You're one of those horse-whisperers?"

"That's me," Tori said. In her mind she suddenly saw Matt's painting of her standing at Hope's stall, the two of them touching, Hope's neck around her body.

"I'm a city guy myself," said Colton. "Never much cared for horses."

Tori glanced at Emma. Emma swallowed and gave an infinitesimal shrug.

"But I think it's *amazing* what you do." Colton seemed to realize his mistake and tried to backpedal. "I could probably *learn* to like horses if I had to. I mean, you know, if..." he coughed and took a drink of water.

Tori looked past him, out the window to the summer's evening sky. It was nearly dark and the lights of the city were beautiful, jewels dotting the landscape. She wished she was at home looking at the stars. Wished she was out of this city.

But part of her wanted to go back to the gallery. To look at the paintings again. To examine them. To see what other parts of her life he had stolen.

The waiter brought their food. Tori tried to listen to Emma talk about the various groups she volunteered with, and the organization she had started. The maple plank salmon Tori had ordered was really very good. She was enjoying her dinner and keeping her mind off of the artist until Colton started asking her more questions. Then she had to pay attention. Where did she live? Did the bed and breakfast bring in a good living?"

"It pays the bills," she said. He asked about her lavender fields. Emma or Brian had obviously told him a lot about her. Emma hadn't told her much about *him*. She felt slighted.

As they finished dinner, Colton told her he had tickets to a musical tomorrow night. "Hamilton," he said. "Third row. I bought them for my mom, but she broke her hip. I was hoping you'd come with me."

He was clearly interested in her, this city-man-who-didn't-like-horses. Hamilton sounded spectacular, but she didn't want to lead him on. Suddenly she was tired. She was angry at Matt for the paintings. She was angry at Matt for never contacting her again. He knew where she lived, after all! And she was angry at Emma for setting her up on date that she claimed wasn't a date.

She felt the anger surge up in her. It wasn't Colton's fault, any of it. Her anger was directed at Matt. But she couldn't help it. She needed this date to end, needed to get out of here *now*.

"There's something you should know about me," Tori said, suddenly feeling ornery.

Colton raised an eyebrow. "Oh," he said, picking up his water goblet to take a drink. "What's that?" He began to look worried.

Tori avoided looking at Emma and leaned back in her chair. "I have a stalker."

Colton choked on his water. "I'm sorry. A *what?*"

"A stalker. He paints me. He knows what I wear. Where I live. Even knows about my favorite horse."

Out of the corner of her eye she saw Brian looking sideways at Emma for confirmation. Emma cleared her throat.

"Well, we *think* he's a stalker," said Emma. She glared at Tori.

"You seemed pretty certain of it in the car," Tori shot back.

"Tori, I don't think now is the time or place..." Emma said.

Tori stood. "Emma, I'm not feeling well. Maybe the fish was bad. Can you take me home?"

"Go ahead," said Brian, standing. "I'll take care of the bill."

"I'm really sorry," Tori said to Colton. "It was nice to meet you."

"Um, yes," Colton said standing. "Same here. I'll call you later about Hamilton?"

"Sure," Tori said. She turned and headed for the door, suddenly needing some fresh air. Seeing the paintings, seeing Matt, this horrible date, it was all too much. She felt Emma's hand on her shoulder.

"Come outside and wait, hon. I'll get the car. I'm sorry. This whole evening was a bad idea. We'll pick up some chocolate chip ice cream on the way home."

Chapter Four

On Saturday morning, there was a small article in the *Times* about Matt's work. Allison had sent him the link. He sat there in his hotel room, sipping his coffee, and read it. It was only a few paragraphs long, under the arts section, but it was there.

Mystery Horse in Cheval Paintings is Real

Artist Matt Cheval admitted to a packed gallery last night that the white mare in his series "The Woman with the Horse" is modeled after a real horse. After years of speculation, it appears that the answer is within the grasp of art lovers who have wondered for quite some time just who this horse is.

The white mare, who appears in no less than 18 of his paintings, carries a "blood-stained" marking on her left shoulder. The marking is known within the circles of Arabian breeders as a rare occurrence, and horses bearing it are said to be courageous and loyal according to an old Bedouin legend.

So that leaves one question: is the brunette woman who appears in most of the paintings with the horse also based on a real person?

Cheval is careful to never show her face, so she remains more mysterious than the horse. One observer last night told a Times *reporter that the woman was at the showing yesterday evening, but that can't be confirmed. Cheval has no comment.*

Matt closed the news app and put his phone down. Allison had been merciless last night in trying to get more out of him on Tori.

"She's a liability," Allison said. "You're only halfway through your tour and a large part of the success of your paintings is the mystery! *Who is she?* Is she going to follow you around? Do we need to worry about her?"

But Matt refused to talk about Tori, and when Allison had left last night she was mad at him. He couldn't blame her. It was her job to make him look good, to protect him from bad publicity, and to promote his work. She couldn't do her job well on limited information.

He took another sip of his coffee. They weren't worried about her suing him. He had the intellectual property rights in this case. He had simply seen something inspiring and painted it. There was no law against what he had done. He had never named her, or the horse, or hurt them in any way.

But he knew the problem ran deeper than that.

He looked at his watch. He didn't have to be at the gallery until noon. Maybe he should find Tori this morning and talk to her. But what would he say? Should he *apologize?* He wasn't really sorry for what he did.

Or how he felt.

He pulled out a brochure and looked at the paintings portrayed in it. Hope was a beautiful horse, and the way he placed her in fields of lavender, and on the Lake Michigan shoreline, just added to the overall feeling of nature and freedom that he was trying to capture. His gift was painting light, and her white coat and the waves, or fields of flowers and silvery leaves, all lent to allowing him to work with light in so many creative ways.

One of his favorite paintings however, which wasn't in the brochure, was of Tori standing outside of Hope's stall, her hand on the mare's shoulder, and the mare's neck wrapped around her in what he'd consider a horse hug. That *moment* was forever captured in his mind. That *day.*

It was the day that had changed his heart. He had gone back to his room after that and sketched the scene before he lost it.

He closed his eyes for a moment, remembering.

It was his second day at the bed and breakfast. The B&B had hosted an artist's retreat, and all of the residents were painters. There were five rooms, and he didn't remember many of the guests, just that he had spent a pleasant few days among peers, on a summer week, painting to his heart's content. He had come because of the lavender fields, and the large sunflower field that surrounded Tori's farm, as well as the beautiful Lake Michigan shoreline. There was fodder enough to keep him busy painting outdoor landscapes forever.

But then the B&B's owner had caught his eye. She hadn't been there when he checked in. An older woman, Phyllis, had checked him in and served the guests their dinner that night. Phyllis had pointed the owner out to them, and he had seen a woman out near the barns, riding horses in the arena. From a distance, he could see that her dark hair was in a ponytail, and she looked graceful as she rode, but he didn't watch her for long. He was there to paint.

After dinner, he and the other guests went outside to paint the sunset on the lake. It was a spectacular event, and he still had the painting hanging in his studio at home. When darkness made it impossible to work any longer, they had all come inside and gathered around the dining room table, talking about their day, and consuming some incredible cranberry muffins that Phyllis had brought out with cups of tea and glasses of milk. He was talking with a man from Atlanta, about his technique of painting light on waves, and the man, a landscape artist, was sharing how he accomplished the same with leaves on trees.

Then Tori walked in.

"Hello, everyone!" she said, smiling. She leaned against the door frame that separated the kitchen from the dining room where they were sitting and pulled off her riding boots. "Yum! I see Phyllis is treating you with her tastiest bedtime snack!"

Tori was now in stocking feet, wearing jeans and a white t-shirt that was streaked with dirt. She also had a smudge of dirt on her left cheek. But it was her smile he noticed. She was radiant.

"I'm sorry I haven't gotten in before now to welcome you here, but I had a new horse to train today." She was in the room now, her boots in one hand and, with the other, she pulled the pony tail out of her hair and ran her fingers through it. The thick, dark waves hung down over her shoulders. It framed her oval face, and he noticed that she had hazel eyes and a few freckles across her nose.

"Phyllis says you all do incredible work," she said. "I'd love to see!"

She strolled over to the table, completely unconcerned that she was in stocking feet, dirty, and had just burst in on everyone. Her presence took up the room, and she walked around the table like she owned it. Which she *did*. But she was so comfortable, acting like they were her family and not guests. She politely looked at some of the sketch books of the other artists, and when she came to him, she asked to see his.

He flipped it open. He had recently been commissioned to paint horses for a calendar, one horse per month, and he had a start here in his sketch book. The horse for January was a tall Friesian, standing in front of a frost-bitten oak tree, some of the leaves still hanging on the branches from fall. February was of a mare and colt standing at a gate, ears pricked, looking forward to the food that they knew would be in the barn.

"These are *incredible!*" said Tori and sat down next to him. She smelled pleasantly of the outdoors and hay. She demanded to see them all. They spent an hour pouring through his sketches, while the other artists finished up their snack and left.

"I like yours best because they have horses in them," she whispered to him after the last person was gone from the room.

He smiled.

"Oh my gosh!" she said, suddenly getting up. "Look at the time! I'm *so sorry* for keeping you!" And she pushed her chair in, picked up her boots, and headed upstairs.

Her absence left a void in the room, taking the energy level down. He suddenly felt empty. It was like her presence had filled him with something he never knew was missing, until he found it.

Matt sighed, coming back to the present. That was a long time ago.

He took another sip of his coffee. It was getting cold. He needed to talk to her. He picked up his phone again and looked up Tori's website to see what her latest book was called.

Maybe she was in New York for a book signing, and he could see her there.

On her website, there was a menu item for *Events*. Even better. He clicked on it. She was hosting a training seminar today at Dixie Briar Farm and signing books afterward from 4–5 p.m. in the farm's conference room.

He was busy today with the showing, but he thought he could escape for a short time.

He called Allison.

"I have to leave for a few hours this afternoon," he said.

"What time?"

"I'd like to be out by 3:30 p.m."

There was a long pause. Then Allison said, "Does this have anything to do with that woman?"

Matt thought about how to answer. Allison was loyal to him, and he valued her deeply. He didn't want to lie. "Yes. I just need to talk to her before she leaves town."

Allison was quite for a moment. Just when the silence was about to become awkward, she said, "Okay. I'll rework your schedule so you give a talk a 2 p.m. and then your last talk at 6 p.m., and then some mingling. Can you be back by then?"

"Yes. You're a dear," he said, smiling.

"I know."

He thanked her and hung up. He'd have to figure out what he was going to say to Tori. But right now, he needed to take a shower and get dressed. Otherwise, he'd be late to the gallery and Allison would kill him.

When he arrived, there was a large crowd gathered outside of the art gallery. He always filled up a showing, but this time, there were more people than he imagined would show, even here in the art-loving Manhattan.

"There he is!" someone said, and the crowd split so he could make his way through.

"Excuse me, Mr. Cheval!" said a young man, no more than mid-twenties. "I'd like to ask you a few questions." He showed his press pass.

"Excuse me!" said a woman in her fifties. She, too, had press credentials hanging around her neck. "I'd like to learn more about the horse."

"Is the woman real too, and was she here last night?" said a smartly dressed woman.

"Is the horse still alive?" said a man with messy gray hair

"Where do they live?"

"Are you in love with her?"

"Is she a long lost sister? I hear you were separated at birth!"

"What?" Matt said, honing in on the last person who spoke. "*No!* I don't have a sister..."

The reporters were all persistent and he just wanted to get inside. As politely as possible, he declined to talk, and invited people to come in to hear his story when the gallery opened at noon.

The gallery owner was there to let him in. He locked the front door behind Matt, and tactfully didn't say anything about the chaos outside. Matt retreated back into the building to the office. Allison was standing behind the desk.

"I guess it's true what they say, that any publicity is good publicity," she said. "The *Times* wants an exclusive interview with you. So does *Horse and Rider* magazine."

"Oh, geez," he said, running his hand through his hair.

"Don't do that. You'll mess it up," said Allison, coming over to him and fixing his hair. "Who is she, anyway?"

"I don't want to go into it," said Matt.

"Well, look, the doors open in twenty minutes. You need to figure out how much you're going to say and how much mystery you are going to leave. I recommend mystery." Allison handed him a card. "I called a lawyer, and like we discussed last night, you're okay with intellectual property rights. You don't owe her a thing for painting her horse, or the likeness thereof. But here's his card if you have any questions."

Matt took it and pocketed it. He thought about the crowd outside and the questions he was going to have to field. He thought about Hopeful Farm Bed and Breakfast, and the still, quiet land around it.

What if people went looking for Hope? He had heard of such things, of famous landmarks having to be moved because of the crowds who came to see them, like the bench in the movie *Forrest Gump*. Would the same thing happen to a horse? Tori had told him how much she valued the peace and quiet of the farm. And her privacy.

What had he done?

Chapter Five

Tori stood at the railing and looked at the horses enclosed in the round pen. The pen stood about a hundred feet from the indoor arena where she'd be training but was set back behind a barn to give the animals some quiet. The government rounded up wild Mustangs from time to time out west so they didn't get overcrowded, and auctioned them off to the public. These horses were from one of those roundups.

Tori's job was to train one of them to ride by the end of the day.

The horses had been here about a week, and gotten accustomed to the noises and the confinement, or, at least as used to losing their freedom as they could get. Still, it was better than starving to death on the prairie, or that's what she told herself. Several of them watched her warily, but many of them munched on the hay that had been tossed to them and ignored her.

People always billed her in the promotions as a miracle worker, a horse whisperer, because she'd take one of these wild animals, who had only been in captivity for about a week and never had any previous contact with humans, and tame it to ride. Most of her audience would be horsemen and women who came to learn her training techniques and take them back to use on their own animals. But she always got some curious onlookers in the crowd who were just there to watch.

This "breaking" of the wild horse was a mystery to many. She hated the term "breaking" or "taming," because in reality, all she was doing was building a relationship based on trust. Once she gained that trust, she could pretty much do what she wanted with the horse. It was all about body language.

If she watched the horse closely enough, she could tell what it was thinking.

She had arrived early this morning to pick out her horse. This wasn't a show where she chose the wildest horse to impress the crowd. Instead, she looked for the horse at the bottom of the pecking order. Horses had a hierarchy, and there was always a leader. Then, the power trickled down through the herd until there was one or two that were subservient to the others, that always got picked on or shoved aside for better grass. Horses weren't cruel, only practical, and if they could bully the horse next to them so that they and their offspring could eat more, so be it. The name of the game in the wild was survival.

She found a small mare who seemed to be at the bottom of the herd. She was pretty, with a brown coat, white stockings, a white blaze down her face, and a black mane and tail. A bay. The little horse was run aside from the hay and nipped at by the others. She wasn't a fighter, and her humble and timid nature made her a good candidate for training. That was the horse that Tori would use.

Roy came over and stood beside her. He was the guy in charge of helping her today, the one the farm had assigned.

"I want that one," she said, pointing. Roy, a seasoned horseman himself, smiled and leaned his arms on top of the railing. "Good choice. And she's a cute little mare. You going to keep her?"

Tori shook her head. She had enough horses at home already. "No. She'll bring in a lot at the auction. They need the money."

Profits from the auction always went back to the Wild Horse Bureau, the government agency that took care of and monitored the mustangs.

"Okay. I'll get her for you when the time comes," Roy said.

"Thanks."

This farm was a big operation just outside of Manhattan. It provided the high-end horse lovers of the city a place to keep their animals and an escape to the "country." It consisted of several white barns, twenty acres of fenced pastures, four outdoor riding arenas with jumps, and a big indoor arena with bathroom facilities, a heated observation room, and plenty of natural light coming from special filtered windows along the top. It was beautiful.

Today, a round pen had been set up inside the arena, and bleachers brought in for the event. Tori would use the arena to train the new little mare she had just picked out.

By 10 a.m., the place was full. She entered the arena to the applause of more than two hundred people and introduced herself. She reminded them to remain quiet while she worked, hold their applause, and try not to scare her horse.

Then, on cue, Roy brought in the mare. The horse struggled against her ropes, but with the help of two more men, they managed to funnel the mare into the open gate of the arena, pull the lassos off her neck, and close the arena. Tori was inside.

The horse trotted the circle a few times, keeping one eye on Tori, looking for a way out. When she discovered she was trapped, she stood with her hind end up against the railing, on the far side from where the audience was sitting. She was watching Tori.

Her eyes were wide with fear, showing the whites. She snorted a few times.

"Hey," Tori said quietly. She began to talk to the mare, keeping her voice quiet. Tori remained where she was, but she pulled a long carrot out of her pocket. She broke a piece off and tossed it on the ground in front of the horse. The horse shied back, but then realized the carrot wasn't coming to get her. She sniffed, then lowered her head and gobbled it up.

"Easy now," Tori said. She held her hand out, palm up, with another piece of carrot on it. She slowly stepped toward the horse, but when she got within touching distance, the mare trotted away.

A rope and the carrot were the only things Tori had with her and the only tools she'd use at the moment. She uncoiled the rope and flicked it toward the horse. Right away, the mare startled and began running around the arena. Tori kept flicking the rope, just a little, just enough to keep the horse moving.

"There's a magic line on a horse's body that makes her move forward or not," she said to her audience. "I draw a straight line from her shoulder to myself. If I move behind her shoulder (that line), she'll feel like I am pushing her forward, which is why she's moving right now."

She let the mare canter about six times around the arena. The horse's ears swiveled, listening to her.

"If I stand in front of that line, she'll stop, and probably turn."

Tori stepped forward, so she was in front of the line to the mare's shoulder.

The mare's eyes were on Tori. She halted, her ears swiveling. Tori gently flicked the rope, driving the mare in the opposite direction. She let the horse canter around the arena, watching her.

"In the wild, the leader of the herd of horses will drive out problem horses, usually those who are young and causing trouble," Tori said. "Horses are herd animals, and dislike being away from the others. They naturally push toward pressure, wanting to return."

Tori watched for the signs that this mare had enough. Her inside ear was on Tori, while the outside ear flicked back and forth, searching for danger. Finally, she started licking and chewing. This was a sign she was telling Tori that she was repentant. Whatever she did or didn't do, please, let her back in the herd.

Until this point, Tori had her shoulders squared toward the horse, her eyes firmly on her. Now, she turned to a forty-five-degree angle, lowered the rope, and dropped her eyes.

The mare stopped. She turned toward the center of the ring, both eyes on Tori. Tori could see her out of her peripheral vision, but she kept her eyes off the horse. The mare took another step.

Tori raised her hand and the mare bolted.

She flicked the rope and repeated the process, driving the mare a few revolutions around the arena until she saw the signs of submission again.

When the mare asked to come in, Tori stopped and dropped her eyes. Slowly, she turned her back. The horse approached her, and Tori responded by moving away.

The mare followed her.

Tori stopped. She felt the warm breath of the mare on her shoulder. She sniffed Tori's shoulder. Slowly, Tori reached her hand up behind her, finding the itchy part on the mare's neck. As she scratched, the mare's upper lip came out in pleasure.

She had gained her trust and made a friend.

She slowly turned and put a hand on the mare's neck. The mare stood still, her nostrils quivering. Tori had completely forgotten the crowd at this point. Her mind was strictly on the horse. She watched until the ears relaxed and the head dipped a little, then, she moved in until she had her hand on the horse's neck. She felt the muscles quiver under her touch, and go ridged in fear, but then, she moved her hand up to the base of the horse's neck, on top by the withers.

She scratched the mare and saw her upper lip quiver a little bit. She had found an itchy spot. Then she used that same hand to offer another piece of carrot. She also had the rope in her hand, loose, but ready to apply pressure if the mare tried to move, to drive her back out of the herd, to teach her that this wasn't acceptable behavior. But the mare remained still.

After a moment, the mare took the carrot from her palm. Things were moving along as planned.

Over the course of the next hour, Tori taught the horse that she was somebody who brought pleasure and not a human to be afraid of. She itched the scratchy parts and fed her yummy treats. After they had made friends, she reached through the fence and got a bridle, and proceeded to put the bridle in the horse's mouth. She rubbed her and made a great deal of fuss over her.

Tori stepped back, behind the point of the mare's shoulder. The mare moved forward, in a counterclockwise circle around the outside of the arena. Tori remained in the center and let her canter for a while. She needed time to realize that she could still move with the bridle on. The reins had been unclipped, so there was no danger of her getting caught up in them.

When the mare slowed down on her own, Tori stepped back, crossing the invisible line from herself to the horse. Now she was in front of the point on her shoulder.

The mare turned to look at her, and Tori crossed that line, pushing the mare forward again. The mare cantered a clockwise circle around the arena.

Tori watched for the signs, and when she saw the mare's tongue coming out, she stepped back on the other side of that invisible line at the shoulder.

The mare stopped and turned to look at Tori.

Tori turned sideways, no longer facing the mare directly.

The mare took her time, but again, she eventually came to Tori. She sniffed Tori's shoulder. Slowly, Tori reached her hand up, finding the itchy part on the mare's neck. As she scratched, the mare's upper lip came out in pleasure.

"We're still friends," Tori said. There was a low murmur of agreement in the audience.

After much petting and scratching, she walked over to the side of the arena and reached for a wooden box, about two-foot by two-foot. She put it in the middle of the arena and sat on it.

"Come here, little one," she said quietly, pulling the rest of the carrot out of her pocket and breaking it. The horse watched, then head lowered, slowly made her way to Tori. Tori fed her, then quietly moved the box to the side of her horse.

She stepped up on the box so she was on the left side of the horse, by her back, and continued with more scratching and rubbing. The mare gave an audible sigh and turned her neck around to nuzzle Tori. Tori gave her the final piece of carrot, feeding her from the palm of her hand.

Then, she gave a little hop, and laid across the mare's back. The horse's head shot up, and her ears swiveled to Tori. But Tori found her itchy spot and scratched some more.

"It's okay," she said. "We're friends now."

She eventually swung her leg over and straddled the horse. She was riding her.

She felt the muscles tighten for a moment, as the mare tried to figure out if this was going to hurt her, and then she relaxed again.

Tori couldn't help the smile that came. She raised a hand to the crowd, sitting bareback on the horse with a bridle on, and no reins for control. The audience remembered not to applaud, for fear they'd scare the animal. But as she looked out into the crowd, she could see the awe on their faces. She didn't understand why people were so amazed at what she did. If people just took the time to becomes friends, most horses were this easy to work with.

She heard the mare chewing on the bit. Then the horse turned her head around and sniffed Tori's boot.

She sat there for a few minutes, rubbing the horse's neck, and scratching her itchy spots. She really was a nice mare. And pretty. If she didn't already have a few horses, she'd take her home. But the show was over, and this mare, at least, had a good start in life with people.

After Tori's training presentation, a veterinarian gave a talk about colic. There was a short break with boxed sandwich lunches, and then another workshop. Afterwards, she made her way to the conference room across the driveway from the arena for her book signing. She had shipped thirty books ahead of her, and most of them were already pre-sold.

The conference room was housed inside a building that had a tack room and a small concession area. The room itself was walled off with two double doors at the entrance—a perfect place for meetings or workshops. Her table was at the back, and a line of customers had formed, leading from her table across the room and out the doors. She sat down and started signing books, taking the time to speak individually to each customer.

Finally, the line thinned and then stopped. She had three books left. Not bad. She looked at her phone and saw that it was 4:45, almost time for her to leave.

A woman came into the room to buy one of her new books. She turned it over, glancing at the author photo, taken just a few months ago.

"You're so pretty, you can wear your hair any style," she said to Tori. "I really like that bob you have in the author photo on your first book.

Tori hated that photo but hadn't been able to get her publisher to change it. Her hair was shorter then. She had cut it that way because Tim had seen a woman with that style and admired it.

"You should do something different with your hair," he had said. He never mentioned her hair, or how it looked, so this was something new. Tori loved her long hair, but she asked him what he might like.

"Maybe something like that," he said. He looked at her then, something he rarely did. "It might look cute."

His comment had more effect than she liked to admit. She had thought about it for an entire week, then went in and got a trim. She came home, fixed his favorite dinner of steak, put on some mascara and lipstick, and waited to show him. She was both nervous and excited to hear his reaction. They had been married for three years, and it was time for a change. Maybe this would put a spark into their marriage.

Tim came home on time for once, gave her the regulatory kiss hello, and started looking through the mail. Tori cleared her throat.

"Dinner smells good," Tim said.

Tori cleared her throat again. Finally, Tim looked up. His expression was a mixture of shock and distaste.

"What did you do to your hair?" he said.

"I cut it," Tori said. "You said I should do something different."

"But it was so pretty before," he said. How long had it been since he had last called her, *or* her hair, pretty? She felt anger rising in her.

"I cut it for you."

Tim looked at it and shrugged. "No matter. It will grow back."

Tori was heartbroken. Her long, beautiful hair. Gone. She had cut it for him.

Never again.

"You're quite an inspiration," said the woman, handing her the book. "Can you make it out to Willa?"

Tori signed the book. After the woman left, Tori stood, stretching. It was finally five, and she was exhausted.

"We'll buy the last two books from you and put them in our tack shop," said Katy, the farm's manager.

"Thanks!" she said. "I'll sign them for you." She took out her Sharpie and signed her name on the inside title page of each.

When she looked back up, Matt was standing at the doorway.

"There's someone else here to see you," Katy said. "Should I let him in?"

"Um, he's...I know him. Yeah, let him in."

"Okay. I'm heading back to the barn," said Katy. "I'll lock up when you're done. It was nice to have you."

They shook hands and Katy left. Matt was still hanging back at the door, and she saw Katy speak to him, inviting him into the conference room. Katy closed the door behind him, leaving him and Tori alone together.

Matt slowly walked across the room toward her. He was wearing a button down, white dress shirt. The sleeves were rolled up, and it was open at the neck, like he had just come from the gallery and didn't have time to change.

As she watched him, she was aware of a small fluttering in her stomach. He hadn't changed much since she had seen him four years ago, except now he had the beard. She hadn't recognized him at first yesterday because of the hat, sunglasses, and facial hair, and because she was so busy looking at those darn paintings.

Thinking about the paintings made her angry again. But she wasn't lost to how good he looked.

"Hey," he said quietly when he reached the table. His eyes were an incredible shade of blue.

She remembered that she was mad at him, and she frowned.

He glanced down at the book on the table.

"Your new one?" he said. He picked it up and turned it over.

She nodded.

He put the book down and met her eyes. "I came to apologize," he said. He shoved his hands into the front pockets of his jeans.

From where he was standing, she could faintly smell his aftershave. It was the same type he had worn four years ago. Her stomach did another flutter.

She crossed her arms. "Apologize for what?" she said.

Matt looked down at the table, considering. Then he looked back up at her. His eyes were soft, honest. "For that day. Four years ago. I had no right."

She swallowed. She remembered it too well. The memories she had tried to repress for so long came flooding back.

"It wasn't entirely your fault," she said. "I should apologize too."

She remembered it as if it were yesterday. They had spent a lot of time together the weekend he was there. He was a total stranger, but she was completely enamored with his horse sketches that Friday night when she first met him. Then, on Saturday morning she had offered to show him around the farm. She had done that for other guests, so she told herself she was just being polite.

She took him to the beach and showed him the gull's nest, and the wooden poles that stood like sentinels along the shore to keep the sand from washing away. She had led him through the fields of lavender, ripe for picking, their scent like a love potion. Then on to the sunflower field, where they laughed and hid from each other behind the large flowers. It turned into a game and they were both sweaty when Phyllis rang the bell for lunch.

After lunch, she stayed with him and the guests and had iced tea out on the lawn under the trees. Matt sat next to her, and they talked about his work. She was drawn to his sensitivity and perceptiveness.

"A picture is like a story without words," he had said, opening up his sketchbook. He showed her a pencil sketch he had done the previous year in Italy. There was a couple sitting at table outside of a little bistro, laughing ad holding hands. Behind them was a cart with a horse.

"They look like they're in love," Tori said.

"They were. They had been married only a short time and were apartment hunting. I think they had been living with his mother."

She looked closely at the sketch.

"How do you know?"

Matt smiled. "I don't, really. They had an apartment guide and were looking through it. That's this booklet I drew here on the table. And they both had rings on. Shiny rings. I just assumed. I made up the story in my head."

Tori looked at it again. "That was a year ago, you said? They could have a child by now."

"They could," he said.

"And what is this?" Tori pointed to the cart and horse behind them.

"A delivery person. He was dropping off fresh flowers, fruits, and vegetables to an outdoor market."

The horse was old, its head down and its back leg cocked in a resting position, while an old man unloaded a wooden crate off the wagon.

"A dapple draft horse," Tori said.

"It was happy. He gave it one of the apples when he was finished."

Tori looked at the drawing for a while. She could almost smell the bistro, hear the jingle of the horse's collar, feel the love of the couple. Matt had a gift. And he had brought this story to life for her.

He closed his sketch book. "I need to go paint," he said. "That's what I came here for."

The other guests had made their way off the lawn to return to their art.

"Of course," Tori said, standing. "And I have to go exercise some horses."

"I'd like to see your horses."

"I'll show you this evening," she said.

All afternoon, she couldn't get the painter out of her head. His blue eyes, his wavy, brown hair that hung below the nape of his neck, his long fingers, his incredible talent. She thought she must be crazy. She told herself to realize it for what it was. Her husband was out of town and she was *lonely*, and Matt was handsome. But that was *all*. He'd be gone tomorrow. She'd show him the horses, and then he'd go back to his room to paint, and she'd go up to her room to read that night like she always did.

Except it didn't happen that way. They walked through the barns together that night after dinner and some of Phyllis's blueberry pie. Tori was feeling pleasantly sleepy and relaxed. She told him the names of the horses, and what she was working on with them, what new things she was teaching each of them. Then they came to Hope's stall, and she saw Matt's eyes light up the way hers always did when she was with her mare.

"She's beautiful," Matt said. He offered Hope his hand, letting her sniff and determine that he was a friend. Then he rubbed her on the neck. He had grown up around horses, he said, and while he currently didn't have any of his own now, he still loved them. Tori was impressed with how comfortable he was around them.

"What's this marking on her shoulder?" he asked.

Tori began to explain the legend behind it. As she did, she ran her hand along the mare's shoulder, tracing the marking with her finger. Hope loved the attention, and closed her eyes, moving closer to Tori until she was right up against her. The mare wrapped her neck around Tori, giving her a horse hug.

"She loves you," Matt said quietly.

Tori pulled away from the horse then, turning toward Matt. "And I love *her*," she said. "She's my hope."

"You have an incredible life here," he said. His blue eyes were staring into hers.

"It has its moments."

There was a breeze blowing in from the west, carrying the scent of lavender on it. She could hear the waves crashing up on the beach. Matt was close to her, and she could smell his scent mingling with the others. They were alone in the barn, and the quiet of the evening had set in. The horses were lazy, well fed and sleepy. A few early crickets chirruped in the fields outside.

She looked up into Matt's eyes. They looked wise beyond his years, and she knew that they saw things the rest of the world couldn't see. They were the eyes of an artist.

Before she knew what was happening, Matt leaned in and kissed her.

The kiss was long and sweet. He tasted like peppermint and his lips were soft, and Tori's stomach fluttered, awakening a desire in her that she had long forgotten. It seemed like forever since a man had touched her. She felt herself putting her hands on his well-muscled biceps and pulling him toward her, and then his hand was on the flat of her back. She was suddenly up against him, the kiss deepening, when she realized what she was doing. She pulled back.

"I'm so sorry!" she said, putting her hand to her lips. "I...uh..."

She backed up, bumping into Hope. The mare shook her head, startled, and retreated into the stall.

Matt had gone pale. "No, I'm sorry. I shouldn't have..."

She twisted the ring on her finger. "I'm married."

"I know."

Then she turned and ran.

"It was my fault. I made the first move." Matt's voice brought her back from that moment to the conference room. He was standing here in front of her, those same, well-muscled arms and deep blue eyes.

"But I kissed back," she said quietly. She'd lived with the guilt of that kiss every day. It ate at her for weeks. *Years.*

"No matter," said Matt. "I'm sorry it happened."

Tori pushed her hair behind her ears, suddenly uncomfortable. "Yeah. It was a *big* mistake. Just too much... lavender and the beach and all." She tried to laugh, but it came out sounding more like a cough.

Matt nodded and looked away. "I just wanted to say, that um...I guess I don't know what to say."

He looked contrite.

He was *sorry it happened?* Had it just been a weekend thing for him? Just a moment in time that he regretted? No, there had been a connection that night. And he hadn't forgotten her after all. The paintings told her that.

After he checked out of the B&B, she had spent weeks trying to forget about him, trying to be a better wife to Tim out of guilt.

And then Tim had died.

Suddenly, she was angry again. "Why did you paint me?" she asked.

He turned red. "You and the horse were great subjects. I guess I just got caught up in what I could do with the light and color. It doesn't mean anything. And it sells well. So it was a right move to use Hope as a subject."

It doesn't mean anything.

"And me," she said.

"Yeah. And you. You made a good subject too."

So she was just a subject to him. And he was just a one-time crush to her, a moment she had gotten carried away with and regretted.

"Well, fine then," she said, her voice snappy. "I'm glad I was a good *subject*. I guess we'll part ways, and we will never see each other again."

"Fine." Matt said crisply. He suddenly sounded mad as well. "I just wanted to be sure you knew I was sorry."

"I do."

"Okay," said Matt.

He stood there for one more awkward moment. She bit her lip, because suddenly the humiliation of it all hit her, and she thought she might cry. She bent her head down, picked her book up, and pretended to leaf through it. When she looked up, he was gone.

She swore under her breath, slammed the book covers together, and gathered her things. Then she looked at her watch and wondered if it was too late to make the *Hamilton* play. She'd call Colton and find out.

Chapter Six

Matt didn't sleep well that night. He kept going over the brief exchange they had at Dixie Briar farm. He didn't know what he expected when he decided to see her. But whatever it was, he hadn't gotten it. Closure? Forgiveness? Love?

He pulled the covers over himself and turned over.

The truth was, he had never gotten over her. He'd heard about love at first sight but had never really believed in it before he met Tori. Then, from the moment she walked into the room his first night at the B&B, he hadn't been able to get her out his mind.

He had felt an instant connection, and when she sat beside him and poured over his sketches, pointing out details that only someone really paying attention would see, she had buried herself deeper into his heart. So, when she asked if she could show him around the farm the next day, he quickly agreed.

She was wearing a wedding ring, but he hadn't seen a husband around. The morning he left, he overheard Phyllis saying that Tim had been away on business, and that's when he learned his first name. He wondered where Tim—and the wedding ring—were now.

He knew Tori used her maiden name, so he wasn't sure how to find Tim on the internet. He had no idea what he did or what his last name was. He could do a little searching online this morning to see if he could find out about Tim, and if they were still married, but that felt like stalking. And he *wasn't* a stalker.

He sighed.

Matt's phone alarm went off, signaling that it was time to crawl out of bed. He felt exhausted. He had scheduled the morning off to attend church, so he didn't have to be at the gallery until 1 p.m. He traveled a lot and was often on the road on a Sunday. He always tried to find a place of worship in whatever town he was in.

He had chosen the Evangelical Presbyterian Church on Broad Street. It was close to the gallery, and similar in beliefs to his own home church. He wasn't concerned with non-essentials. He just wanted to worship with people who loved Jesus.

Maybe attending the service would get his mind off of Tori.

He showered and shaved, carefully trimming his short beard. Then he put on blue jeans and a collared, button down shirt in burgundy. With his dark hair and blue eyes, his mother had always told him that burgundy and blue were his two best colors. He tried to wear them when he was doing a gallery showing. Of course, she had also told him he should wear a suit with those shirts, but he preferred jeans, cowboy boots, and his black Stetson.

Allison let him "dress down" because she said it was a "good costume" to create a "brand" with. She used those fancy words to mean that he was appealing to the audience that loved his horse art by keeping up a certain persona. But he was really just wearing what made him the most comfortable.

He caught a taxi to church. Traffic was heavy. He arrived four minutes after the service started.

An usher helped him find a pew. Everyone was standing, singing a praise song. He slid in next to an elderly couple, who smiled at him.

He picked up a hymnal and was leafing through it, trying to find the page, when the song ended. He was too late.

The pastor came up to the pulpit to pray, and after the prayer, everyone sat down.

As people sat, Matt saw someone three pews ahead of him that looked familiar. He could swear it looked like Tori. There was a woman sitting next to her with a blond bob, and a man next to that woman.

It *was*. It was Tori and Emma.

Oh no. Matt felt a wave of panic. They'd think he was stalking them for sure!

He was trying to figure out if he should leave or simply move to the other side of the church, when Emma stood, excusing herself past two people to reach the aisle. She must be going to use the bathroom.

He quickly opened his church bulletin and looked down, hoping she wouldn't recognize him. But then he heard a sharp intake of breath.

He raised his head and there was Emma, staring at him. When their eyes met, she frowned and pointed her finger at him, crooked it, and then motioned for him to follow her.

He reluctantly got up and followed her out into the atrium. As soon as the doors closed, she rounded on him.

"*You!*" she hissed in a whisper. "What are *you* doing *here?* Did you come here to watch her worship? You really are some kind of a creep!"

"I'm not a creep!" said Matt. "I just wanted to go to church."

"This is *my* church!' said Emma, and she actually stomped her foot, which was encased in a very expensive-looking heel.

Matt met her eyes. "Are you saying I'm not welcome here?"

That gave her pause. "Well, I mean…it *is* a church," she said. "But it seems awfully coincidental that of all the churches in Manhattan, you are attending this particular one."

"It's close to the gallery," Matt said.

Emma considered.

"Well," she said. "I'm going to tell Tori. There's a security team here. My husband's on it. I think we may ask you to leave. For safety reasons."

That miffed Matt a little bit. He had been maligned as the "bad guy" since he had first met Emma. He was about done with that.

"Go ahead," he said stubbornly. "Meanwhile, I'm going to go back in there and worship my God. You're going to throw me out of a church and you call yourself a Christian?" He raised his arms above his head. "You want to pat me down?"

Emma frowned. She looked like she was actually considering it.

"And go ahead and tell Tori about me. She *knows* me. It isn't like we haven't met before." He realized after he said it that he shouldn't have opened that can of worms.

Emma latched onto his words, aware that this was her chance to get more information.

"About that," she said, her eyes narrowing. "How *did* you meet her? If your stories match, I'll know you're telling the truth, and I'll let you go back in there and you can worship all you want."

Matt wondered how much Tori had told Emma about them.

"We met when I was staying at her B&B," he said.

"I know that already," Emma said. "Give me more."

Matt glanced through the glass in the doors into the worship service. He could see the back of Tori's head.

"I can't," he said. Tori had been married when they kissed. It was just a kiss, hadn't gone any further, but it was a kiss all the same. It was her story to tell.

Matt thought he'd try to get some info as well. "Where's her husband?" he asked.

There was a flicker in Emma's eyes when he asked the question. She fell silent, which he knew by now was unusual for her. "Never you mind," Emma said. "Go ahead inside. But I've got my eye on you." She held up her phone and started texting.

He hesitated, wondering if it was worth it just for a church service. But he was stubborn. He decided to go in. He took a seat in his earlier pew next to the elderly couple. Then he saw Tori turn around and look in his direction. Emma must have texted her. Tori frowned at Matt.

Then, suddenly, she was making her way back and sat next to him.

"What are you doing here?" she whispered. "You really *are* following me!"

"I'm not," said Matt. "I'm here to worship, same as you."

"But it's awfully convenient that you're at this church," she said.

"I've already had this conversation with Emma."

The elderly woman leaned over. "Can you two keep it down? We're trying to listen."

"Sorry," whispered Matt. He looked over at Tori. "We can talk after the service."

Matt tried to follow the sermon, but he was having trouble paying attention. Tori was dressed in a turquoise sundress with white sandals. Her arms were tanned, probably from all the time she spent outdoors with the horses. Her hair was loose across her shoulders. He glanced at her hand, and again noticed that she wasn't wearing any rings.

She saw him looking at her, and she frowned at him. He turned his attention back to the pastor. The sermon was a message on having hope, based on Jeremiah 29:11 and how God has plans for us, for good things for our future. Matt hoped God was going to work *this* out so the frowning woman next to him didn't kill him. He sighed. Out of the corner of his eye, he saw the elderly woman glance at him again.

At the end of his talk, the pastor gave the benediction, and they made their way out the door, shaking his hand as they left.

Once they were out in the atrium, Tori turned to face Matt. "Well, *that* was a timely sermon," she said, a bit of sarcasm in her voice. "On hope and all. Seems my horse is a theme this weekend. An interesting coincidence. Just like you being here with me is a coincidence."

"I don't believe in coincidences," he said. "Maybe God's at work."

She watched him closely for a moment, thinking. "Did you really just *show up* here?" she asked.

"Yes, I really did," he said. "I had no idea you'd be here. How could I?"

She looked at the ground and shuffled her feet a little bit. He felt his heart tugging at him. He still had feelings for her, that was obvious to him now. All those years he had spent thinking about her as he painted. And here she was.

"Fine," she said. "Maybe you *didn't* plan it."

He saw Emma coming down the aisle. She and her husband would be there in a moment. He didn't have much time left. He may never see Tori again, so he decided to take a chance.

"You're not wearing a wedding ring," he said.

She glanced at her finger as if she was surprised. Then she nodded. She looked up at him.

"He died."

He hadn't expected that. Divorce, maybe. But not death.

"I'm so sorry," he said, meaning it.

"Four years ago," she said.

Emma burst through the door, shook the pastor's hand, and headed straight for them.

"Tori, is he bothering you?" Emma asked.

"No, Em. I'm fine. Why don't you go get some donuts?"

Emma looked at Matt, then back to Tori. "Are you sure?"

"Yes." Tori raised an eyebrow. Emma caught on, took her husband by the arm, and guided him toward the kitchen area where coffee and donuts were being served.

"Look," Tori said. They were standing apart from the other churchgoers, the voices around them a muffled white noise. Matt forgot there was anyone else in the room. All he could hear was his heart hammering. "I don't know what happened between us four years ago, but it's okay," she said. "I'm okay. I just…" her voice trailed off. She looked away.

He couldn't tell what she was feeling, but he didn't want the conversation to end.

"When I got home from that weekend retreat, I pulled out my sketch book and saw all of the sketches I made of Hope, the farm, the fields, the sand dunes," Matt said. "I made paintings for weeks of those things." He wanted to tell her that he couldn't stop thinking about her after that weekend, of how the one thing he hadn't sketched was the most beautiful image on the farm- her.

Of how he regretted it.

Instead, he said, "But I hadn't sketched *you*. So, I sat down one day and sketched you from memory, but only in profile. Your hair, your hat, was always covering your face, keeping it hidden. Then, from that sketch, I made the painting of you standing next to Hope at her stall door."

Because that was the day they had kissed. That was the day that he never forgot.

Tori was blushing now, but she met his eyes.

"Then I added your likeness into one of the paintings with Hope already in it—the one on the beach. And after that, I made another. You in the fields with her; you lying across her back; you riding bareback across the pasture."

She was watching him intently. He couldn't read her eyes, but she hadn't stopped him, so he continued.

"I tried to protect you. I knew you were married, and I know it was just one day, *one moment*, and that you had probably forgotten me. So, I never showed your face. I didn't intend for this series to become such a big hit, but it did. It meant a lot to people, and because I wouldn't give up names, there was mystery surrounding it. Who was the horse? Who was the woman? But I never told. Not even Allison. And I never contacted you again because you were married. It wouldn't have been right."

Tori was staring at him. Her eyes were filling with tears. He wasn't sure if that was a good thing or a bad thing.

She opened her mouth to say something, but her phone beeped with a text. She glanced at it.

"It's Emma," she said. "We've gotta go or we'll be late for my plane." She sent a text back.

Matt had one last chance. "Okay," he said quietly, wanting to keep her here. "I just wanted you to know why. Why I painted you and Hope."

She nodded.

He saw Emma heading their way. "One last thing, Tori."

He fell in love with her that day. That's what happened. That's why, even now, his heart was hammering in his chest.

She was watching him, waiting.

But he couldn't tell her that. As he paused, searching for words, she looked up at him sharply.

"You stole my world," she said. "If you learned anything about me that day, you know how much my horse and my privacy mean to me. And you gave that away."

He felt the sting of her words.

Emma was on them then. "We're going to be late," said Emma. "There's a backup on the freeway." Her husband held up his phone as confirmation. There was a solid red line on the streets of his app.

Tori nodded. He couldn't read what she was thinking.

"I've got to go," she said, wiping away a tear that had escaped down her cheek, and she allowed Emma to pull her away. As they hurried toward the door, Tori glanced back one last time. Then she was through the doors and outside. Gone. Matt was left standing alone in the atrium, wondering if he had just made a fool of himself.

Chapter Seven

The first thing Tori did when she got home to the farm was change out of the turquoise dress into a pair of soft blue jeans and a faded t-shirt that said "Hopeful Farm Bed and Breakfast." The t-shirt was light purple and had a sprig of lavender flowers under the wording. They sold them down in the living room, which doubled as an office.

"Welcome back!" Phyllis stepped through the open bedroom door, a laundry basket of clean sheets in her arms. "I heard Hope whinny when you got out of the taxi. That's how I knew you were home!"

Her housekeeper had a smile on her face. Phyllis was always cheerful. In her mid-fifties, and formerly an innkeeper, she helped Tori with everything from office work to making beds. She also did most of the cooking for the guests.

"Hi, Phyllis," Tori said, offering her a smile in return as she sat down on her queen-sized bed. Simon, who had been twining through her legs, jumped up beside her for petting.

"Looks like everybody missed you," Phyllis said.

"It's good to be missed."

Phyllis asked her a few questions about how her weekend was, how many books she had sold, and then she hustled off to make beds. Tori gave Simon one last pat on the head and then headed out to the barn.

The sun was warm, but there was a cool breeze coming in from the lake. Tori called to Hope as she approached the gate, and the mare raised her head, her nostrils flaring, then slowly made her way toward her master. They met in the middle of the field. Tori wrapped her arms around her horse and laid her head against her warm neck. Horses had the perfect sized necks for hugging.

"It was a rough weekend, girl," Tori said.

Ever since she was little, she had always brought her problems to her horses. Growing up on her parents' horse farm, the barn had provided a refuge when she was hurting, and an escape from the pressures of school and social obligations. Near her horses, she could relax and be herself, spilling out her problems. She figured she had probably saved thousands of dollars on therapy by talking to her horses.

She walked back to Hope's left side, put her hands on the mare's back, and hopped up. Straddling her, Tori lay forward on her stomach, resting her head on her mare's neck, and letting her arms stretch down. She put her palms against Hope's warm shoulders.

Hope turned her head back, nuzzling Tori's boot, then put her head down and resumed grazing. Tori closed her eyes and lay there, feeling the comforting warmth of her horse under her. For a while she just let her mind rest, taking in the distant sounds of the shore, the birds in the trees around the field, the gentle breeze rustling the grass. The soft, warm body of Hope, who moved along slowly, grazing, felt like a massage to Tori's tired muscles. Why was she so tired, anyway?

Stress. That's why.

The weekend had been full of unexpected things. Some of them fun. *Hamilton* had been a blast, and the energy of the music and dance had taken her mind off of Matt. Colton had been pleasant. He was nice enough, but they really didn't have anything in common. Both of them agreed they'd get together when she came to town, but that neither were interested in commitment at the moment.

Matt. Now *he* was another story and was confusing her emotions. She remembered that weekend he had visited her bed and breakfast, and had an awful time letting it go. After that kiss in the barn, she had run to the house, locked herself in her room, and didn't come down for the rest of the night. Then, she had gotten up very early the next morning and taken Hope for a long ride down the beach, not returning until after 11 a.m. check out. She had even called Phyllis from her cell to be sure everybody was gone before she returned.

And Matt had never contacted her again.

He had signed in under a different last name. Matt Jones. She knew because of the hours she had spent trying to find him on the internet the following evening. And then the guilt afterwards. What was she doing looking him up? She was *married*.

Tori sighed. Hope lifted her head and did the same. Sometimes, Tori felt that she and her horse were connected emotionally. Actually, she *knew* they were.

Her cell phone vibrated in her back pocket. She considered letting it go to voice mail, but she was running a business, and Phyllis needed to be able to get in touch with her. She sat up and pulled it out of her jeans. It was Emma.

"Hello!" Emma's voice rang out when she answered it. "I just wanted to be sure you got in safe. You forgot to text me."

"I'm sorry," Tori said. She *had* forgotten. "My mind is on other things."

"Like Matt?" There was teasing in Emma's voice. "Or Colton?"

"I told you, Colton and I are just friends," Tori said.

"I know. I'm just teasing you. I wanted to check on you. It was a pretty tough weekend. Are you okay?"

"I am now," Tori said, rubbing Hope on the neck. "I have my Hope."

"That's *so* nice," said Emma in a dreamy way. "You know Tim will always be with you in some way, when you're with her."

Hope had been a surprise wedding gift from Tim. Before they married, he had bought Tori a horse farm on Lake Michigan, and when they came back from their honeymoon, Hope was waiting in the barn. There was a red ribbon tied on the stall door, and her registration papers were framed and hanging next to it. "Victoria's Hope" was her full, registered name, one Tim had come up with. She was a purebred Arabian, and rare because of the marking on her shoulder. Tori had no idea what he paid for her, but she knew horses well enough to know it had to be in the tens of thousands.

"Because I want you to always have hope," said Tim.

Tori had warmed to him then, after the cold honeymoon, and thought things were going to get better. The honeymoon had been awful. He had been on his phone for business the entire time, it seemed, and she had spent most her days alone, strolling along the shops of Milan and eating in small Italian restaurants by herself.

"It's business, honey," he had said.

But it was always business. From the honeymoon on, it had always been business.

"Tor?" Em's voice startled her.

"Yes, it will," said Tori. "Tim's memory will always be with me. I need to go, Em. Lots to do."

"I understand. Love you."

Tori hung up and closed her eyes. She had never told Emma about her marriage problems. Everything else she had shared, always, with her best friend. But not Tim. Not their problems. Not how she felt when she was with him.

Because she had never really been sure how she felt until he was gone.

She laid back down on her mare and relaxed. She let the sun wash over her and listened to the rumble of her stomach. She hadn't eaten anything since this morning at Emma's house, before they left for church.

Thinking about church reminded her of Matt.

I never contacted you again because you were married. It wouldn't have been right.

Was that the only reason he hadn't contacted her?

The look in his eyes while they were talking seemed much more than an artist interested in a subject. It had taken her right back to that day they spent together. He hadn't forgotten her after all these years.

I sketched you from memory.

He had painted all of those paintings of her, and she had always been on his mind.

And now...now she was free.

Phyllis had homemade clam chowder soup on the stove and a fresh baked loaf of bread on the counter.

"Hungry?" she asked Tori.

"Starved."

"Me too."

Tori got two bowls and filled them with soup, while Phyllis cut them each a large chunk of bread. They ate at their usual spot, at the little kitchenette instead of the large dining room table. Phyllis said grace for them.

Today was Sunday and the house was empty. Checkout was at 11 a.m. and most of the guests had left for their homes and jobs.

"Anybody still here?" Tori asked.

"There's a couple still checked in, the Gaberdeens, but they're in town somewhere, sight-seeing. Another couple is checking in tonight, but not until after 7 p.m."

Tori nodded and dipped the corner of her bread in her soup. In the quiet of the house, she could hear the grandfather clock ticking in the next room.

Phyllis had been hired two years into her marriage, when Tori decided to turn the farm into a bed and breakfast. Tim was never home, she was lonely, and she thought the B&B would be a good distraction. But then she had needed help around the house so that she'd have time to work with her horses. At that point, she'd had five in training: Hope, two young Arabians she was starting under saddle, and two lesson horses that she used for teaching both kids and adults to ride. She said she needed a housekeeper to run the B&B, and Tim didn't hesitate to pay when she asked him for one. The income from guests would offset what his salary didn't cover.

She put out an ad and Phyllis answered. She had been a Godsend, taking care of the place when Tori started traveling, and taking great care of Simon, her cat, when she was away. Phyllis had recommended William for the barn work. He was an older gentleman, in his sixties, but strong as an ox. He knew horses, and Tori felt comfortable leaving them and the barn in his care. She rather enjoyed sleeping in some days and not having to worry about shuffling through the snow in the winter mornings to feed, like she had done the first few years here, and for most of her life on her parents' farm before she met Tim.

It was nice to have money.

But she would rather have had love.

"Something troubling you?" Phyllis asked casually. Phyllis was sharp. She had never married, but she was a people person and loved working with Tori. She had her own place about two miles south, and went home in the evenings after snacks were served. But she was here again the next morning bright and early.

Tori stirred her soup to bide her time. She needed to talk about Matt, and Phyllis was the right person.

"Yes, actually," she said. She looked up and across the table at her friend. "I met someone in New York who stayed with us once," she said. "His name is Matt. He was here that weekend four years ago when we hosted the artists."

"I remember Matt," Phyllis said, "Longish hair. About your age."

"You *remember* him? We've had so many people come through here I didn't think you would."

"But not that many people that you give private tours to, or spend so much time with." Phyllis raised an eyebrow, then got busy breaking off a piece of her bread.

"What do you mean?" Tori said, feeling her cheeks grow red. "I was *married*."

Phyllis frowned and made a pffft sound. She had never liked Tim. "Well you aren't now. Did you invite Matt to stay with us again?"

"No," Tori said. "The whole thing is kind of weird. He has been painting pictures of Hope, and the thing is, he's kind of famous. And so is this series."

"Painting pictures of Hope?"

"And me."

Phyllis stopped eating and put down her spoon. She got a thoughtful look. "Did you take pictures?"

"I have a brochure." Tori got up and went to her bedroom to dig the brochure out of her purse. She returned with it and handed it to Phyllis. She sat and finished her soup while Phyllis carefully studied the brochure, taking her time looking at each painting.

"You didn't know about this?" Phyllis eventually asked.

"No. Not until Emma took me to the art gallery. We had no idea. We just thought it was some random guy painting horse pictures."

Phyllis flipped it over to the back and continued to read.

"Creepy, huh?" Tori said.

Phyllis carefully put the brochure down on the table between them. She folded her hands in her lap and looked at Tori. "Looks to me like a man in love with a woman," she said quietly. "I think it's romantic."

Tori swallowed, again remembering Matt's words.

I never contacted you because you were married.

How did she feel about him? She remembered the guilt after that kiss, the fear that Tim would somehow find out. The sleepless nights that following week, and the hours during the day when she wanted to call Matt. The search for his number. And then, Tim's death.

She didn't think she'd ever have called Matt then, because she strongly believed in fidelity. But she wanted to see where he lived, and what he was up to. Just one last time. Just to know he was okay.

Now she had his number.

"So you think I should call him?" Tori asked.

"Well, what did he say when you met him?"

Tori hesitated, playing with her soup. But this was Phyllis. Phyllis didn't judge.

"He said he never called me because I was married at the time," she said quietly.

Phyllis smiled. "Honey, you deserve to get out and have some fun. You paid your dues. For Heaven's sake, give him a call!"

Chapter Eight

Matt's crew had packed up his paintings, and the paintings were in the truck and on their way to the next showing, which would be at an art gallery in Ohio. He had just settled in his Jeep and was buckling in for the long drive. He preferred to drive himself from town to town, instead of flying or relying on a bus. The long hours alone gave him time to think of his projects, and the evenings in hotel rooms offered him the chance to sketch those ideas out. The real painting was done at home in his studio in Northern Michigan.

He had the two-day gallery stop in Ohio, followed by a three-day weekend in Detroit, then to Traverse City and onto LA for a short, west-coast tour.

His cell phone rang. He glanced at it, and saw it was an unknown number. He almost didn't answer it, but thought maybe it was one of the gallery managers needing to get a hold of him.

"Hello?

There was a brief silence, and then a soft voice.

"Hi Matt. This is…um…"

He knew right away who it was.

"Tori," he said, recognizing her voice. He suddenly felt uncomfortable. He remembered spilling his guts to her at the church and wondered how she felt about it. She had seemed angry, left abruptly to catch her plane, and he hadn't heard back from her. He was sure Emma had taken one of his business cards, and he was easy to find online, so Tori should be able to find his number. But he figured she didn't want to talk to him.

"Yes," she said. "It's me."

There was a brief silence while he waited for her to say something. When she spoke, her voice trembled a little bit.

"I was calling to see if maybe you wanted to come out to the farm some time," she said. "Or we could meet in town for coffee. Or we could—"

"Yes." He interrupted her. "I would. I'd like that a lot."

He shouldn't have added "a lot" onto that sentence. It made him sound overly eager. He remembered Emma calling him a stalker. "I mean, whenever you have time," he added.

"I have time whenever," said Tori. "Or rather, when I'm not on the road. Which is for the next few weeks. I thought you could come and see Hope."

"Okay. That would be great." He thought about his schedule and cursed the fact that he had to go to Ohio first. "I'll be in Detroit on Friday for the weekend. What if I stop by next Monday?"

"Um, okay," Tori said. "You can stay here if you need a place. I think we have one room open. Or there's the guest room. We have an actual guest room that's not for guests. I mean, *paying* guests."

He thought of the small town she lived just on the outskirts of. A sweet touristy town with nice history. The weekend seemed like a lifetime away.

"Okay. I'll be there around 5 p.m. on Monday."

"Yes," she said. "That would be nice. Phyllis and I will have dinner for you."

He remembered the round housekeeper she had employed when he was there. She had been friendly and a wonderful cook, making their stay a very pleasant experience.

"Okay. I'll see you then."

"See you," said Tori.

And then she hung up.

Matt sat in his jeep looking at his phone, his heart hammering in his chest. He reviewed everything he had just said to her and wondered if this could be real. After years of not being able to get her off his mind, he was finally going to see her again. At *her* invitation.

He was excited and also afraid he'd mess it up. He had no idea what she expected from him. Perhaps she just wanted to be friends? Maybe she wanted to talk about the paintings. Or what if she was inviting him there to chew him out? But no, he had seen something in her eyes yesterday before the sudden turn to anger, before Emma pulled her away to go catch her plane. There was a flame that night they had kissed in the barn, and he was pretty sure it was still there. He was willing to bet his life on it.

Unless he had extinguished it by painting Hope.

There was an unusually large crowd at the Ohio gallery showing. Cleveland boasted a few tourist places, such as the Rock & Roll Hall of Fame, the Cleveland Museum of Art, and the Great Lakes Science Center. He had visited them all before on previous tours, and knew that Ohio folks liked their cultural events, but never had he seen such a crowd for his *own* work.

He made his way through the thick crowd that had already been let in to his gallery showing, and saw that Allison and the gallery manager had corralled them up front. He had been here last night to help set up the large rolling partitions covered in black cloth. They were arranged at the opening of the exhibit to block the view of "The Woman and the Horse" paintings inside. His larger than life poster was hanging there, along with the canvas of the black stallion he had painted several years ago.

There was a murmur, and then a temporary hush as he pushed through the crowd and was recognized. When he got to the other side, he ducked under the rope barrier that was hooked across the entrance, then turned to the crowd. He smiled and gave a slight tip of his hat before he continued around the corner.

"Nice," said Allison. "I like the hat touch."

"What on earth is happening?" Matt said, following her back to the make-shift office space. "Am I suddenly famous?"

"Honey, you've *been* famous. You're just *more* famous now."

"Why?"

In answer, Allison brought out three newspapers and laid them on the desk in the office. "Cleveland has been waiting for you."

The Cleveland Journal had a story on the front page titled "Artist Matt Cheval Brings Mystery Horse to Ohio – She's Real!"

The two other papers had similar stories. Allison handed him her phone. "Scroll through the photos."

He did. There were four screenshots of websites carrying the story locally.

"Wow," he said quietly.

"Yeah," said Allison.

He wasn't sure how he felt about it. He had suddenly been thrust from *kind* of well-known to *really* well known, all because of Hope and his statement that somewhere out there was a real horse.

"I've had several offers for sales. Some of them would set you up for retirement," said Allison.

Matt felt his chest tighten. "The paintings aren't for sale. Not yet."

Allison shrugged. "It's up to you. But best to sell while they're hot. I can arrange it so that we get to keep them through the rest of this tour."

Matt shook his head. "We can talk about it later." He was willing to part with a few of them...just not right now. These particular paintings had always been personal for him, and suddenly, they seemed more important to him than ever. It felt like if he let them go he would be letting go of Tori. Which was crazy.

He took his hat off and smoothed his hair down, then put it back on. He needed to get his mind off of Tori so he could work.

The gallery manager poked his head in the office and held up his wrist, tapping his watch. "You have ten minutes before you're on," he said.

"Okay, thanks," Matt said.

"You all set?" Allison asked. Matt nodded.

"I'm going to go check on the hors d'oeuvres," said Allison, and disappeared out the door, leaving Matt alone.

He sat down in the office chair behind the desk. When he had started painting as a small boy, he had never dreamed he'd be sitting here today getting paid to do what he loved. He sold enough paintings regularly to cover his living expenses and gave talks and workshops for additional income. He was also commissioned to do calendars and other horse art, such as the horse art that appeared on wrapping paper and wallpaper, as well as china plate designs for collectors. He also had been commissioned for a few "living room" paintings that were reproduced in bulk for big box stores. He would never get his own designer label for home decor, but his work appeared in quite a few places, and for that he was grateful and well paid. He was quite comfortable. And now, it appeared, his work was even more in demand.

He would spend two days here in Cleveland, then, on Thursday, he'd head toward Michigan. It would be several more days before he'd see Tori, and he was filled with mixed emotions about the whole thing. He had thought about calling her just to talk, but what would he say? Waiting until he saw her in person would be best.

He had thought long and hard about her invitation for him to stay at her B&B and decided against it. It just seemed like a bad idea. He had booked a reservation at the hotel in St. Ives. She was less than fifteen minutes out of town, so it would be a short drive. That way, if things didn't go well, he'd have an escape.

One of his brochures was sitting on the desk, and he took it and opened it. Hope's big, black eyes started out at him from under her long, white forelock.

"Hey girl," he said, and ran his finger across the picture of the horse. "Looks like we get to see each other real soon."

He remembered her gentle muzzle, and the playful bump of her nose against his arm the night he and Tori had kissed. Tori had fled to the house, and he had stood there in the growing darkness of the barn, wondering what to do—wondering if he should pack up and go home, or run after Tori and apologize.

While he stood there, deciding, Hope had stuck her head out of the stall door, and he felt her warm breath on his arm. Then she nuzzled him, and he turned toward her.

"Hey girl," he had said then. As if knowing he needed comfort, she pressed her forehead against his arm and closed her eyes. He took his other hand and gently rubbed her behind the ears. Hope stood there letting him pet her, and he felt his heartrate slow and his breathing calm down.

"Thanks," he had whispered to her, and let his hand fall away from her ears. She stood there, still, against him for a moment, then she opened her eyes and gave him a playful bump with her nose as if to say, "I want more!"

He had laughed and given her one more pat, but then he went inside. He had stayed in his room, thinking long into the night about Tori and the kiss, and when the first light of dawn rose, he got up and heard Allison telling someone that Tori's husband was out of town.

Matt had packed his bags and left.

Chapter Nine

Tori led Hope into her stall, careful that the mare didn't bump into the door on her way in. She took the halter off of her, kissed her on the muzzle, and said goodnight. Hope nuzzled her softly, then held her forehead against Tori's for a moment before moving on to her hay.

Tori closed and latched the stall door. Her barn helper, William, had left a few hours ago. The night was warm, the stars were out, and the crickets chirruping. The wind was blowing in from the lake, and she heard the swell of the waves on the beach in the distance.

She took a long, deep breath, and thought of her brief conversation with Matt a few days before. When she had told Phyllis that Matt was coming to visit next Monday, and that he would stay for dinner, Phyllis didn't tease her, but she had worn a smug smile for the past couple of days. She also went shopping and bought some supplies to make up her best blueberry cobbler and chicken pot pie. Tori knew the guests would be in for a treat as well, but Phyllis was baking it for Matt, because the pot pie was a lot of work and was only made on special occasions.

She wondered how Matt really felt about her. He hadn't confessed any undying love, or love at first sight like heroes did in the movies. But Matt's eyes said more than his words. Or maybe he was just obsessed with her, and that wasn't the same thing. She had no idea what to think. *Tim* had said he loved her, had in fact *sworn* to love her forever on their wedding day. But she had never really *felt* loved.

Would she even recognize love if it came to her? After what she had been through with Tim?

She sat down on a bale of hay across from Hope's stall and leaned her back against the cool, wooden wall. She placed her hands on the thighs of her soft jeans and rubbed them, as if cold. Every time she thought about Tim, she got a little uneasy.

It seemed like just yesterday, instead of seven years ago, that they got the diagnosis of Hope's disease.

"She's going blind," said the vet. Tori had called him after noticing for a few weeks that Hope was stumbling frequently, and twice had bumped into the side of gate on her way into the pasture.

"It starts with the peripheral vision," the vet had said, "and advances rather quickly into full blown blindness."

It was one of the rare days when Tim was at the barn. He had come down to hear the vet's diagnosis.

"Oh, hon," Tim said, putting his arm around Tori. "I'm so sorry."

The vet said that many horses did fine with blindness, and that Tori would just have to give her special attention.

"Make sure she's always out in a familiar pasture, and keep her in the same stall every night," he said. "Stuff like that."

"Maybe we should have her put down," Tim said. "It's cruel to let her go on like this."

Tori was reeling from the news of Hope's disease when Tim said that to the vet. The vet, bless his heart, shook his head.

"Not necessary," he said. "She's perfectly healthy otherwise. The disease will run its course, and she'll be okay. She won't be a show horse any longer, but she'll still be a great pleasure horse with a rider she trusts. Nice long walks along the beach. That sort of thing."

"Tori can still *ride* her?" Tim said, shocked.

The vet nodded. "If they go slow."

After the vet climbed in his truck and drove down their long, winding driveway, Tim hugged Tori again. "I think we should have her put down," he said. "I don't want you riding her. What if she stumbles and falls? You could get hurt."

"You heard what the vet said," said Tori, fighting back tears.

"Still. I'm not sure," said Tim. "I think you should let this one go. I'll buy you another horse."

"No," Tori said firmly, and that was the first time she realized that the familiar feeling in the pit of stomach was fear. "No. She'll be fine. *We'll* be fine."

Tim didn't press the issue, but it had unsettled Tori.

Tori stood up, shaking the memory from her mind. She headed toward the house, hoping that Phyllis had something good cooked. She was starving.

They had two couples there for dinner that night. Tori had time to shower and change before dinner, and then joined them at the table. One couple was on a tenth anniversary trip and away from the kids for the first time in a while. They were in their thirties, but giggly like school kids. She thought it was sweet how he kept holding his wife's hand, and she kept giving her husband little looks across the table. It was obvious they were in love.

The other couple was here on vacation. Just a fun week in St. Ives.

"This roast chicken is incredible," said the giggly man. "I'll have to try to duplicate it."

"Nobody can duplicate Phyllis' magic," Tori said.

"He will try," said his wife. "He loves to cook."

Dinner was roast chicken with herbed potatoes, green beans with almonds, and a garden salad with dried Traverse City cherries. To top it off, Phyllis served it all with her warm home-baked bread. Peach pie with vanilla ice cream was for dessert.

Tori often wondered how she wasn't fat, because she ate like this most days.

They had great conversation and talked about a lot of different topics. Both women at the table were avid readers, and they launched into book discussions with Tori, who also loved to read.

The couple who was on their anniversary clasped hands on the table.

"That's sweet," Tori said. "You two seem *so* in love."

The woman blushed and leaned her head on her husband's shoulder. "He's the best. I will always be grateful for him. He is definitely a gift from God."

Tori smiled, and the woman continued.

"My first husband was abusive. Not physically. But he cut me down a lot and took me for granted. I didn't realize that was abuse, but the constant negative words and attitude…" She looked at her current husband. "I didn't realize what love was until I truly found it."

Tori looked at the woman's bright face, and intelligent eyes, and had a hard time imagining her as a victim.

The conversation switched then to Lake Michigan. Tori told them a few shipwreck stories. Guests loved to hear about those.

When Phyllis started cleaning the table, Tori suggested that both couples go for an evening walk on the beach. "It's a beautiful evening," she said. "Not too windy, but you still might want a sweater. The temperature is always cooler near the shoreline."

Tori helped Phyllis clear the dishes and load the dishwasher. Then, she wiped down the table and put the white table runner across, setting a vase of fresh flowers in the middle.

Afterwards, she stretched her arms above her head and yawned. It had been a long day outside with the horses, and she was sleepy. She pulled out a chair and sat down. When she did, she saw the dent on the edge of the table. She had been helping Tim carry in the nightstand that sat near her bed now. She had accidently bumped the kitchen table with it.

"I *knew* I should have hired a professional to help me," Tim had said. He hadn't raised his voice, but the disappointment was evident. Afterwards, he had come back downstairs and ran his finger across the dent, shaking his head. "You need to be more careful," he said.

Tori ran her finger across the dent. She had dismissed his condescending comment at the time, like she had so many others. But it hurt.

Phyllis came into the dining room and turned out the light. They could see outside now, through the large dining room window, into the darkness behind the house. A blanket of stars filled the nighttime sky. It would be dark down at the beach. Tori was glad she had given the couples some flashlights.

Phyllis pulled out a chair and sat down at the table, beside Tori.

"I remember that day," she said, touching the dent. "You were bringing in that antique bedroom suite the two of you had gotten at the market."

Tori nodded.

"I said it was too heavy for you. Tim said you could do it. And of course you could, because you can lift forty-pound bales of hay, one in each arm. But I didn't want you working with him. He was always so critical."

Phyllis didn't usually talk about Tim.

"It was just his way," Tori said, automatically defending him.

She had been out riding when the phone call came from the hospital. Tim had collapsed from a heart attack. Sudden, swift, and deadly. One moment, he was questioning a witness, the next he had toppled over in the court room and died.

A coronary embolism is what they told her. A blood vessel in his heart had burst. It was probably a defect he was born with, and undetectable. It was just one of those things.

Tim had been well loved in the community. A young lawyer, handsome, and from the top of his class, he had joined a law firm in St. Ives and was beloved by his clients. In the summer, he had helped business owners and the hospital defend against tourists who tried to sue for one reason or another. In the winter, he spent more of his time helping the local folks with things like real estate issues, wills, probate, and trusts. He also did volunteer work in town, helping the Rotary with fundraisers and installing handicap ramps for people. When he died, there wasn't enough parking at the funeral home.

Afterwards, support poured in from all over: cards, letters telling how great of a lawyer he was to this client or another, casseroles from women at their church. Men he had worked with on charity events called to see if she needed their services plowing snow, mowing the grass, or any other handy service that they imagined Tim had done for her.

Tori retreated to her room and stayed there. Phyllis brought her meals. But Tori wasn't mourning. She was racked with guilt.

She had kissed a man less than two weeks ago, and now her husband was dead.

And the terrible thing was, she didn't miss him.

Instead, Tori had felt a sense of relief, something she couldn't explain. And the shame and the guilt of that relief had also eaten at her, so she had never told a soul. Not even the grief therapist who the church pastor said she should see.

"Four years," said Phyllis.

"What?" Tori said, not sure if Phyllis meant four years since Tim's death or four years since Matt had visited.

"That's time enough to grieve. He would want you to move on."

"I know," said Tori. But there was something nagging at her. Something she had never thought about before. It had been there since the honeymoon, in the back of her mind, this little feeling that something wasn't as it should be. But she had never been able to name it.

She traced the dent in the table with her finger again, rubbing it softly. He had been upset with her for an accident. An *accident*.

It was just his way, she had said to Phyllis.

But *was* it? Everyone else loved him. Why didn't Tori?

She thought of what the woman at the table had said. Her husband had never hit her. And yet...

Tori stood, suddenly needing to move. "I should go do the evening barn check," she said.

Phyllis stood as well. "Yes, and I need to get snacks ready. They'll be back in an hour or so, I suspect, hungry. I want to prepare the quiche for breakfast as well."

Later that night, after checking on the horses and filling water buckets, Tori slid in between the soft, silky sheets of her bed. Her room was at the back of the house, on the first floor, overlooking the horse pastures. Beyond them was the shore of Lake Michigan. If she slept with her window open, she could hear the far off, hypnotic sound of the waves lapping on the beach, lulling her to sleep. But tonight was warm, so she had the windows closed and the air on. The room was cool and dark.

She thought about Matt again, and that kiss so long ago. What would have happened if Tim hadn't died just a little less than two weeks later? Would she have found Matt and realized that what she currently had with Tim wasn't true love? Would she have divorced?

No. She had stayed with Tim. Her Christian upbringing told her that divorce was wrong except in the cases of abuse or infidelity. Tim had neither hit her nor cheated on her. She had mentioned to a church friend once that she though she should leave Tim, that she thought the relationship was harming her.

"I'm so stressed," said Tori, even though she couldn't put her finger on why. "What if he doesn't love me?"

"He loves you," the friend had said. "Look at everything he has given you! And besides, if there is a problem, your God is big enough to fix it. Have faith."

After that, she had never complained about Tim to anyone again.

Tori woke the next morning with a plan. There might be a way she could keep Matt in her life, and her privacy as well. She'd do a little research on him this morning, and then run her plan by him when he came.

He had said he wanted to protect her, which is why he never gave up her name to his fans. So, her well-being was obviously on his mind. He'd listen to her logic and understand that what she was saying made sense. Then he'd pull his paintings from his tour before people found who she and Hope were. She was sure of it.

Chapter Ten

Matt's show in Detroit had been even crazier than the one in Ohio. It appeared he had even more of a following now. The newspapers were carrying the story about the "horse reveal," although he refused to talk about it again. Because he had admitted that the horse was based on a real horse, everyone was trying to figure out who it was. And now, as well, everyone wanted to know about the mystery woman

Matt used the same lines he had always used to deter the questions. When asked if he knew her, he'd smile and say, "Doesn't everybody have a secret love? We *all* dream of true love. I just haven't found her yet!" And he let it go at that.

For the most part, the crowd was polite. Most of them were there to see the art, and he had other paintings besides "The Woman and the Horse" series. Nobody got too obnoxious, and he and Allison were enjoying the extra attention and resulting sales of his other works. He was also commissioned to do a horse calendar again, which he was looking forward to.

He thought about calling Tori a couple of times over the course of the week, but he wasn't sure what he'd say to her. He reminded himself that anything they had to say to each other was better said in person.

His showing ended Sunday afternoon, and he had to do some paperwork. On Monday morning he supervised the loading of the paintings. They were being shipped off to Traverse City, his next stop after he visited Tori, and the last one before a break at home.

He was eager to be on the road. He had about a five-hour drive, and he told Tori he'd be there by dinner.

He left the Detroit area, and then headed west, toward the coast, and then north. He was a little anxious. He had decided on a soft blue t-shirt to go with his khaki shorts, and Allison said he looked amazing. She had a smirk on her face when she said it.

"It's not like that," he said.

But it was. It was totally "like that." He had spent extra time on his hair today and made sure he got in a good shave. He felt like a 16-year-old schoolboy instead of a 30-year-old man.

He only stopped once, and he arrived at Hopeful Farm forty-five minutes earlier than the 5:30 arrival time he had expected. He had texted Tori when he was about ten minutes out, so she'd be expecting him.

He stopped the car at the end of the driveway and took in the view. A white, wooden sign hung between two posts, swinging a little in the breeze, and welcomed visitors to *Hopeful Farm Bed and Breakfast*. The name was in Tori's signature font that she also used on her t-shirts (he had bought one when he visited last time), and there was a sprig of cut lavender tied with a bow painted underneath the wording.

He had picked up a bouquet of flowers in town. They sat on the seat beside him, a mix of daisies, carnations, and other summer flowers. He wondered if the flowers were a mistake, if it looked too much like this was a date. But no, it was polite to bring something when one was invited to dinner. That's what his mother had taught him. He needed to quit second guessing himself.

Please, God, don't let me mess this up, he prayed.

The winding drive was about a quarter of a mile long, and then split off in two directions at the top. If he went right, the drive would take him to the old two-story house where Tori lived, and the seven rooms that comprised her quarters and the bed and breakfast rooms for guests. The house was beautiful, sitting up on the top of the sand dunes. He remembered that there was an old-fashioned widow's walk across the back, looking out onto Lake Michigan several hundred yards behind.

If he turned left at the top of the driveway, it would take him to the barns. The main barn was a long, white gabled building with a roof that peaked in the center and had a horse weathervane on top of it. There was a main doorway in the middle and stretching out on either side of it were rows of stalls.

If he remembered correctly, there were ten stalls on each side (five across from five), along with a tack room, grooming stations, and a room that stored the feed. If he walked straight through the middle, a hallway led into an indoor riding arena with a heated observation center. It was top class, and would make a wonderful competition facility, but the last time he had been here, all Tori used it for were her five horses.

Matt took a deep breath and drove toward the house. As soon as he pulled up to the parking spaces near the house, the front door opened, and Tori walked out onto the big, white wrap-around front porch.

She had her arms around herself, like she was cold. But the day was warm, in the seventies, so it was more likely she was nervous.

Matt climbed out of the car, leaving his bag and other stuff inside. He hadn't been to the hotel in town yet to check in.

He walked up the steps, and Tori met him on the porch.

"Hi," she said shyly. She smiled a little.

"Hi," he said, handing her the flowers.

Their eyes met and held, but before he could say anything else, the front door swung open and her housekeeper came out with a tray.

"I brought iced tea and some cakes," she said. "I'm Phyllis. Not sure if you remember me."

Matt nodded as Phyllis handed the tray to Tori, and Tori handed her the flowers in return.

"How pretty. I'll put them in water." Phyllis nodded toward the swing. "I thought you might enjoy sitting on the porch swing while I finish up dinner."

Just as swiftly as she entered, Phyllis left, shutting the door behind her. They were alone together on the porch.

Tori walked over to the porch swing. It was white with a floral cushion. She sat, and Matt sat down, leaving some space between them. He was nervous, and felt his palms sweating. She handed him a glass of iced tea, then placed the tray on a small table beside the swing.

Tori was wearing a simple yellow sundress, and she looked gorgeous in it. The straps revealed her tanned shoulders. She had her hair pulled back in a loose ponytail.

He took a sip. It tasted good after his long drive. "Thank you," he said.

Tori gave a little push with her bare feet, to start the swing moving lightly. "I read in the news that the paintings are bringing you some attention," she said.

So, she was going to talk about the paintings.

"Yes," Matt said. "It seems interest has picked up."

"I appreciate you not telling people who I am," she said.

"Of course."

He wondered where this was going.

"Do you want some cake?" Tori leaned over and picked up the plate that held two small pieces of vanilla cake with some sort of red berry filling in between the lawyers, and white frosting on top.

"Sure," he said, and reached over to take one. He bit into it, and it was delicious.

"Dinner is at six," Tori said. "So only eat one. Phyllis tends to overfeed people. How was your drive? Was traffic bad?" She was just making small talk. She seemed as nervous as he felt.

"The drive was good," he said. This was painful. He needed to figure out where he stood with her.

"About the paintings…" she said. "I don't want to come across as ungrateful. When you were here four years ago…" Tori started. "Afterwards…" Her voice trailed off.

After *what*? After he left? After her husband died?

"I looked for you on the internet. But I couldn't find you."

"I signed in under a fake name," he said. "I didn't want the publicity here. I just wanted a quiet retreat."

"I know. You used Jones as your last name."

"My mother's maiden name."

"Then I was hoping you would call." She dropped her eyes to her hands in her lap.

"I didn't know," he said, a sudden lump in his throat. So many years lost. "You had a husband."

"When Tim died, I was so…I felt so…" She couldn't finish. "Anyway, here we are now."

This was moving faster than Matt had imagined, and he still wasn't sure where it was going.

"I didn't know how you felt about me," he said.

She met his eyes again.

"I'm still not sure," she said.

"I'm not asking you for anything," he said.

"I know."

He set the cake on the napkin she had given him earlier, and laid it on the swing beside him. Then he took her hand and held it in between his. She didn't pull away. Her skin was warm. He had no right to touch her. Not yet. But the moment he did, a tingle ran through him.

"We hardly know each other. But I'm grateful you invited me here to dinner. It'll be good to catch up."

He didn't want to let her go. He thought about leaning over and kissing her, right here, right now. But then the front door opened.

"Dinner!" chimed Phyllis.

Tori quickly jerked her hand away from Matt's. "Coming!" she said, and stood up, smoothing her dress. "Let's go eat!"

The house hadn't changed and looked exactly as he remembered it. The dining room table was reserved for the guests, who were eating tonight at 7 p.m., so Phyllis led them through to the kitchen so they'd have more privacy. The small table was set for three, he noticed, and wondered if Tori had asked Phyllis to join them just to keep things safe.

The kitchen smelled wonderful.

"I have the guests' food warming in the oven, and will have to go serve them soon," said Phyllis. "But I'm going to grab a bite to eat with the two of you first."

As she dished out some fantastic smelling chicken pot pie, Phyllis had questions about his drive up and his work, keeping the conversation blissfully free of the specific paintings of Hope and Tori.

"Where do you live?" asked Phyllis.

"North of Traverse City," said Matt. "I bought a place up there shortly after I stayed here. I fell in love with the Lake Michigan shoreline, so I moved from the middle of the state out here. I love it."

"Do you have a place on the water?" Tori asked.

"No. I'm in town, but within walking distance of the shore. The houses that sit right on the lake are a bit out of my price range." He made a good living as an artist, but not enough to live on Lake Michigan itself. Land was at a premium, and prices were astronomical.

Dinner was delicious, and when they finished Phyllis suggested they go for a walk on the beach. "I'll clean up after I serve our guests. But come back later for dessert."

Tori grabbed a sweater from a hook near the back door and motioned for Matt to follow her. She was barefoot, so he took his shoes off as well.

The sun was low above the lake when they started their descent down the dune. Sea grass lined both sides of a stone walkway that led down to the lake, and there wasn't much of a wind coming off of Lake Michigan tonight. Seagulls flew overhead, their calls filling the air.

Since his arrival less than two hours ago, the whole night had seemed like a dance around topics. He had imagined it going differently. She would either yell at him about the paintings or she would throw herself into his arms. Neither had happened.

They reached the shoreline and Tori turned left, walking south down the beach, which would bring them behind the barns. The water lapped around their ankles, sparkling in the setting sunlight. It was cool, but not unpleasant, against his bare feet. He spent countless hours walking just like this on the beach in his own town. There was something relaxing about the water, and it erased most of the stresses of life for a while.

He noticed the colors of the sky, the yellows, pinks, and blues. Sometimes, when the sun was almost set below the water, a green halo appeared around it. This was an optical illusion, caused when a layer of warm air trapped cooler air and moisture close to the surface. He had captured a photo of it once and painted the phenomenon.

Neither of them spoke, and he wondered what Tori was thinking. When they were down the shore quite a distance away from the house, she turned and walked up the sand dune toward a pasture that ran along the ridge. Matt followed her up, and she stopped near a gate, let herself through, and whistled.

The wind stirred the quiet breeze, and all Matt could see was a rounded hill, and behind that, the top of the barn.

Tori whistled again. Matt heard a subtle rumbling, and then Hope appeared over the hill, trotting in their direction. He would recognize her anywhere by the marking on her shoulder. She was still as beautiful as he remembered.

"Hey, girl," Tori said as the mare stopped near them. She grabbed a handful of mane and gave Hope a little tug. Hope followed as Tori led her through the gate. She locked it behind her, then turned and hoisted herself up on the horse, pulling her dress up her thighs a little way so she could straddle the mare.

"A sunset looks better from horseback," she said, smiling down at him. Suddenly her shyness was gone. Her eyes sparkled as she held a hand out for him. "Come on."

"Um…" Matt had on shorts, and he wasn't at all certain he could get on the back of the horse behind Tori.

"Hold on," Tori said. She nudged Hope with her legs and moved the horse over near a rock. "Climb on behind me."

Matt went over and climbed up on the rock. He hoisted himself up behind Tori with what he hoped was a bit of grace. Matt's parents had owned a little farm for a while and some horses, so he had grown up riding, but it had been a few years since he had been on a horse. He put his arms around Tori's waist and closed his eyes as Hope made her way carefully (and blindly, he reminded himself) down the sand dune. Once they were at the bottom, he opened his eyes again. They stood on the beach, and Tori turned Hope to the right so they were headed north.

"Wrap your arms around me and hang on," said Tori. "But if you're going to fall off, don't pull me off with you," she said, laughing.

"How are you controlling her?" he asked.

"Through my body pressure," she said. "Leg pressure for turning, seat pressure for speed."

"I see."

He didn't really see at all. But his worries were overcome with the fact that his arms were around Tori. There wasn't all that much room on Hope, so Matt was pressed up against Tori's back, and he could feel the warmth of her body through her thin dress. Her hair smelled like lavender, and the back of her neck was the same tanned color as her shoulders and arms.

Hope walked slowly forward, and he felt the familiar sway of the horse under his thighs. The slight rocking motion and warmth of the animal, the silky hair against his bare calves, all made him wonder why he hadn't taken the time to ride in so long.

And Tori. Here. In his arms.

They walked, silently, up the beach until they were well past the house. He felt a slight shift in Tori's weight, back against him, and Hope stopped. Then Tori applied some light pressure with her right leg, and Hope turned so they were facing the sun. Its big, round globe had just touched the water.

"Let's watch," Tori said.

The color was spectacular. Matt wished he had paint with him so he could capture some of it. But then, no, his arms were busy at the moment. He realized he probably didn't need to hold on while they were just sitting there, so he reluctantly let go of Tori and put his hands on his thighs.

"It's beautiful," he said.

A few gulls flew past, one silhouetted in the sunset. The sun went down quickly, and within minutes they were left with a darkening sky streaked with purples, pinks, and oranges.

"I never get tired of watching that," said Tori. "In the winter, we get some really pretty ones too. But nothing like this."

"I try to watch every night," said Matt. "I can walk a few blocks to the beach from where I live."

Hope snorted and tossed her head up and down, as if she knew the sunset was over and they needed to be on their way home.

"How does she get around if she's blind?" he asked.

"She trusts me," said Tori. "She knows I won't run her into anything."

"But what about her footing?"

81

"I keep her on smooth ground. She trusts me for that too. And she knows the area she lives in, her pasture, and where her stall is. You ready to go back?"

Matt wasn't. There was a lot he wanted to say. He wasn't sure how to start, but he needed to know what she was thinking.

"Tori," he started to ask.

"Hang on tight," she said. "This part is fun."

Matt wrapped his arms around her as she turned Hope back toward the barn. She leaned forward slightly, which pulled him against her tighter, and suddenly Hope took off in a canter. The wind rushed at them, causing his eyes to tear. The sand sped by under him, and suddenly, he felt like he was flying. The three-beat gait was so smooth that it was like sitting in a rocking chair. He could hear Tori laughing and saw Hope's ears flicking back and forth. He glanced behind him; her tail was up in a banner. Hope was having as much fun as they were.

Matt briefly wondered how on earth Tori would get Hope to stop, but as soon as they reached the area below the barns, she shifted her weight back. Matt felt her back arch into his chest, and Hope slowed to a walk. Then Tori turned her, and she took them up the sand dune. At the top, they stopped. Matt dismounted, then offered a hand for Tori. She took it and gracefully slid off of the horse. Her dress was wrinkled, and much of her hair had come loose out of her ponytail. Her smile was radiant.

"Did you like that?" she asked.

"Yes," he said as he watched her open the gate and let Hope back in. She locked it behind the horse, then turned to Matt. The sky was almost completely dark.

"I'm sorry," she said.

"For what?"

"For calling you a stalker," she said. "It's just…it scared me."

This was the opening he was looking for. It saddened him that she had been afraid.

"What were you afraid of? Are you afraid of *me*?"

She shook her head. "No. Just the opposite."

He wanted to say more, to talk about the paintings. But standing there with the sound of the waves and the subtle scent of lavender mingled with hay grass, his senses were in heaven. She was looking at him intently, like she wanted to tell him something. He wondered why he had never looked her up. What would have happened if he had contacted her one, or even two years after Tim died? He had buried his feelings for her for so long, but it was clear they were still there. And now that she was free, he had a chance.

He wanted to kiss her.

He had no idea how this was going to end. But he knew for certain that he'd never be able to go back.

Chapter Eleven

Now seemed like a good time to ask Matt for the favor. She had gone over how to say it so many times before he arrived, and now that they had established a friendship, it felt like the right time. She was feeling good after the ride on Hope, and Matt looked relaxed here on the beach.

"I need to ask you for something," Tori said.

"What?" Matt said. "Anything." He reached out and took Tori's hands. His touch was warm, inviting. For a moment, she thought he was going to kiss her. She swallowed, not sure how to say what she wanted to say, not sure if she wanted to tarnish this moment.

But what did she want?

"I wanted to ask you…"

He was watching her expectantly in the darkening light.

"I need for you to take the paintings of me and Hope out of the art show."

His eyes registered shock, and he dropped her hands.

"What do you mean?"

She swallowed, rubbing her hands together. They were cold now. "I'm afraid of the publicity they are going to bring to me and my horse," she said. "Or have already brought to us. I don't want to be popular."

"But you write books!"

"For a small, very select group of people. *Horse* people. I only get write-ups in small-town newspapers, and I don't have a huge following. When I go do a horse seminar, mostly horse people show up. I'm only well-known in my peer group. You…well, you have been on national television and radio."

It was true. She had watched some of his interviews this morning on the internet.

"You do art showings in *Manhattan*," she said. "You're *famous*."

Matt turned to look at the lake, and put his hands in the front pockets of his pants. He stood there, quiet for a moment, thinking.

Had she made him angry?

"Tori, do you realize what you're asking me to do?" He turned back to her. "That's my livelihood. Those are my most popular works, and I have an entire six more months of showings booked out all over the United States. I have been commissioned to do several more paintings based on that work. Those paintings are my best. I'm proud of them."

"But they are going to end up hurting me," Tori said. "I just know it."

"How?"

This wasn't going smoothly. She took a deep, calming breath. "By bringing attention to me and Hope. People will want to see my horse. They will want to see *me*. I don't want to be seen."

"It'll be good publicity," Matt said. "For both your training business and your B&B."

"I don't want any publicity. Things are going fine the way they are."

The wind was playing with the loose waves in his hair, and she longed to run her hand through it. She saw the tension in his shoulders, which hadn't been there before, and she wanted to tell him that it would be okay.

"You can make *new* paintings. And you have others. That one of the stallion is gorgeous."

"And it's three years old," Matt said. "People want to see new stuff. They want to see this series."

Tori was starting to feel frustrated. "But I don't *want* them to see it."

Matt sighed. "Okay. Let me sleep on it. Now probably isn't the best time to talk about this. It's late and we're both tired. Can we discuss it more in the morning? I'm sure we can come to a compromise. This evening has been so fun. Let's leave it that way."

Tori nodded. *Tomorrow.* Did that mean he was coming back?

Tori had been *so* nervous to see him again. Her feelings were a mixture of guilt from the first kiss when she was married, to desire for him, to anger because of the paintings. She had no idea how she felt about him. But her body apparently did. She longed to touch him.

"I think we should get back to the house," she said, pushing her feelings down. She untied the sweater from her waist and put it on. She had goosebumps all over. She wasn't sure how much of it was from the cold and how much of it was from excitement at being so close to Matt again after all these years.

"Sounds good," Matt said. "You look cold. I don't have a jacket to offer you." He put his arm around her, and they turned and walked along the sand dune, being careful of the rocks since they were barefoot. When they came to the house, they stopped.

"I need to go lock the horses up," Tori said. "You want to come?"

They stopped back at the house and put their shoes on, then he followed her to the barn. Hope was already at the gate, waiting to come in.

There were three other horses waiting in a separate pasture.

"This is Brownie," she said, pointing to a solid bay. He was a tall gelding, with black legs, mane, and tail. "He's William's horse. William is my barn helper. This is Queenie." Queenie was a beautiful golden palomino mare. She looked like she was of Arabian descent because of her dished face. "Queenie is a rescue that I am training and plan to sell. And this is Jax and Flip." These two were young, each only about three years old. Jax was a deep red chestnut, and Flip was a bay like Brownie, only with white markings on his legs. "I'm starting them under saddle for two separate owners. They aren't mine."

Matt helped her put halters on them and lead them in to their stalls. He filled up the water buckets while she distributed hay.

When the horses were settled and eating, she sat down on a hay bale across from Hope's stall and motioned for Matt to sit next to her.

His thigh was brushing hers because there wasn't much room on the bale of hay. It felt good to have him beside her. She remembered the ease of their relationship four years ago, how they just fell into a comfortable companionship. She had likened it to finding a best friend as a child, and that wonderful feeling of "belonging" to someone who understood you.

She wondered if he was seeing anybody else.

"Are you in a relationship?" she asked. It was a bold question, but she wanted to know if he was involved with somebody else while pining for her. While painting her.

"No," said Matt. "I've been involved a few times but nothing serious. Nothing now."

He was so *handsome*. She wondered who these women were who had let him go.

"I haven't had anybody since my husband, Tim," she said.

"If you don't mind me asking, how did he die?" Matt said.

She told him briefly of the heart attack. She left out the details.

"I'm so sorry."

"It's okay. He wasn't…"

He wasn't what? she wondered. *Attentive? Caring? Loving?*

She thought about the words the guest had used last week, about being a victim of abuse. She had never thought of herself as a victim.

But what about the time that Tim had accused her of spending too much time with the horses? He had just come home from a weekend golf trip after a seventy-hour work week at the law firm, and here he was accusing her of not dropping everything the minute he arrived and spending time with him? She had been so angry at his remark and they had argued. She had fled out of the bedroom and slipped on the wooden floor. She had cracked her wrist. He took her to the emergency room. Instead of showing concern for her, Tim was upset that the rest of the evening had been ruined. Her wrist was put in a cast and she was off work for six weeks.

"He wasn't *what?*" Matt asked gently.

Tori turned her attention to Hope, who was happily munching hay. "Tell me about yourself. What do you do besides paint?"

Matt laughed. "That's about it. That and travel around with the paintings. Nothing too exciting. I grew up with horses, as I told you once before. I love them but haven't taken the time to get myself one since I've been grown. I love blueberry pie and listening to baseball on the radio in the summer while I paint. I have one brother, who is two years older than me and lives near the middle of the state by my parents. About an hour from here. They were a bit upset that I moved out of their town, but once they saw how close I was to the lake, the drive got shorter. They visit me a lot!"

Tori laughed. It was still so easy sitting here talking to him, like it had been the first time. That one day they had spent together was one of the best days of her life.

"I love blueberry pie too!" she said. "I'm an only child. My parents live here in town, in St. Ives, and still think Tim was the greatest man alive."

That slipped out before she thought about it.

"Wasn't he?" Matt said.

"He was a lawyer," she said. "Graduated the top of his class and opened his own law office here after finishing law school. Everybody loved him. He was chosen number one lawyer in St. Ives county area his last year by his clients."

"Oh," Matt said quietly. "But I didn't ask for his resume."

"He started work here in St. Ives so I could be close to my parents. That was nice."

Phyllis had once suggested that Tim came to St. Ives because of his ego. She said he needed to be somewhere small so he could feel big.

Tori didn't know what else to say. She hadn't told anybody much about her marriage. Not Emma. Not even Phyllis. And she didn't want to destroy the image her parents had of Tim. They would be devastated if they had known how miserable she really was. She wanted them to be happy.

She remembered all the Sunday dinners with her parents and now deceased grandparents she had missed because of him. She had wanted to go, but he was always tired and wanted her to stay with him. When she did, he was usually watching a game on television. She wondered why he needed her at home.

"He was ten years older than me," she said. "We met at a charity event in New York. Emma had taken me there to help her stuff bags full of goodies for the dinner guests coming that night to pledge. And Tim walked into the room. He was the guest speaker for their cause, which was raising money for a women's shelter. He was young and cocky and full of himself, but he took a shine to me and took me out to dinner the following night. We had a blast." She pulled a stem of hay out of the bale and began to fiddle with it. "Tim had this charisma about him, which is why everybody loved him. He could make you feel like you were the only one in the room. We dated for a little over a year, and then married in the spring, right after he graduated from law school. I was only twenty-one. He bought me this farm and moved us here. It was like a dream come true."

"Was it?" Matt said.

"No," Tori said quietly.

It was like Tim had claimed his prize and moved on. Once they married, he became busier than ever and didn't even seem to notice that she existed half the time. He was on the phone during most of their honeymoon, but she had let that go because he had just started his new job at the law firm. But then it never stopped. She'd cook dinner for him, and he'd never come home. He would usually call, but he wouldn't give her much notice. She often ate alone.

He'd come home late and crawl into bed beside her, waking her with a kiss. But then he'd set his alarm and say he had to get to sleep, not even wanting to take the time out for sex.

She had wondered what was wrong with her. Why didn't he want to spend time with her? Or make love to her? Wasn't he *in love* with her?

She tried to make tastier dinners and picked out sexy nightgowns, but he didn't seem to notice. She bought tickets to his favorite music group when they came to town, but he had an important business meeting that weekend. He pushed himself too hard, and when he was tired, he became even more critical of her.

Tori remembered the interest Matt had shown in her horses that weekend, the questions he asked about her job. He had even found one of her books in the living room the night they had met and took it up to his room to read. He told her the next day what he had learned. She thought about how he looked at her when she spoke and paid attention to the details of what she said and did. She had been starving for that kind of attention. That was part of the pull he had over her, she believed. He was actually *interested* in her.

She wanted to take Matt's hand, to feel its strength and warmth here in the dark of the barn. But she kept fiddling with her piece of hay.

"People think I loved him," she said. At the words, she felt a crushing wave of guilt.

Matt was quiet.

"But I didn't. Not there at the end," she said. "I barely knew him." She turned to Matt. "Isn't that awful?"

"No," Matt said. "Not if he wasn't kind to you."

And here was Matt. She was still attracted to him after all these years. She thought about the paintings again. Phyllis thought it was romantic. In a way, it was. It was flattering to have someone paint her. She knew that asking him to stop showing the paintings was a huge thing to request. But it was the only way she'd feel safe. And she hadn't felt safe with Tim for years. Not really.

"He wasn't kind," she said. And her stomach got that strange, sick feeling that it always had when she talked about Tim. The feeling she had grown to understand was anxiety.

She looked across the aisleway at Hope's stall. That's where Matt had kissed her. Leaning her head back against the wall, she wondered again how her life might be different if Tim hadn't died. If she hadn't kissed Matt and run from him.

But that's not what had happened.

She began to tell Matt a little bit about her marriage. She said just a few things, but it felt like the lifting of a burden she hadn't even known she as carrying. The more she said out loud, the clearer her marriage suddenly became.

Chapter Twelve

Matt listened as she talked about her marriage to Tim. The things she told him sounded like emotional abuse. When Tim was around, he nitpicked at her. He didn't like the dress she had on or the meal she had cooked for him. He sounded like he was overworked, and when he was home, he was tired, and took it out on Tori.

She didn't go into details, and Matt didn't ask. But the few things she told him, about the dent in the dining room table, and the fact that he wanted to put Hope down, didn't sound good. If that was the way Tim treated Tori all the time, it was no wonder she hadn't loved him. And then to have him go and die had left her in a confused, guilt-stricken mess.

He listened quietly and let her talk. After a few minutes, she stopped, and looked at him. "You probably think I'm awful, don't you?" she asked again. "He *died*. Everybody loved him."

But instead of responding to the question, he asked her one. "Why haven't you told your parents these things? Or Emma? Emma seems like a good friend. She certainly had your back in New York."

That got a smile from Tori. "Yes, *Emma*. Oh, I don't know. I guess I didn't want anybody to know. Honestly, I always thought it was *my* fault. I figured I was doing something wrong. If only I could be prettier or nicer or *something*. I came into the marriage with great self-esteem, so I'm not sure what happened."

"It's called emotional abuse," said Matt.

Tori looked across the aisle at Hope.

"That's the second time this week I've heard that term. But he wasn't abusive. He never shouted at me or hit me."

"Doesn't matter," Matt said. "For starters, he wasn't around much and when he was, he withheld love from you. I'm not a psychologist, but when kids are pulled out of a home situation, it's because of *neglect* or abuse, so neglect can be a form of emotional abuse. Think about it. He kept from you the nurturing you needed, the love, the feeling that you *mattered*. Babies *die* from that. We all need to know we matter. We all need to be touched. And that feeling you got when he was around? What was *that*? You said your stomach did something."

"Yeah," she said. She closed her eyes, thinking, and put her hand on her belly. "It was like nerves…"

Suddenly she opened her eyes, and laughed, dismissing it with a wave of her hand. Then she stood up, pushing her hair away from her face. "I'm *so sorry*," she said. "You came for a visit, and here I am dumping my baggage on you."

"Not at all," said Matt. He didn't want the moment to end. But she walked over to Hope's stall. The mare came to her, and Tori put her arms around her. "Tell me more about *your* life."

"My life," Matt said. "There's not much else to tell. As I said, no special relationships with women that made me want to marry, so I'm still single. But I had a great childhood. I still get along well with my parents. I like my brother. We're best friends. And I love my job. Painting is my passion. I get paid to play, basically. It's not all bad."

She was quiet, her face buried in Hope's mane.

"Tori?" Matt said.

"Hmmmm?"

"We should talk about the paintings."

"I'm not going to sue you, if that's what you're asking," Tori said, her face still hidden. "Legally, I don't even think I can. Emma looked into it."

"Of course she did," Matt said, laughing. "She's something else."

"Yeah. Oh, believe me, you *don't* want to go against Emma. She'd make a *great* lawyer!"

"I can imagine." Matt smiled. Then he steered the conversation back to the paintings.

"But I think you believe I invaded your private life, and in a way I did. I'm sorry and I need to know that you're okay with that. And you said you aren't."

She patted Hope on the neck and turned around. In the dark of the barn, he couldn't see the expression in her eyes, but when she spoke, her voice was soft.

"Phyllis thinks it's romantic," she said.

"But what do *you* think?"

"I have to admit, it creeped me out a little bit when I first saw them, and I was *really* angry. Part of me still is. But Matt, I never forgot you either. Come. I want to show you something."

He got up and followed her out of the barn and toward the house. Inside, they took their shoes off in the mudroom and went through to the kitchen. There was a note on the table, next to a blueberry cobbler.

"Phyllis has left for the evening," said Tori, reading the note.

The house was quiet, peaceful. He imagined the guests were either still out or in their rooms, reading or sleeping. "Do you ever get afraid, staying here alone with strangers?"

"Guests," Tori corrected. "And no. We've never had a problem. I probably need to get some security set up, but since every guest is free to come and go, we couldn't figure out how to do it. So we just have keys."

She motioned for him to follow her up the stairs and into a bedroom at the back of the house.

"This is my room," she said, turning on the lights. "Don't get any ideas," she said playfully." Matt smiled. "But I want to show you something."

The room was light and airy and very tidy. Her bed had a white comforter and yellow pillows on it, and there was a fresh bouquet of daisies on her dresser. She went over to her closet and stood on tiptoe, reaching for a box.

He saw a Bible on her nightstand, along with a book on horse training. There was a pair of jeans thrown over the foot of the bed, and a pair of socks on the floor, but other than that the room was clean.

"Can I help you with that?" Matt said.

"I got it," she said, bringing it over to him. It looked like a fancy shoebox, like the ones his mom kept photos in. It was deep yellow in color and had a flower pattern on it.

"What's this?" he asked.

"This is where I keep my favorite things," she said secretively. She sat down on the bed and put the box on her lap. She opened the lid and pulled out some dried grass. Matt walked over and stood in front of her.

"Remember this?" she asked.

He bent over and took a closer look at it. It was a bracelet of dried grass, braided together. Suddenly he remembered making it for her.

"That's when we were sitting on the dunes and you were telling me the stories of women waiting for their husbands to arrive home safely from their fishing trips," he said. "You kept it all these years?"

Tori nodded. "That was the best day of my life."

The sun had been out, warming the day to just the right temperature. She'd had on a straw hat to keep the sun off of her head, and wore a light pink t-shirt and faded jeans with sneakers. He had spent the entire day with her, listening to her tales of Lake Michigan, shipwrecks, horses, and stories about some of the guests that had come to the bed and breakfast over the years. She had been full of life and was an excellent story-teller. He usually carried a small, pocket-sized sketch book with him, and he remembered regretting he didn't have it with him that day so he could sketch her.

"Wow." He couldn't think of anything else to say. So she *had* thought of him all of these years.

He thought about kissing her, then. Her lips looked soft, and she smelled wonderful. He was standing close. All he'd have to do was lean down a little bit

Tori suddenly stood, put the bracelet in the box, and closed the lid.

"Do you want to stay here?" Tori said. "We have an extra room."

Matt did, very much. And he wanted so much more. But he thought it would be better if they got some distance from each other so their heads could clear. He didn't want her to have any regrets.

"I'd love to," he said. "But I have a hotel room in town. I think if I stay here…" He didn't finish.

She nodded.

"But I'd love to come back tomorrow, if that's okay?"

Tori smiled. "On Tuesdays, Phyllis makes excellent strawberry Belgium waffles. Breakfast is at 8 a.m."

"I'm definitely coming back for those. I don't have another showing until the weekend." He smiled, wondering what to do next. He couldn't figure out where to put his hands, so he stuffed them in the pockets of his pants. "I've had a great time."

"I'm so glad you came."

He felt something soft around his ankles and looked down. An orange cat was twining itself around his legs. The cat looked up at Matt with big, yellow eyes and meowed.

"That's Simon," said Tori. "It seems he likes you."

Matt leaned down and scratched the purring cat behind the ears. Then he followed Tori out of the room and toward the front door.

She stood in the doorway and watched until he was almost at the end of the driveway, then he saw the door close and the living room light turn off.

He drove to his hotel room, his heart full. She was as remarkable as he remembered. In the morning, he'd explain to her how important it was for him to keep the paintings on tour. He'd promise not to reveal who Hope was, and that way she could keep her privacy. Tori would understand.

He couldn't wait until morning so he could see her again. It seemed like the last piece of his life was finally coming together.

Chapter Thirteen

Tuesday dawned warm and sunny. Tori helped William feed the horses, then came inside, showered, and put on a yellow sundress. She took some time on her makeup and realized she was humming as she brushed her hair out. She pulled it back into a neat ponytail, then observed herself in the mirror. It looked like she was trying too hard. Hmm. What if she pulled a few strands loose to soften her look? That worked. Then she blotted her lipstick off. A simple gloss was better.

Satisfied, she walked out of her bedroom and to the dining room, still feeling a little uncomfortable with her looks. Maybe Phyllis wouldn't notice the makeup.

The guests were trickling downstairs and Phyllis was putting out the bottles of real maple syrup that they bought from their neighbor every year.

"You look extra pretty today," she said to Tori.

"I have plans," Tori said mysteriously, trying not to blush. Just then, there was a knock at the door and she skipped over to open it.

Tori naturally had a happy disposition. She was always a "glass half full" kind of person, but she felt more alive and happier this morning than she had in a long time. She had awoken at first worried that she had shared too much about her marriage with Matt, and a little embarrassed. But she had kept the details out, and the fact that he had listened to her, really listened, drew her to him as it had before. He had such a gentle, loving disposition. And she had to admit it helped that he was attractive. That dark, wavy hair. His blue eyes. And he definitely worked out.

She tried to wipe the silly grin off her face before she opened the door.

She shouldn't have worried that she'd taken the time to look good for him. Matt showed up wearing an amazing blue polo that brought out his eyes, khaki shorts, tennis shoes, and white socks. He was freshly showered because his dark hair was curling just a little bit as it air-dried. He had given his short beard a trim. She wanted to run her hands over it. She couldn't get over how handsome he was.

"Good morning," he said.

Like an excited child, she grabbed his hand and pulled him through the door. "Wait until you taste breakfast," she said. "Phyllis is quite the chef!"

Tori sat at the end of the table, her usual spot when she dined with guests, and Matt sat to her left. Phyllis brought out steaming plates of waffles and fresh strawberries. Then, she poured coffee for those who wanted it. Matt, it seemed, was a coffee person, and Tori noted that he took it black. No cream or sugar.

She herself didn't like coffee. She had enough energy without it.

She introduced Matt to the guests as her 'friend' and everybody talked about their plans for the day. When the guests settled into talking to each other, she turned to Matt. "I have some plans for us today if you have time," she said.

"I have all week," he said. He reached over and squeezed her hand.

"I'd love to take you into town, and we can look around. I'll give you the native resident's tour of St. Ives. Then we can have lunch at this little café I love, and when we come back, I need to start training a young horse. I'd like for you to help. Or watch. Or whatever makes you the most comfortable."

She realized she was rambling. "I'm sorry. I—"

Matt laughed. "Don't apologize. There's nothing I'd love more than the 'native resident's tour' of St. Ives," he said, making air quotes with his fingers. "But only if you let me buy lunch."

"It's a deal."

After breakfast, she climbed in his car, and they headed off toward town.

"Let's talk about the paintings later," she said. "I want to show you around first." She knew they needed to have a discussion, but she was confident that Matt would see her side of things. He didn't have another showing until the weekend, so she felt they had plenty of time.

"Sounds like a plan," Matt said.

Hopeful Farm was about twenty minutes outside of St. Ives. Tori still had a St. Ives mailing address, but was away from the hustle and bustle of town and the many tourists it brought in every summer.

She had him park near the harbor. As they got out of their car, they saw a mix of fishing boats, charter boats, and yachts heading out to the lake. Coming along at the rear was a big sailboat, its green and yellow sails catching the morning sun.

"It's beautiful here," said Matt. He pulled out his phone and took a photo of the sailboat. "In case I need inspiration for a painting later," he explained.

She took his hand. It felt so natural to touch him, like he had been a part of her life forever.

She led Matt up a hill and along the shoreline.

"Where are we going?" Matt asked.

"Up this hill," she said. She had taken her sandals off in the car and slipped into some white tennis shoes. "I hope you're in shape." But it was only a small dune that rose just above the harbor. They were at the top in about five minutes.

On the dune stood a gray statue of a woman, the edges of the stone softened from weathering. The woman's long dress billowed out behind her, caught permanently in the wind. Her hands were folded together in a position of prayer. Her head was bowed, but her eyes looked up over the vast expanse of Lake Michigan.

"Here's the best place to start your private tour," Tori said. "Right here with St. Ives herself."

Matt looked at the statue, which was about the height of two men. It has been erected one hundred and three years ago, and at the statue's feet was a plaque.

St. Ives
Patron of sailors
Prayer warrior of the town

"Is she a real saint?" Matt asked.

"Not at all, at least not officially," said Tori. "Her name was Mary Ives. She lost her husband and only son to Lake Michigan when their fishing boat sailed off and a sudden storm came up. They, nor the boat, were ever seen again. But Mary came up here every day to pray and gaze out over the lake. After more than a year passed, she accepted their deaths and had a gravestone erected it the town cemetery with their names on it. But she continued to come up here every day, praying for those who were out fishing. The town at that time was just a harbor with no official name. Its residents made a living by fishing. Mary became a well-known figure and there wasn't a day that went by that you couldn't look up on the hill and see her praying. It comforted those who had loved ones out on the water.

"They say she was out here in any kind of weather, and that you could hear her pleading with God during storms. But I don't know how much of that is true."

Matt shook his head. "Seems to me she could have gotten struck by lightning."

"Hey! Don't mock our history," said Tori, feigning insult. "She came up here until her death at the age of eighty-eight. Some say she died here on the hill praying, but I looked her death record up and she died of pneumonia during the winter in her bed."

"Hmm."

"If people were lost during the storms, she'd take their grieving widows and children baskets of food. She was a town icon. When she died, so many people came to her funeral that there was standing room only in the church. The line strung outside and wrapped around the building."

"That's amazing," said Matt. He took a few photos.

"So, the townsfolk erected a statue and named the town after her," said Tori. "St. Ives."

She saw Matt looking intently at the statue and then beyond it to the lake.

"I'd love to paint this," he said.

"Maybe we can come back up here another day," said Tori. "I'd love to see you work."

He ran his fingers over the stone, tracing the billowing dress. "I've often wondered how sculptors do it. It looks so real, like it really is blowing in the wind. Maybe I'll try working with clay someday."

They walked back down to their car. Tori asked Matt to drive them a few blocks into town.

"Turn here," she said as they approached MacIntosh Street. She pointed out the red brick building that was her high school.

"This your school?" Matt asked.

Tori nodded. "I was on the homecoming court. Didn't quite make queen. But I had the most *gorgeous* dress!"

He slowed down, and she explained where the gym was, and the theater, and which window led to her favorite teacher's classroom.

"Did you have a high school sweetheart?" he asked.

Tori shook her head. "I dated a few guys and went to prom with a guy named Joel," she said. "But I didn't have time for them. Horses were my life."

She asked him to turn left at the next street and circle back into the downtown area. "When we met, Tim had no idea I was just nineteen. He showed interest in me and I just went along. It was flattering that an older man was flirting with me. Then we went on a date. Then another. Because I didn't go to college and was working, he assumed I was at least twenty-three. And by the time I told him my age, it didn't matter. We were in love. Oh! Turn here!"

"You didn't go to college?" Matt asked.

"No," Tori said. "I didn't need to. I knew exactly what I wanted to do, and I had a great job as the head trainer at Prescott Stables, just north of here. I trained their Arabian show horses. Emma didn't go to college either. She volunteered for a non-profit over the summer after her senior year, and it turned into a paid position. Then she met her husband,

100

married, and went off to New York to run charity events as a volunteer. She loves it."

"I went to the University of Chicago," Matt said. "Art School."

"Have you always known you wanted to be an artist?" asked Tori. She had always known horses were her thing. Her dad used to read a story to her about a horse who couldn't neigh. It was a funny picture book and she had loved it. She'd asked for it every night and her dad had memorized it.

"Yes," Matt said. "My mom and dad got me an art kit when I was five, and I started sketching everything I saw. I was hooked. It had a bunch of freshly sharpened colored pencils in it, some ink pens, paper, chalk. Everything. I love art supplies, and this might sound really geeky but office stores and craft stores are one of my favorite places to shop because of all the different colored ink pens. Art stores are great too, but there's more variety in the other stores because they have art for everyone. I still love to open a fresh box of crayons."

"The big one with the pencil sharpener in the back!" said Tori. She used to sit for hours and color with her mom.

"Yes!"

"Park here," she said, pointing at an empty spot in front of the town's soap and candle shop. It was unusual to find a spot during tourist season. Matt pulled in and shut off the car.

"My lavender fields produce the oils that go into Camilla's soaps and candles," said Tori. She loved the smell of Camilla's store.

She took him in. The mixed aroma of lavender, vanilla, and citrus greeted them. It wasn't overpowering; just enough to let them know they were in a shop that sold scents. Tori took a deep breath, inhaling the smell and feeling the lavender working its relaxing magic.

A woman about Tori's age stood behind the cash register. Her short, dark hair was cut just above her shoulders, and she had big, round blue eyes. She heard them come in and turned her head, her long, dangling earrings swinging.

"Tori!" she said, coming over to give her a hug.

"Cam, this is Matt," Tori said. "He's a friend of mine. And an artist."

"Welcome!" Cam said, then had to turn her attention to a customer.

Tori showed Matt around the shop, stopping to hold up candles and essential oils for him to smell. "The lavender all comes from my fields," she said happily. "And we ship all over the United States."

"Do you harvest it yourself?" Matt asked.

Tori shook her head. There was no time for that with running the bed and breakfast and training horses. "I hire the work out. And then sell it to people like Camilla here who make their own products. Her line is called 'Heaven Scents'."

"Very cool," Matt said.

Tori took him in a few more of the little shops, telling him about the owners and the wares. He seemed to be enjoying himself. "Most everything is locally grown," she said. She felt her stomach growling. "Hungry?"

He nodded, so she walked across the street to Louie's Sandwich Shop.

"Have the local homemade clam chowder," she said.

"I wasn't aware clamming was a thing here in St. Ives," Matt teased.

"Louie is from Boston. The clams are probably from there as well, but we don't ask because it's so good."

"Lots of myths in this town."

"Mmmmhmmm."

They sat at a little table near the window. The sidewalks were busy with people walking around, carrying shopping bags or holding ice cream cones. The restaurant was busy too and they were lucky to have gotten a seat.

She ordered a cup of the clam chowder and a turkey breast sandwich. He ordered the turkey club and a big bowl of clam chowder.

"You're going to love it," she said.

She smiled at him, happy to be here. The sun was coming in, making a streak of light in the middle of their table. While they waited for their food, he pulled a small sketch book out of his pocket and opened it. Taking out a charcoal pencil from the pages, he looked up at her and started to sketch.

"What are you drawing?" she asked, trying to see. But he blocked it with his hand.

"You."

She felt a little bit self-conscious as she tried to sit still for him.

"Relax," he said. "You can move around. It doesn't bother me."

The waitress brought them their drinks. Iced tea with lemon slices. She opened a packet of sugar and stirred it in.

By the time their food came, he was finished. He turned the book around and removed his hand.

The picture was breathtaking. Tori saw herself mirrored on the paper, her eyes bright, a smile beginning on her lips. Her hair was pulled back with a few strands loose from the band. He had added dimension to her cheeks and somehow captured the natural light from the sun, making her skin glow. All in pencil.

"Wow," she breathed. "It's beautiful." She lifted a hand and self-consciously smoothed her hair. "Kind of like how those models have their faces air-brushed."

"I beg your pardon," Matt said, smiling and leaning back in his chair. "I drew you *exactly* how you look. No need to air brush lines here."

She glanced down at it again, then back to his face. It was an amazing drawing and he had done it so quickly.

"You're good."

"You're beautiful," he said.

Her heart rate picked up. She realized he probably had been sketching her for years. She wondered how many sketches of her he had in his studio back home.

"Do you have a lot of these back home?"

"Of you?"

She nodded.

"No," he said quietly, folding his notebook closed and putting it away. "None. I never wanted to try to capture your face. I kept it in my memories, afraid if I tried to put it on paper, I'd lose it somehow. Without you there to draw it from."

She swallowed. It was so personal, being sketched. Like he looked at her and really *saw* her.

"Now," Matt said, picking up his spoon. "I'm going to try this clam chowder and let you know if it's up to par. I've eaten clam chowder all up and down the east coast."

Tori laughed, glad he had lightened the mood. "You won't be disappointed," she said. Then, she bit into her sandwich and silently thanked God for bringing this incredible man into her life.

Chapter Fourteen

Dinner was seasoned fried chicken, cornbread, and a garden salad with dried cherries. Matt thought he could live here forever if Phyllis was the cook. The woman had a gift in the kitchen.

He enjoyed visiting with the guests. One guy named Ted was a photographer, and he and Matt got in a great discussion about light. Matt saw Tori drift off, losing interest, and she began a conversation with Ted's wife Tina about the antique shops in town.

Matt was full when he pushed aside his dessert plate, leaving only a small bite of the cherry pie and vanilla ice cream. "I'm going to get fat if I eat here all week," he said.

"Nonsense," said Tori. "I've eaten this way for years, and I'm not fat."

Tori was slim and the muscles in her arms and legs were well toned. She also had a healthy tan from all the work she did outside, but she always had a hat on then. He supposed it was to protect her face from the sun.

"You'll have to teach me your secrets," he said.

She got up and stretched as one couple retreated into the living room to sit.

"Grab a magazine, Tina!" Tori shouted from the kitchen. "There's a new *Country Market* out there somewhere. Check the coffee table. You'll love the section on antiques."

He noticed that she treated her guests casually, like family. Like they lived here. He figured that was one of the appeals of the place and why she had so many repeat guests. She told him that she and Phyllis gotten to know some of the guests over the years and looked forward to their return every year.

105

When the other couple decided to go down to the beach, Tori reminded the woman to grab a sweater. "There's one of mine on the back porch if you don't have your own," Tori said.

Matt was being treated as family as well. Only in a different way—in the kitchen.

"Help us clean up," said Tori. "And then I want to show you something."

He didn't mind helping at all, and it felt good that she assumed he would. Just like he belonged here. For a brief moment, he let his mind wonder what it *would* be like to live here. With Tori.

Afterwards, she took his hand and led him to her bedroom. As much as she pulled him into her bedroom, a guy could get the wrong idea. But it did seem like the only really private spot in the house.

"There's an easier way to get to this," she said, "but the stairs are broken. So I go this way." She pushed open her bedroom window and climbed out.

"What are you doing?" he asked, then remembered the long stretch of widow's walk.

"Come on!" she said.

He climbed out her window, standing beside her on a narrow walkway with a railing. The wind was blowing her hair back and billowing her dress. Standing there, she reminded him a little bit of the statue of St. Ives.

"Look," she said, pointing.

He looked out across Lake Michigan and the sun set, which was deepening into a brilliant orange.

They stood there together, watching, as the giant orb dipped into the water, and a soft twilight started moving up the beach.

She looked so pretty. He tried not to stare.

"This house has had three generations of women living here, standing here, watching for their lovers to come home," she said. "I can't imagine living like that, always wondering. It would be terrible."

"Do you believe in love at first sight?" Matt asked quietly.

She hesitated. He saw her swallow. "Yes," she said in a whisper. "Sometimes."

The scent of lake water and lavender mingled up from the ground, caressing his senses, and he closed his eyes. He felt like he belonged here, in this house, with this woman. It felt like he had finally come home.

He wanted to tell her, but he was afraid to.

"Look," Tori said.

He opened his eyes. She nodded toward the sky, and he looked out toward the beach. The stars were coming out against the fading colors of the sunset. The sky was incredible.

"God's amazing handiwork," he said, turning. Their eyes met. A soft shaft of light drifted out from her window, probably from the dining room downstairs or a night light somewhere. It cast a silvery glow on her hair, outlining her cheekbones and putting a sparkle in her eyes. He pulled out his sketchbook.

"May I draw you?" he asked.

She laughed gently. "Right now?"

"Don't move."

She looked embarrassed, but also pleased. She stood still while he captured the light and the way it contoured around her. After about five minutes, he closed his notebook.

"Can't I see it?" she said.

"I don't usually share my work so early in the process."

He liked to sketch ideas and let them stew for a few weeks before painting them on canvas. This nighttime image of her was definitely something he wanted to capture in color.

Also, there was an intimacy to his work that few people understood. When he drew what he saw, it was also what he *felt*, and sharing it was like exposing a part of himself that he didn't let people see. Even with his finished paintings, there was always a vulnerability when he displayed them. Art was a part of him, a manifestation of his inner thoughts, dreams, and desires. Sharing his art was openly putting himself out there for criticism.

"Please?"

After a moment, he flipped opened the notebook and handed it to her. After all, he owed her. He had painted her many times without her permission. He watched her face as she carefully looked at the sketch, or what she could see of it in the dim light. Slowly, a smile appeared on her lips.

"I never realized I was this beautiful," she said. Her voice was full of wonder. "You've made me pretty."

"*God* made you pretty," he said. "I just captured it on paper."

She looked up at him. "It amazes me what you can *see*. I never realized I had this dimple. And the sketch you did today in the restaurant...you found just the right light to make me...*glow.*"

"I just draw what I see. It's all there. People just need to look."

"Sight is obviously your gift."

She handed it back to him. "I know what would be fun," she said, suddenly excited. He loved how quickly her enthusiasm rose. "Would you be willing to teach a class for a few hours to our guests this week? It's supposed to rain tomorrow morning, and it would give them something to do."

Matt had taught countless workshops across the country and even one in France a few years back. He could probably pull together a one or two-hour workshop here. Actually, it would be fun.

"Sure," he said. "I'll have to pick up some art supplies."

His phone buzzed. He ignored it.

"There's an art store in town. I think they're open until 9 p.m. tonight."

His phone buzzed again.

"You can answer that," Tori said.

Matt shook his head. But whoever had called hung up, then called again. He pulled it out of his pocket. It was Allison.

"It's the boss," he said, hitting the talk button. "Hey, Allison. You're on speaker phone."

"Matt! The *Washington Post* and the *New Yorker* both want to interview you! It can be done remotely, over the phone."

"Wow!" His career was sure taking a turn for the better. He glanced at Tori. Her eyebrows shot up.

"Should I set it up?" Allison said. "How's tomorrow morning?"

"That's great," Matt said. "Make it early. I have a painting class to teach later." He winked at Tori.

They settled on 8 and 9 a.m. He and Tori decided the class would start at 10 a.m. and she'd inform the guests at breakfast.

"Maybe you can talk to the reporter about your *other* work," Tori said. "Not about me and Hope."

"Maybe." That would be hard to do, but he'd give it a go. For Tori.

Then, he and Tori drove into town to get some art supplies.

The interview with the *Washington Post* was first. Matt sat at the small desk in an empty guest room and sipped a hot cup of coffee that Phyllis had given him.

"Tell us when you first saw the horse," the reporter said, starting right away on the topic of Hope. Matt had given countless interviews. They usually started with his current work and his how got started as an artist. This man, whose name was James, was jumping right in.

"Well," Matt said, stalling for time. He and Tori had talked further last night, and he agreed not to mention Hope's name or location, but that he could admit that his work was based on a real horse. "I saw her one year when I was on vacation."

"Up north?"

"Someplace quite remote," Matt said. That was all this guy was getting. "I was on an artists' retreat. A weekend getaway."

"Who else was there?"

"Some of the more well-known landscape artists," Matt said. To give names might offer too much information for a web search. Matt would have to be careful.

"Did you spend a lot of time with this mare?"

"I just saw her from afar," said Matt. Which was partially the truth. He had never ridden Hope, back then, or been into her stall, exactly. "Her beauty is what captured me."

"And the lavender that is in many of the paintings," said James. "I imagine the smell was incredible."

"It was," Matt said carefully.

"Let's talk about the woman," James said. "Who is she?" James was direct, that was for sure.

"Everyone has a dream woman," said Matt. "She's mine."

"*Is* she real?" James persisted. "I assume this is the horse's owner?"

Matt didn't like to lie. He had grown up in a family that counted trust and truth paramount to anything else. It only took one lie to break down trust, but a lot of truths to build it back up. *If* trust ever *could* be built back up. His mother had pressed that into his conscience since he was very young.

He remembered when he was four years old, he had lied to his mom. She had told him not to take a second cookie for dessert and had set the cookie jar up high. Later, when she walked outside and down the driveway to get the mail, he saw his chance. He dragged a chair over to the counter, took out not one but *two* cookies, and shoved them in his mouth. They were the best things he had ever tasted, and he felt mighty proud of himself. He pushed the chair back to the table, still chewing, and was sitting on it, hands folded, when his mother returned with the mail.

"You got a letter from Grandma!" she said, handing him a red envelope. His birthday was in three days and he'd be five. He tore it open, and five one-dollar bills fell out. He knew then that everything was going to be okay. He had clearly sinned and nothing bad was happening to him. No repercussions! As a matter of fact, he had gotten *money!* He was having a bonus day!

The afternoon wore on, and his mother never missed the cookies. He had almost forgotten about them when she came in his room just before dinner.

He was sitting on the floor playing with his toy dinosaurs.

"Matt? Did you take more cookies?"

He looked up at her and shook his head no. He hadn't left any evidence. He had this covered.

"Hmm," his mom said. "Because there were four left, and I was planning on them for dessert tonight. One for me, one for your dad, one for your brother, and one for you."

He hadn't known there were only four left. Now there were only two. That was a problem.

"Oh," he said, and shrugged.

"Are you *certain* you didn't have any?" his mom asked.

He couldn't look at her. He only nodded.

She left, and later they ate dinner. After dinner, she set the cookie jar on the table.

"There are only two cookies left," she said. "Two of you can have a cookie and two of us will have to go without."

Matt's little brother, only two-and-a-half at the time, grabbed a cookie before anybody else could move.

"Okay," Matt's mom said. "Larry has one. Is anyone willing to go without?"

Matt swallowed. He loved his parents very much.

"I can go without," his dad said.

"I guess I can too," said his mom. She handed Matt the last cookie.

This was working out well. He not only got away with stealing two cookies earlier, but now he was getting a third.

Bu he couldn't eat it. He looked at the people he loved, sitting across the table from him, without a cookie. The guilt was strong.

What could he do?

Then, he broke his cookie in two, handing half to his mother and half to his father.

"Oh, what a good boy we have!" his mother said.

They looked so happy to have a piece of cookie, and they praised him over and over until the guilt was too much. Matt confessed. He told them all about his cookie theft. Then his parents explained to him about how hard it was to rebuild trust once broken. He never forgot that lesson, nor how sad he had felt knowing he had hurt his parents.

Lying didn't work for him.

When he got older, he realized that his mother had probably played up that whole role, knowing the entire time that Matt had stolen and lied. But that didn't change the fact that he had learned a lesson. He hated to lie.

"Matt?" James said again. "I asked who the woman is?"

Matt cleared his throat. "She's not my lover, if that's what you want to know. Let's move on to the next question. I'd like to tell you how I work with light and give you a few examples of the uses in some of my newer paintings."

The interview didn't finish well. James was only interested in two things: the identities of Hope and Tori. When he didn't get these, he ended the interview.

The *Washington Post* interview went similarly. Only he *did* take the time to ask Matt about his upcoming shows.

Matt hung up and stretched. He was disappointed in both of the interviews. He felt like he had wasted the morning and now it was almost ten o'clock. At least *now* he could go do something he was good at—teaching art. When he walked into the dining room, he was pleased to see that four of the guests were there, sitting in chairs in front of their canvases.

"How did it go?" Tori asked.

"It went okay," he said.

"Did you talk about me and Hope?"

"I skirted the issue."

"Good. Thanks." she said. "I can't stay for the class. I have some work to do in the barn."

She smiled, unsure, and he felt like she wanted to give him a kiss goodbye. Then she left. He stood in front of the small group and pushed the nagging thoughts of the interviews to the back of his mind. Now it was time to do what he loved.

"All right," he said, clapping his hands together. "Let's get started!"

Chapter Fifteen

Tori was bummed she had to miss Matt's class, but she was quite behind on her work with the horses. She spent the morning in the barn, then had lunch with Matt and the guests. Matt got several more phone calls from Allison, which he stepped out of the room to take. The guests were all talking about their own paintings from his class, and the artwork was quite pretty, sitting on easels, drying. After lunch, Matt went upstairs to work in an empty guest room that Phyllis provided him for the day, and Tori went back to the barn.

It wasn't until after dinner that Tori finally got some time alone with him.

"I'm so bummed that I had to miss your class!" she said.

"I have a solution to that," Matt said, and cheerfully led her through the house to the mudroom, where he had a packed canvas tote bag. "Get your shoes on, grab a sweater, and let's go!"

She followed him down the dunes and north up the beach a little way, to the private spot they had found earlier in the week. He found a clear, sandy spot that was a little sheltered from the wind by some driftwood and surrounded by tall grasses. Then he reached into the bag, unfolded an easel, put a canvas on it, and handed her a brush. He opened a case of paints that reminded her of the ones that came in paint-by-number sets. There were twelve colors, linked together in little tubs. Then he positioned her in front of the canvas, on a tall stool that he had carried down.

"We're going to paint the sunset," he said.

The day had cleared up by noon, and the sun had come out. Tonight's sunset was beautiful. She gazed across the water at the deep purples and swirling clouds and saw a bird fly across the giant orange orb that was just above the water's edge.

Matt had prepped the canvas by painting it blue, the color that the sky was now.

"Paint," he said. "Just a circle, like you see the sun."

She found the color orange and painted a big circle in the middle of her canvas.

Matt poured some water from a plastic bottle into a small container and told her to rinse her brush. Then he set it down next to her paints.

"Now, add some color," he said.

She dipped in some purple and began painting it along the top edge of the sun, trying to capture the clouds she was seeing. But her work looked stilted and the edges were hard.

"Like this," Matt said. He stood behind her and took her right wrist in his. Leaning into her, he moved her arm up and around, swirling the purple into the top of the orange ball she had painted. His abs were tight, and she could smell his aftershave. Something subtle; woodsy with a hint of musk. She was acutely aware how close he was.

Then, holding her hand, together they carefully dipped her brush in the water, rinsed, and then he added some blue. As he showed her how to blend the colors, the painting transformed into something that was quickly resembling the sunset. Moving down to the bottom of the painting, he guided her hand in quick strokes, creating the water's surface. They rinsed again and added some white, swirling until the blue and white turned into waves. All the while, he held her wrist in his hand, his body up against hers.

They rinsed in water again. The sun was halfway down now, just a half pie shape resting on the water. "Let's capture the color before it's gone," Matt said. Dipping into red, he leaned into her and guided her arm in a circular motion, mixing into the still-wet orange, blending. The warmth of his body felt good up against hers as the temperature dropped in the air.

He leaned into her, his arm outstretched along hers, moving her arm in sweeping motions. His chest was against her, the steady rhythm of his heartbeat pulsating. She closed her eyes and let him guide their movement, as together they created something beautiful. She realized she was breathing with him, like she had done so many times on horseback with an animal she was bonded to.

She pressed herself back against him and she felt him pause. He released her arm and put the brush down. He sat down behind her on the small stool, pulling her against him and wrapping his arms around her waist.

"It's beautiful," he whispered into her ear.

"Yes," she said, still not opening her eyes.

His touch was filling her senses, his breathing, his heartbeats, in sync with hers. Their bodies fit together perfectly, with her back against his chest in a slight, soft curve, like spoons. She leaned more into him and felt a deep hunger inside her, awakening something that had been asleep for so long. Or maybe forever.

Then he was kissing the back of her neck. She leaned her head back against him, her neck exposed, and felt his soft beard caressing it as he kissed her more.

"I love you," he said.

His words didn't surprise her. This man, who had turned her world upside down twice now, who had never forgotten about her, felt like a gift brought to her after so long alone.

"I love you too," she said. And she meant it. She had never felt like this before, *ever.* She thought of soulmates and wondered if this was what it was like to have one. She felt so at home, so comfortable with Matt, like they had known each other forever.

His long fingers found her hand and clasped it, entwining his fingers in hers. Those fingers that brought life to canvas, that had revealed his love for her long before he expressed it in words.

A gull cried somewhere in the distance, and she could feel the last rays of the sun on her face, warming her before they disappeared.

Then a voice called to them, loud, harsh, down the beach.

"TORI!"

She opened her eyes, sitting up straight, as Phyllis's voice jerked her back to reality.

115

"One of the horses has colic! It's not Hope, but we need you!"

Tori stood, waving at Phyllis. "I'll be right there!" she shouted down the beach.

She turned to Matt. "I gotta go," she said. "One of the horses is sick."

"Sure," he said. "I'll pack up. You go on ahead."

She gave him a quick kiss on the check, reluctant to leave, then turned and ran up the beach toward the barns.

It was one of the young horses she was supposed to start training with this week. The vet came and gave a painkiller and offered the usual prescription: walk him until he poops.

Colic was gastric distress, and horses had sensitive stomachs, so it wasn't uncommon. Because horses can't vomit, the problem had to be relieved through the back end. In some cases, it was merely gas or constipation, or they had eaten something that didn't agree with them. In more serious cases, the colon could twist, and that almost always meant death.

To promote a bowel movement (which could unplug the problem or release the gas), one had to walk the horse, sometimes for hours, and not let the animal lay down. Because of the stomach pain, most horses wanted to lay down and roll, but that could only create more problems, usually a twisted gut.

So Tori spent the next two hours walking Jax around. Matt took turns with her. It was nearly midnight before she felt comfortable putting the colt in his stall.

"I'll spend the night in the barn," said William, because Jax couldn't be left alone. "When Phyllis called me, she said it would probably be an all-nighter, so I'm prepared to stay. I know you have other things to do tonight."

"No, I can stay. He's my responsibility," argued Tori.

"Phyllis insisted," said William. He cocked his head in the direction of Matt, who was down the aisleway filling water buckets for the other horses. "Enjoy yourself, Tori. Go tend to your guest."

Tori was grateful. They went inside, and there were cherry scones on the table with a note from Phyllis to enjoy them. The guests were all in bed. Matt picked one up and took a bite.

"Perfect snack after an evening of walking."

"I really appreciate your help," Tori said. "We got our exercise in tonight." She felt oddly shy in front of him, after their encounter on the beach. And yet she wanted more.

"We did. And I'm glad the colt is feeling better."

He turned to her and took her hands in his. "I should go. All of my things are at the hotel."

Tori nodded.

"I'll see you tomorrow?" Matt asked.

"Yes," she said. "How about I teach you to start a horse? Since you taught me to paint?"

"Is it going to be as much fun?" he asked.

She giggled. "I can *make* it fun."

They kissed goodbye, and Tori watched his car work its way down the driveway and turn onto the road. The headlights disappeared into the darkness.

She sighed and closed the door, locking it behind her. She felt light, happy and free. She went upstairs and got ready for bed.

On the nightstand lay her bible. She opened it. On the first page, written in her mother's handwriting, was a verse:

"For I know the plans I have for you," declares the Lord, "plans to prosper you and not harm you, plans to give you hope and a future."
Jeremiah 29:11

How many times had she read that verse? All those years with Tim, all the time lost to fear and anxiety. Then the years of guilt following his death. But now, maybe the Lord was letting her live again. Maybe he had brought Matt into her life so she could finally have love.

She lay there for a few minutes, pondering this new love, and reliving the moment on the beach.

Thank you, God, she prayed. *Please let this last.*

Then she closed her eyes, imagining Matt's arms around her, and soon she was fast asleep.

Chapter Sixteen

Matt called before breakfast to say he wouldn't be there until after lunch. He had to take care of some paperwork, and he wanted to get started on the painting of Tori in the moonlight. Plus, he knew that he was keeping Tori from her work.

She sounded disappointed, but she agreed. They both had stuff to do.

"I love you," he said before they hung up.

"I love you too."

He couldn't believe how happy those words made him.

Because of the pickup in business, Allison had things for him to sign, and she wanted to tweak his tour schedule. Apparently, a few more cities wanted him to visit.

"Allison, about that," he said. "Tori wants me to pull the paintings from the tour."

Allison was a woman who was usually careful with words. He heard the long pause and knew she was weighing how to respond. Finally, she said, "I was afraid this was coming."

He didn't answer. Delaying gave her time to think. Matt had already thought it through and knew what her answer would be.

"Does she also want to pay your bills?" Allison said, a little sharply. "Because if you pull those paintings, you'll lose bookings. Probably *all* of them."

"You think?" he said. He remembered Tori's touch on the beach. The trust in her eyes. The love.

"Definitely," Allison said. "I *know*."

She was right. He had been in this business long enough to know that when you had something hot, you played it out until the end. And this series of paintings was hot. If he

118

canceled, he'd anger the gallery owners who were counting on his showings and probably still demand he pay in full for the rented space. He'd lose fans as they lost interest in *him*. And the work he was most proud of in his life would do what? Sit in a closet somewhere?

"She has no legal grounds to make you," Allison said. Then her voice softened. "I know Tori means something to you, Matt. Can you try to talk her out of it? If you explain to her that it's your livelihood and she would be destroying you, she may understand. If you mean as much to her as she does to you, she won't want to hurt you. Right?"

Matt thought about Tori. He didn't doubt she cared for him. This week together with her was the best of his life. He knew he couldn't live without her, but she was asking a lot of him to remove them.

"Let's at least confirm our bookings," Allison said when he didn't answer. "We can always cancel later. You have until the weekend before the Traverse City showing."

"Which doesn't give us much time," Matt said.

"Then you need to talk to her now. I'll go ahead and book the new offers while your work is still hot."

He agreed and spent the morning on the phone with Allison, setting up flights and his schedule. Then he had a little time left over, so he started prepping the canvas for the painting of Tori in the moonlight.

When he finally pulled into the driveway of Hopeful Farm, he was wearing his most comfortable jeans, western boots, a gray t-shirt, and his Stetson. Basically what he wore to art gallery showings, minus the button-down. He knew he looked cool, (confirmed many times over by Allison) and he wanted to impress this cowgirl of his.

Tori was at the barn, leading the bay colt out of his stall.

"This is Flip," she said, introducing him again to the colt. Brown, with black legs, a black mane and tail, and a white blaze, Flip was all inquisitive eyes and ears. He reached his nose out to sniff Matt, then gave him a playful bump. Matt rubbed him between the eyes.

"How's Jax?" he asked.

"He's better. He was banging his grain bucket around this morning, demanding food."

Tori led the Flip out to the round pen. Once she and Matt walked through with the colt, she closed the gate and took off Flip's lead rope.

She moved to the center of the ring, and Matt stayed beside her. Flip tried to follow and she waved him away.

"There's a magic line on a horse's body that makes him move forward or not," she said. "Standing here, draw a straight line from his shoulder to you. This is the line you're going to use. So, if you stand behind his shoulder (this line), he will feel like you are pushing him forward. If you move in front of that point, you can get him to stop and turn."

She made a clucking noise, stepped behind the point of his shoulder, and just as she had predicted, Flip moved forward in a counterclockwise trot around the rail. The colt's inside ear was cocked toward her, listening. She kept him trotting around the perimeter of the ring a few times, then she stopped moving, stepped in front of him, and said, "Whoa."

Flip stopped and turned to face her.

She moved to her left, which put her on the other side of that "magic line" with him. He turned, and she clucked again. He started trotting clockwise.

She didn't have a rope or any other method for controlling him. She just used her body language. Matt was fascinated.

She stepped on the other side of the magic line, and Flip stopped. He turned to face her, pricking his ears and watching her.

"He's asking me what I want him to do next," said Tori. "I'd let you try, but at the moment, I've established myself as the head. I'm in charge."

"Aren't you always?" Matt teased.

In less than an hour, Tori had the horse responding to her body language and voice signals to walk, trot, and canter both ways of the ring. He would also stop on command and come into the center of the ring to stand next to her.

The horse had a light sweat on him, and Matt was feeling warm in the sun. He was glad for his hat. Today, Tori had on a Kentucky Horse Park baseball cap, her hair pulled back in a ponytail. He had always found women in baseball caps attractive. Maybe because he loved baseball. Tori wiped her palms on the front of her jeans. She was sweating as well.

"Pay attention to the horse," she said, giving Matt a gentle nudge with her elbow. He realized he had been staring at her.

"Sorry," he said.

Flip was standing next to Tori, his muzzle against her side.

"He's different than working with a wild horse," she said. "He grew up trusting people, so really, I am just teaching him stuff today. Because he's been here a few weeks, he knows me." She scratched Flip on the withers. His upper lip curled in blissful response. "I don't have to earn his trust first. So this next part will be easy."

She brought in a small box about two-by-two-foot square and set it in the middle of the ring. Flip sniffed it, then looked bored.

Tori moved him so that his back was lined up with the block, and then she stood on it. That way, she was tall enough to lay across his back. She gently lifted herself up and onto her stomach, and stretched across him, her arms dangling off one side, her legs the other. Flip turned to sniff her boot.

"Shouldn't you have a bridle or some sort of control?" Matt asked.

"I have plenty of control," Tori said quietly. "We're friends, Flip and I." She made a show of patting his sides and wiggling around on him. When the movement didn't seem to faze him, she swung her leg around and sat up, straddling him.

"And now he has his very first rider," she said, a big smile on her face. "Ta-da!" she raised her arms over hear head in triumph. Flip craned his neck around so he could sniff at her boot again. She told him what a good boy he was, and rubbed his neck, finding his itchy spots and scratching them. The horse was in ecstasy, thoroughly relaxed and enjoying this.

Tori wiggled around on her seat some more, rubbing him with her hands, sliding her legs back and forth against his sides, shifting her weight. None of it fazed Flip.

After a while, she slid off. Then she pulled some carrots out of her jeans pocket and handed them to Flip.

As the horse was munching them, Matt put his hands on her waist and pulled her to him, kissing her. "That," he said, "was one of the coolest things I've ever seen."

"You think *that's* cool," she said. "Wait until you see me ride a wild mustang."

"Seriously?"

"Yeah."

He kissed her again and felt Flip give him a playful nudge with his nose.

"Somebody's jealous," Matt said.

His phone vibrated in his pocket. He pulled it out.

"It's Allison. Do you mind if I answer this?"

"No," Tori shook her head. "Go ahead. We're finished with Flip."

"Hi Matt," Allison said. "Have you spoken with Tori yet? I need to confirm Traverse City."

Matt stepped over to the side of the arena, out of earshot.

"I'm working on it," he said quietly.

"I have to get moving on this." Allison's voice was gentle, but firm. "You need to talk to Tori *now*."

He hung up. Tori was rubbing Flip's neck.

"What's up?" she said, her expression worried. His face must be giving him away.

"That was Allison. She needs to tell the Traverse City people what to expect this weekend."

Tori brushed a stray lock of hair behind her ear. "Tell them you'll have all the *other* paintings on display and show them a wonderful example of the use of light," she said lightly.

Matt put his phone back in his pocket. "You realize what you're asking of me?"

Tori nodded. "I'm sorry, Matt. It's just…I don't want the publicity."

"It won't be publicity, Tori. I won't ever reveal your name. Or Hope's."

"That's not the point," she said. "You won't *need* to. These things have a way of getting out. Someday, someone will see Hope in one of my books, and match her up with the horse in your paintings."

"Tori, I'm booked for the next several months, here in the Midwest and then later on the west coast. This is the biggest tour I've ever given, and I'm getting paid work because of it. A *lot* of paid work. Do you have any idea how difficult it is for an artist to survive? These paintings have *made* me."

Tori turned to Flip and busied herself with smoothing his forelock down. Matt couldn't see her face.

"So what you're saying is they're more important than *me?*" Tori said quietly.

"No."

"But you *are*," she said. She snapped the lead rope to the horse's halter and turned back to Matt.

"Tori—"

"Matt, *no*. Look, I was trying to be nice about this, because you...you mean something to me. And I understand that those paintings mean something to *you*. And yes, I know what I'm asking of you. I'm not an idiot. But this is one time you need to think about someone else."

He felt a flare of anger. "I *do* think of people other than myself. I thought of you for *four whole years!*"

"And I never asked you to paint me! *Never!* I never wanted any of this!"

So there it was. This was how she felt.

They had both raised their voices. Flip didn't like it. The colt snorted, shaking his head.

"I can't do what you're asking," Matt said, more quietly.

Tori folded her arms across her chest, one hand still holding Flip's lead rope. "So this whole week has been a waste."

Matt felt the pang of hurt, like she had stabbed him, then angry at her words. "A *waste?* Is that what this week was about? To soften me up, so I'd pull the paintings?" He remembered the porch swing and how she had skirted around to different topics. How she had avoided the issue several times. Was all the good food and...and...*flirting*...just for the sake of manipulating him?

"Is that what you think?" Tori said. "That I was playing you?"

"I don't know what to think!" he said.

Tori frowned. "Well, whatever. Just don't you dare put those paintings in the Traverse City showing!"

"Or what? You'll call Emma?"

That made her mad. He saw the hard set to her jaw, and she spun and took Flip into the barn. He followed her and stood by her as she hosed the horse off, and scraped the extra water off of him.

"Are you going to pay my bills?" he asked. "When I go broke?"

"You're exaggerating." She wouldn't look at him. He felt her closing herself off. Part of him knew it was a protective measure, probably because of what she had been through with her husband. But he couldn't seem to focus on that right now.

"Not really," he said. "I can't pull them. I can't."

She put Flip in his stall, and latched it. Then she turned to look at Matt.

"I think you need to leave. I should have known this couldn't work. I never should have kissed you four years ago. I was married, and stupid, and now everything is a mess."

"You want me to *leave?*" He felt the joy of the past week slipping away. She had only been after one thing.

He was deeply hurt. He had already put himself out on a limb several times, rushing here to see her, confessing his love to her. He had made a fool of himself painting her, obsessing over her.

And apparently she didn't care. Her love was conditional. Angry, he turned on his heel and walked quickly out of the barn. After a minute, he heard her coming after him.

"Matt, wait!" Tori said.

She followed him up the drive, to the front of the house where his car was parked.

"I can't believe you were *using* me," Matt said, "pretending to care in order to sway me!"

He jerked open his car door and got in.

"No! That's not true!" Tori said. "But *you* were using *me* to make money! And apparently that's more important to you than my privacy!"

Without looking at her, he started up the car, and turned to go down the long, winding drive. At the end of the driveway,

124

he glanced back and saw Tori standing at the head of the driveway, watching him. She had her arms crossed over herself. Matt faced forward and drove, not looking back again.

Chapter Seventeen

Tori bit her lip, trying not to cry as she watched Matt's car pull out of the driveway and disappear. Then she ran upstairs to her bedroom, shut the door, and lay down on her bed. She remembered the many times she had cried into her pillow because of Tim. And now Matt.

She hated herself for falling in love again.

She understood he had a valid point. Painting was his livelihood, and she was asking him to cancel his tour. But didn't he see the greater harm it was doing, exposing her and her farm to the world? She wanted to keep the privacy and serenity of their farm. That's why she lived so far out in the middle of nowhere. And the quiet was part of the charm of the B&B and why her guests kept coming back.

Simon appeared from somewhere and curled up next to her, washing himself. His purr was comforting. She put her arm around him.

After she had cried herself out, she started to think about the moment on the beach, and Matt sketching her in the café. His feelings for her were real. She *knew* they were. She should never have accused him of money being his prime motivation. All she had to do was look into his eyes, or see the emotion in the paintings of her and Hope, to know he ran deeper than that. He truly loved her. The paintings told the story.

"Oh Simon, I've really messed things up," she said.

Matt had *told* her he loved her. And she had said it back. She thought about those words, and what they meant. It felt so natural to be with him, so comfortable. All these years she had thought she was fulfilled, working with her horses and running the B&B. But she had been missing something. Missing Matt.

She felt more complete when he was near her.

She realized then, how true it was, and how much she meant the words. She *loved* him. She had never felt this way about anyone else, not even Tim. She and Matt clicked in so many ways, and when he was with her it just felt *right*. It felt like she had found her best friend, and a big hole in her soul had filled.

And she had gone and ruined it. All over some future worry that may never come to pass. He wasn't *that* well known. People would probably never connect Hope to the horse in the paintings. And what if they did? She'd maybe get more B&B customers? What was she so afraid of? She was overreacting.

She didn't want to lose Matt. Not again.

She needed to call him now, before it was too late.

Her call went to voice mail. She left a message, apologizing and asking him to please call her. Then she went down to see if she could help Phyllis with dinner and saw the painting of the sunset. He had set it in the living room to dry.

"It's pretty," Phyllis said behind her. She jumped.

"Oh, Phyllis, I really messed this up."

Phyllis stood beside her, looking at the painting. "I saw him leave. You want to talk about it?"

"No."

"It'll be okay. Don't lose hope," she said.

Tori nodded, and they went into the kitchen to get dinner ready for the guests.

"I really don't want to talk about it, but I accused him of loving his work more than he loves me," Tori said. "I'm terrible."

Phyllis put her arm around Tori's shoulder and gave her a little squeeze. "No, not terrible. I think you're in love. Love scrambles your brain. And I truly think Matt loves you. I can tell by the way he looks at you. Come on. Let's get dinner ready."

Later, she tried Matt's number again, and a few more times before bed. It always went to voicemail.

She lay in bed, restless, thinking too much about Matt. Around midnight she finally fell asleep.

Tori awoke to a knock on her door.

"Tori," Phyllis stuck her head into the room.

Tori looked at her phone. It was 8 a.m.! She had forgotten to set her alarm, and thought gratefully of William, who would be feeding the horses. The guests would be having breakfast too.

"I hated to wake you, but Matt is here."

She sat up. "He's *here?*"

"Yes. Get dressed and come down. I'll get him some coffee to stall while you get ready."

Tori jumped out of bed and used the small bathroom that was part of her suite. She quickly brushed her teeth and ran a combo through her hair, pulled on a pair of jeans, her bra, a t-shirt, and ran downstairs barefoot, afraid he'd leave.

She stopped at the foot of the stairs. He was standing at the front door, holding a steaming mug of coffee.

Phyllis saw Tori and brought her a mug of tea. "Why don't you two take a morning stroll on the beach?"

Matt was wearing faded jeans and a polo. There were bags under his eyes, like he hadn't slept. She knew he had to drive up to Traverse City this morning and get ready for his showing tonight.

She accepted the mug of tea from Phyllis and walked toward him.

"Hi," she said.

"Hi," he said.

Neither of them said anything as they walked around the house and headed down one of the dunes. When they got to the water, Matt reached down and unlaced his tennis shoes and pulled them off.

"Let's walk," he said, nodding toward the water.

The water was cold on Tori's feet, but she was used to it. She wondered what he was here to say. Her heart was hammering and her stomach was knotted. It was good that at least he *was* here. But was this goodbye?

"Matt," she started.

"No, let me talk," he said. "I came to apologize. I can't cancel this weekend's art show, because of all the advertising that the city has done, and it would hurt a lot of people other than me. But I can cancel future ones. You matter the most to me. I'm passionate about my work, but Tori, I'm more passionate about *you*.

"We've really only been together a week, and I've been pushy. I painted you, I've confessed my love to you, and I shouldn't expect you to feel the same way or be caught up. I've thought about you for years. Not in a creepy way, but in the way that I knew my heart was always somewhere else. That was stupid, but I couldn't help it. I feel in love with you that day we met, four years ago, and I've never been able to feel the same way about another woman."

He wasn't looking at her. He was concentrating on the beach ahead. The gulls were out, fishing, and their cries were echoing. The wind was blowing, and the waves were erasing their footprints behind them as they walked.

"I said I don't expect anything from you. But the truth is, I guess I did. And I need to leave shortly to go to work, so I won't see you for a while. I just wanted you to know that I'm sorry, and that I am going to give you the time and space to figure out how you feel about me, or if you feel anything at all. And it's okay if you don't. And either way, I'll remove the paintings of you and Hope from my tour after this weekend. Or cancel the tour."

He stopped walking and turned to look at her. He met her eyes. "It's okay. The last thing you need is more guilt piled on you. So it's okay if you don't feel this way about me too. But I love you."

His blue eyes were searching hers, and she knew he was uncertain, and maybe even afraid.

The wind was playing with his hair, lifting the soft curls. He watched her, and she knew she had to say something. She had to set the record straight.

She set her mug down in the sand, then reached for his and placed it next to hers. She put her hands on his arms and felt the solid muscles underneath her palms. But it was his eyes she was searching.

"I love you too," she said. "I've never felt the way I did that day four years ago until now. This past week has been the most amazing week of my life. I love you, Matt Cheval. I love you with every inch of my heart."

His eyes lit up and a smile crossed his face. She pulled him to her then, and they kissed on the beach. He wrapped his arms around her, warming her, and she felt like she had finally come home.

Tori walked on air the rest of the morning. Matt had left shortly after the kiss on the beach, because he had to be in Traverse City by noon. She had explained, the best she could, that maybe she had over-reacted about the paintings. Maybe he could keep them in the shows. Maybe. They'd discuss it more after the Traverse City show. Matt promised to call her during the weekend, and they would make plans to see each other again.

She spent more time working with Flip that morning and was humming as she helped Phyllis with lunch. Then, she put the bridle on Hope and took her for a long ride bareback down the beach.

She was gone for several hours, just relaxing and thinking about Matt, knowing that she'd have to work horses on Saturday to make up for her lack of work this week. But she was so happy she could barely focus.

When she rode Hope up the sand dunes to the barn, there was a red car in the driveway. She wondered if they had an inquiring guest; they'd be disappointed because they were booked through Sunday.

She stopped Hope in front of the barn. The mare turned her head back to nuzzle Tori's foot. She bent down to pet the mare on the shoulder, and when she straightened, William was walking toward her with a man.

"This is Tori," William said. "She's the trainer you were asking about."

130

The man smiled, running his eyes over Hope. "She's beautiful," he said. "Is this your horse?"

Tori patted Hope on the shoulder. "Yes, she is. This is Hope."

The man was dressed in a t-shirt, blue jeans, and boots. He had a Detroit Tigers baseball cap pulled down on his forehead, shielding his eyes from the sun. He looked to be in his forties. He squinted up at her.

"How can I help you?" Tori said.

"My name is Brent Simmons," he reached up and offered his hand. His grip was strong.

"He has a young Arabian he wants started," William said.

Tori looked him over. He was dressed for the farm but had the look of a city guy. She had gotten good over the years at sizing up her clients. "You know anything about horses?"

He shook his head. "Nope. My daughter shows and one of our mares had a foal a few years back. My daughter needs help training him. He's a three-year old. Well mannered. We just need to teach him the basics."

"Sure," Tori said. "I'm finishing two young horses right now, but I have room to start a third. Maybe I can come by sometime next week and take a look?"

Simmons nodded. "We live just south of here." Then he dropped his eyes back to Hope.

"This is the mare from your book," he said.

"Yes."

"She's blind?"

"She is."

"I've read your book. It's pretty amazing how you use trust to work your horses. How you ask instead of tell."

Tori was a little impressed. Most people who stopped by hadn't taken the time to read her books. The ones who did usually trained their own horses, so she was surprised this inquiring dad had cracked open one of her covers.

"My daughter is fascinated. Maybe you can teach her some things at the same time. Hey, do you mind if I take a picture of Hope? For my daughter?"

"Not at all. You want me to dismount?"

Simmons shook his head. "This way my daughter will know what you look like when we meet." He pulled out his phone and snapped a few pictures. Hope posed, pricking her ears toward the sound of his voice and the camera.

"She sure is pretty," Simmons said.

"Thanks."

"How long have you had her?"

Tori thought about that. Tim had given Hope to her just after they married. "Eight years."

"Is she the horse in the paintings?"

Tori froze. Her heart started hammering.

"What paintings?"

"Those paintings by that artist Matt Cheval. You know, it's all over the news. She sure looks like that horse."

Tori swallowed, taking in a slow, deep breath so her discomfort didn't show. Hope shifted uneasily under her. "I don't know what you're talking about."

Simmons shrugged. He looked at his watch. "I need to get going. I just wanted to stop by and meet you. I'll be in touch."

Tori nodded and watched him get in his car. He gave one last wave as he drove off. The conversation had unsettled her. She looked at William. "What do you think?"

"I think you don't need more horses," said William. "But you've never listened to me." He winked at her, wiped his hands on the towel he was carrying, and headed back into the barn.

Tori sat there for a moment, letting the uneasy feeling in her belly settle. Then, she shook her head. It would be okay. It was only natural that he would recognize Hope. She was in Tori's book, and now the paintings were in the news. "Hope, I'm just weird," she said. "Too much emotional stuff in one week."

She got off her mare and led her toward the barn. Hope reached over and nuzzled Tori's arm, then gave a heavy sigh of contentment. All was well with the world.

Chapter Eighteen

There were tons of people at Matt's Friday evening showing in Traverse City. The gallery was along the main street, with the windows in the back opening up to a view of Grand Traverse Bay. The place was packed, and there were more people outside, waiting to get in.

He was always a little nervous about unveiling new work, but this was the first time he was nervous about a show that had been on the road for a month or two.

"Did you see the t-shirts?" Allison asked.

"What t-shirts?"

Allison pulled him over to a window and opened the blinds a crack. There were several people outside wearing shirts that said, "Who's the Mystery Horse?"

"You've got to be kidding," said Matt.

"This is great!" Allison said. "We've never had such attention. Even the mayor is coming tonight for your 6 p.m. talk."

Matt nodded, but he felt uneasy. This was too big.

"I hope none of this falls back on Tori," he said. "She doesn't want any attention." They had never finished the discussion about what to do with his future shows. He was holding out hope that she would tell him she would change her mind.

The gallery owner opened the ropes and people flowed in. Allison went out to work her magic. Matt stayed in the back room, watching through the slatted blinds as people browsed his work. There was security to make sure no one defaced anything, or that no crazies came in. He saw several people wearing the t-shirts.

Soon, it was time for his talk. He took a look at himself in the mirror, adjusted his hat, and went out in the crowd. Several reporters rushed over to him, flashing their credentials and asking questions that he wasn't ready to answer. He smiled and nodded politely the way Allison had taught him, but made his way through the crowd to the podium without talking.

When he was behind the mic, the crowd gathered around to listen. The doors were propped open in the back, so the people outside could hear. He wondered what the air conditioning bill would be after this.

The mayor came up front and stood next to Matt. He said a few words about the town and how grateful they were to have an artist of Matt's credentials here for three days.

Then Matt started talking, giving his spiel about his work. When he came to the part about "the Woman and the Horse" series, he stuck to the script he had memorized.

The crowd was polite. He relaxed and told them his story and the legend of the bloody-shouldered Arabian. As he wrapped up his thirty-minute talk, he asked for questions and braced for the usual "Who is the mystery horse/woman?" inquiries.

But that's not what happened. Instead, a man in the back raised his hand.

"Yes, sir?" Matt pointed to him.

"I know who the mystery horse is!" he announced. He began making his way to the front of the crowd. He looked to be in his forties, with short, graying, sand-colored hair. When he got to the front, he stood next to Matt. This had never happened before, and out of the corner of his eye, Matt saw Allison stiffen.

"I'm a reporter with the local paper, and we're about to make national news. The mystery horse is none other than Victoria's Hope, owned by Victoria Reynolds of St. Ives, MI."

Matt felt ice in his stomach. The man held up his phone, displaying a picture on the screen. The crowd leaned in to get a closer look. It was a picture of Tori on Hope. It looked recent.

"I never said that," Matt said, trying to save the moment, to protect Tori, to protect Hope.

"But it is," the man said. He had a brown envelope under his arm and opened it. He pulled out some eight-by-ten photos of Hope with Tori on her. "Here they are!"

There was murmuring in the crowd. Matt motioned for security, but the man side-stepped away and held up his phone. "We're going live now!" he said, and pushed a button. The security was on him then, their hands on his shoulders, escorting him outside.

"Is it true!" someone said. "That horse in these photos looks exactly like the one in the painting! Is Victoria Reynolds the mystery woman then?"

The crowd got noisy. Phones came out, with everyone taking pictures of Matt, of his paintings. Matt felt hands on him. It was Allison, pushing him toward the back, toward the safety of the office.

He heard people talking, people shouting. One person said Tori's name very loudly, and someone else said, "Let's get a comment from her!" He heard cameras going off and nearly stumbled in the flash of lights.

"Twitter is exploding already," said the gallery manger, his phone in his hand.

Allison pushed Matt into the office. "Call Tori," she said. "Call her now. I'll go fix this."

And she disappeared, closing the door behind her. He locked it, pulled his phone out, and looked at his Twitter account. The hashtag *#mysteryhorse* was trending. He already had twenty-five comments directed to his Twitter account. Same with his Instagram.

Panicked, he dialed Tori's number. He had to tell her before she found out any other way.

"Hello," she answered. Her voice was happy, sweet. He was about to upset her and he regretted it.

"They've figured out who Hope is," he said.

"What? How?"

"I don't know. There was a reporter here who announced it. He had a picture of you on Hope. It looked recent."

He could hear Tori take in a deep breath. She was a glass-half-full kind of person. Maybe she wouldn't be upset. Maybe she'd see how this was a good thing, how it could bring notoriety to her bed and breakfast. In his head, he was going over all of the ways that this could benefit her, so he could convince her that it was okay. It had to be okay.

"What did he look like?" Tori asked.

Matt described him.

"That's the man who was here today asking about my training!" she said, her voice rising in anger. "How dare he! He took pictures of Hope. He said it was for his *daughter!*"

"Twitter is exploding," Matt said. "It's going to be all over the news soon."

There was a pause. He could imagine Tori looking through her social media pages. "Matt, this is awful! What does this mean?"

"Well," he said, trying to think. "I'm not sure. Allison is doing damage control. I need to get back out there, but I wanted to tell you before you found out through social media."

"I'll bet he followed you."

"The reporter?"

"Yes. There should be no way people can connect us. Someone had to have followed you out to the farm. Were you careful?"

Matt thought about it. He hadn't seen anybody that seemed suspicious, but then again, he hadn't been *looking* for anyone. But he had never *had* to look behind him before. He should have been more careful. He should have known.

"He was driving a red car. Something sporty," Tori said.

Matt tried to think. He didn't remember a red car following him out to the farm from town. But again, he hadn't been paying attention.

"I don't remember seeing a red car," he said.

Tori sighed, sounding frustrated. "Okay. Well, the damage is done. I guess it doesn't matter how he found me."

"There are pictures of Hope in some of your books. Somebody could have matched the picture to the painting."

"Yeah."

Tori's voice was now quiet, almost a whisper, like she was exhausted. That horse meant the world to her.

"It'll be okay," he said.

"It will. Phyllis is always reminding me that God is in control and that nothing happens that He doesn't allow."

In Matt's experience, God could allow some pretty scary things to happen. He didn't mention this to Tori.

"I gotta go," Matt said.

"Okay. Love you."

"I love you too."

He hung up the phone just as Allison came through the door. "I have an idea," she said. "We need to stay ahead of this thing, so we'll act like we planned it. Like *we* revealed it. You must always appear to be in charge." She was all business. "Here's what we're going to do, and we need to do it as soon as possible."

Chapter Nineteen

It wasn't okay like Matt had promised. It wasn't okay at all.

Saturday morning, Tori woke at 6 a.m. to find her front yard full of reporters. There were at least a dozen out there.

Tori stuck her head out the front door, and cameras snapped, and several people started asking questions. Three of them were on the porch.

"You're trespassing," she said. "Get out of here."

They ignored her, so she called the police. She saw William's car. He was having trouble getting up the driveway because of all the cars. He crawled along slowly, weaving onto the grass several times, parked near the barn, and made his way in. He shut the gate behind him. At least no reporters were trying to get past the gate into the area near the barn at the moment. There was still some of decency. Tori thought about mobs she saw on television. If anybody went toward Hope…

She called William to ask if Hope was okay.

"She's happily eating her hay," he said. "No worries, Tori. I'm brandishing a pitchfork."

She tried to smile, but the reporters kept shouting questions at her from her front lawn. She stayed inside, just peeking through the front door a crack, and using her foot to keep Simon inside.

It was 6:30 a.m. when the two squad cars finally arrived. They beeped their sirens and fielded people out of the driveway. Phyllis arrived just behind them. Tori could see her surprised expression through the windshield. She rolled down her window.

"What's going on?" she asked as Tori made her way past to the police cars.

"Come on. I'll fill you in."

Phyllis got out of her car, and Tori was grateful for her presence. She explained to the police and to Phyllis about the "mystery reveal," and how she and Hope were now famous.

"What are we going to do? I can't run a business with this going on," Phyllis said, her hands on her hips.

Tori's phone rang with an unknown number. She answered.

"Tori, it's Allison, Matt's PR person."

"I'm being hounded by reporters!" Tori said.

"We're going to do a press conference," she said. "Matt and I will come down there to the farm, and you can show off the horse. He'll officially announce that his paintings are of Hope, then the hoopla will be over. Otherwise, you're going to have curious onlookers trying to figure out if it's her or not."

Tori looked around her at the reporters. Right now, it was manageable with less than a dozen. She knew people were curious, and that her farm could soon become one of those places of interest on a circle Michigan tour. "Stop at the farm to see the famous horse!" the signs would read.

She didn't want that. They already had plenty of bookings for the B&B, and she didn't want tons of people at her farm, especially ones who were overly interested in her horses. But if she took the *mystery* out of it, made Hope seem like a *normal* horse, maybe it would all go away.

"Okay," she said. She didn't really want to do a press conference, but it seemed like the best plan. Allison was supposedly a professional at this PR stuff. "When?"

"Monday," Allison said.

"*Monday?* Are you *kidding* me? I can't get through today and tomorrow like this!"

Allison's voice was confident, and firm. "You'll be fine. I want you to announce to those who are there that we'll have a photo opportunity on Monday at 4 p.m. and they can ask all the questions they want. Tell them Matt is coming down to talk. Until that time, the farm is off limits. The police can tell them that trespassing is a crime."

"Monday at 4 p.m.," Tori repeated, wondering if she could last that long.

"Yes."

Tori thought about her schedule. She was supposed to meet with Flip's owner then. It wasn't like she had time to do these things, and the interruption made her mad. But, on the other hand, it meant she got to see Matt again in just two days.

"Okay," she said. "Monday at 4 p.m."

She hung up, and explained Allison's plan to the police and Phyllis. Then, she turned to the reporters and told them what was happening.

"Until then, I need for you to respect my privacy," she said. "This is a bed and breakfast, and we are booked full-up next week. People come here for a peaceful experience. I don't want my guests harassed."

"Are you the mystery woman?" someone asked.

"I promise that all of your questions will be answered on Monday," she said.

The police helped her usher the reporters away. As she watched them go, she wondered if her life would ever be the same. She felt violated, like a special part of her had been put on display for all the world to see. She was used to controlling what the public knew about her. She didn't like this new development at all.

Tori was stressed out all weekend, a knot of unease growing in her belly. She attended the little church in town on Sunday morning, and listened half-heartedly to the sermon. The other half of her brain kept worrying about Hope and the farm. She was a private person, despite her books and bed and breakfast. She liked peace and quiet.

She opened her Bible several times and re-read the scripture that her mom had written inside, the one she had memorized. But it made her feel good to see it in her mom's handwriting.

Hope and a future.

God was in charge. He only had plans for her *good*. She had to remember that.

On Sunday afternoon, she called Emma and told her the entire story, including her feelings for Matt.

"I *knew* he was trouble!" Emma said. "But he's cute enough to be worth it. Tell me more! What's he like? What is he interested in? Is he a good kisser?" and a few more inappropriate questions.

"Emma! The rest is none of your business!" Tori said, laughing. Emma could always make her feel better.

"Well, does he have *money?*" she asked.

"Emma!"

"Seriously. He could be a gold digger. But he's not. I'm Googling him now. It says on the internet that he is a well-known artist and has done some commission work for several big companies. I'd say he's doing okay."

"A gold-digger? You're crazy," Tori laughed. She had money, left by Tim, and her businesses were doing well. But she wasn't *that* rich.

"But that's not why I called," Tori said. "I'm worried about Hope."

"It'll all be okay," Emma said. "You'll see. Give it to God. He's not going to let anything hurt you."

"That's not scriptural," Tori said. She was always prepared for the worst.

"It's close."

Tori didn't say anything, but she knew that God let bad things happen. She had lived that proof in her marriage, and with Tim's death. Sometimes God had a different plan than what she prayed for. Tori found that trusting Him was not always easy.

"I've gotta run," Emma said. "I have an event to get to."

Things had remained calm the rest of the weekend so far. Allison had done her job well, announcing to the world that there would be an official "reveal" of the mystery woman and her mystery horse. That seemed to satisfy most people. There were still some cars that slowed down in front of the B&B, looking. And they had had a lot of extra phone calls. She had answered twelve herself yesterday, of people wanting rooms. She appreciated the extra bookings, but she knew it was due to curiosity. People wanted to see Hope.

Because of this, she turned Hope out into the back pasture all weekend, out of sight of the road.

"It'll all settle down soon," Phyllis had said. "People are just excited. Next week they'll have moved on to something or someone else. Fame is fleeting."

Tori tried to believe that. When she went to the barn on Monday morning to feed Hope, the mare nuzzled her calmly. Her horse, of course, had no idea the stir she had caused locally, and in the world of art news.

She tried to go about her chores as usual, but she was excited to see Matt again, and nervous about the press conference. She was having trouble focusing, and the young horses she was working picked up on her nervousness.

At lunchtime, Emma called.

"I've thought this over and you should use this to your advantage," Emma said. "With all the charity work I do, I know how important exposure is. It's also hard to come by. You know this from your book signings. But here's the thing—you are about to have *huge* coverage of your horse, of your skills, and of your bed and breakfast. I'd say, since it has come this far, to go with it. *Use it*, Tori. Play the part, get in the game, and use this publicity to bring in more sales, more bookings, and more work. I think you're holding a golden goose egg here."

Emma's phone call made her feel better. But she still couldn't let go of the nagging feeling that this wasn't going to turn out well.

At 2 p.m. she gave Hope a bath, and when the horse was dry, she brushed out her white mane and tail until they flowed like strands of silk. The red mark on Hope's shoulder stood out in stark contrast to the rest of her white coat. Hope was beautiful. There was no arguing that.

Tori traced the marking with her finger. "You're supposed to bring me luck," she said. Hope turned to nuzzle Tori, her soft breath tickling Tori's arm. She gave her horse a hug before she left.

Tori went upstairs to change. She pulled off the faded jeans with holes in the knees that she wore to bathe Hope and put on some newer ones. She chose a pastel, floral print t-shirt to wear with them. Then, she put on the straw hat that was featured in the paintings. Might as well play the part, like Emma said.

She saw her Bible on her dresser and opened it to read the scripture in her mother's handwriting. She read the Jeremiah 29:11 verse again.

Hope and a future.

God was offering her hope. But what did that mean?

She'd have to trust God. Like Emma said, it would be okay. She'd choose to believe that.

She took a deep breath and went downstairs to face the day. Her guests had all returned from their day excursions into town, or wherever, to watch the event unfold.

Several of them wished her good luck. She nodded, then saw Matt's car pulling up the driveway. She went out to greet him.

He stepped out of the car, wearing his normal attire of jeans, a light blue button-up, and his Stetson. The sleeves of his shirt were rolled up. He had on his western boots. A few of his dark curls were peeking from underneath his hat, and he had on aviator sunglasses.

At the sight of him, her heart beat a little faster.

She ran to him and threw her arms around him.

"I missed you too!" he said, hugging her back, then kissing her. For a moment he just held her quietly, and she could feel his heartbeat. She closed her eyes, breathing in his scent, and feeling the tension of the past few days melt away. It felt good to be in his arms.

But then he pulled away. "I'm so sorry this has happened," he said quietly. The anxiety crept back into her stomach.

"It's okay," she lied.

Allison had come with him, and finally emerged from the car carrying paperwork, a pin-on microphone, and a cloth bag filled with something. A few cars were already pulling up into the driveway.

Tori glanced at the cars, then back to Matt. "I gave Hope a bath. She's all ready."

"You look gorgeous yourself," he said, brushing her hair away from her face. She had chosen to wear it down, covered by the hat.

"Thanks. So do you."

"Do you like my curls?" he teased. It had curled in the humidity.

"Very handsome," she said, laughing, and felt her shoulders relaxing. She realized that she felt better *with* him than without him. That was something she wasn't used to with Tim. He had always made the anxiety come, not leave. She had always been so on edge before, so careful of what she said and did. This was different.

"So here's the plan," Allison said, all business. "We're going to start with Matt talking, and then Tori will lead Hope out. The crowd will go "aaahhhh" and then Matt can talk some more and answer questions."

Allison looked at Tori, who nodded to signal she was on board.

"Then, Tori, if it's okay, Matt will tell people you're the woman in the paintings. We thought it would be best if he revealed it, instead of letting it get out. Because it *will* get out."

Allison looked her over. "I'm glad you wore the hat. Nice touch."

"I do marketing of my own," said Tori. "I know the game." She had her own "persona" to think about, with her books and professional training status. She figured this might even help her book sales. "And I was wondering if you can mention what I do?"

Allison nodded. "Already planned on it. Matt will introduce you as an international bestselling author and horse trainer. And he'll plug the Bed and Breakfast."

"Perfect," said Tori. It sounded like it would all work out. She said a quick, silent "thank you" to God, and turned it over to Him.

Chapter Twenty

Matt could tell that Tori was nervous, and he hated that he was doing this to her. But she mentioned how this would be good for her business, and she was right. Publicity was almost always a good thing. It was certainly helping *his* career. He hoped she could use it to her advantage as well.

Between the time he arrived at 3 p.m. and the time the press conference was to start, which was now, the place had become packed. Cars lined the driveway and the road, and there was a good crowd of over a hundred people on Tori's front lawn. They were standing, because Allison said that putting out chairs only encouraged people to linger. She had also stopped Phyllis from offering water bottles and iced tea.

"Don't encourage them to stay," Allison said firmly.

He could tell Phyllis was uncomfortable about not playing hostess. She stood on the front porch, fiddling with her apron, as if unsure what to do with her hands now that they weren't busy.

Tori was in the barn, waiting. Matt stepped up to the "podium." Allison had decided that the best place to speak was in front of an arched trellis covered in wisteria, on Tori's front lawn. To the right of him, the lawn opened to a backdrop of lavender fields. It would be the perfect spot for Hope to stand for photos.

"Welcome!" he said. The microphone squealed, and Allison made some adjustments. "Welcome," he said again. This time it worked. He started off by introducing himself and talking briefly about his work.

"But I know you are all here to see the mystery horse," he said. "For years I've kept the horse's identity a secret. Mostly to protect her. She's very rare and special. Let me tell you why."

He then went on to tell the story about the bloody-shouldered Arabian.

"They are known to be the most loyal and courageous of horses," he said. "And I think Hope fits that description well. She's blind, but her owner is still able to ride her and treat her like any other horse. She's very brave and trusts her owner completely."

The crowd murmured and ooohed.

"Now for the moment you've been waiting for," Matt said. "Tori, can you bring Hope out to us?"

From inside the barn, Tori appeared on Hope. She had a thin bridle on the horse, and she was sitting on her bareback. Tori wore her hat and a dark pair of sunglasses. Hope's coat glistened in the sunlight. The breeze coming up the dunes from Lake Michigan played with her mane and tail, creating a shimmer in the sun as she walked.

There was a gasp from the crowd. It was truly a beautiful sight.

"Ladies and gentlemen–Victoria's Hope!" Matt waved his arm toward the horse. "The Arabian from my paintings!"

Tori rode Hope over to Matt, then around to his right side, where the horse stood against the backdrop of purple. Matt wished he could stop and take pictures, to capture this later in paint.

Tori nodded to the crowd, smiling radiantly.

Hope pricked her ears toward the crowd and jumped a little bit at the sound of the camera's clicking. But Tori put her hand on Hope's neck, and Matt saw the mare relax.

They gave the reporters some time to take photos, and then Matt spoke again.

"And today we want to unveil the mystery woman as well," he said.

Tori took her hat off and pushed her sunglasses up on her head. She squinted in the sunlight. Dozens of cameras flashed and clicked and Hope again danced nervously.

"This is Victoria Reynolds," Matt said. "She's the most incredible woman I have ever met." Matt glanced at Phyllis, who was smiling.

The crowed oohed again, and some of Tori's guests clapped. Matt's words set off a flurry of questions, reporters asking if they were dating, was she his lover, and more.

"You may have already heard of her." He said, not answering the questions about their relationship. Instead, he told about her training and her books. Building her up wasn't hard because she was so accomplished. He felt the pride swell in him. She knew what she wanted and she went after it. She was good at what she did, despite what life had thrown at her. He couldn't imagine how Tim had failed to value her.

Tori spoke a little bit and answered questions about herself and her horse training. She allowed photos to be taken of her and the horse. Then Allison stepped up and told everybody the show was over, and that they could get more information at the table.

She had a folding table out on the lawn, up near the front porch, filled with Tori's business cards and information on the bed and breakfast, Matt's brochures, and t-shirts that said "I know who the Cheval mystery horse is!" Tori had also included her B&B t-shirts in the mix, as well as some of her books, signed. Phyllis came down off the porch to handle the sales.

They sold out of everything.

The whole thing lasted under an hour, and people were polite enough to leave when Allison said it was time to go. The woman was a marvel. Matt was glad he had hired her when his business was really taking off. She had made a big difference, handling things like this so he could focus more of his time on painting.

"I insist that the two of you stay for dinner," Phyllis said as they were packing up the last few things. "We can eat in the kitchen, away from the guests. I want to learn more about this marketing stuff you're all so good at."

Dinner was delicious, and Matt was scraping the last of the peach cobbler of his plate when Tori asked if wanted to go for a walk. Phyllis and Allison were engaged in a lively discussion about marketing.

"Sure," he said, glad they would finally have time alone together.

"I think this was a good thing," Tori said, taking Matt's hand and leading him outside to the backyard. Her touch was warm. She had really relaxed since the press conference. "The answering machine has been lighting up, and I just checked our website–lots of bookings into next year already!"

He was glad. He had been worried this would tear them apart. He couldn't lose her. Not now.

They slowly made their way down to the beach together, hand in hand.

"So you're okay with this?" he asked. "All of it? The exposure. The press conferences. *Us?*"

She turned to him. The night was warm and the stars were out. The waves lapped at his bare feet.

"Yes," she said. "You've brought so much into my life in just one week. I don't know what I'd do without you. Can you stay a little while?"

He kissed the back of her hand. "I have to get back to Traverse City," he said. "We didn't get time to pack up the paintings from the gallery. Then I need to drive home and check on things before I head to LA. But I'll be back. "He gave her a long lingering kiss. "I promise."

"This all turned out okay after all," Tori said, resting her head against this chest. "I was worried for nothing."

He closed his eyes and held her against him, the scent of her lavender shampoo mixing with the fresh smell of the lake. The soft sound of the waves was hypnotic, and, for a few moments, he just let himself be, here, with the woman he loved.

"I'm the luckiest man in the world." He hated to go, but he knew Allison was waiting. He gave Tori one last squeeze, then they turned to walk up the dunes toward the house.

Chapter Twenty-One

On Tuesday morning, Tori woke while it was still dark out. The room was cool from the air-conditioning and she lay there in the quiet, her comforter snuggled up under her chin. She thought about Matt and the press conference.

Hope had handled all of the excitement well, which didn't surprise her since she had ridden the horse in front of crowds for workshops before. She wondered why she had been so worried about this new kind of attention. She supposed it was because she *knew* horse people, and understood them. This different world of art critics and art collectors was one that she wasn't used to. She didn't speak their language.

She looked at her clock and saw it was only 5:30 a.m. She sat up and stretched, and thought she'd go for an early morning ride before breakfast. William would be here at 6 a.m. to feed, but she could be gone before that. She and Hope would eat when they returned.

She pulled on a pair of jeans and slipped out of the house. None of the guests were up, and Phyllis wasn't due until 7 a.m.

Tori loved the quiet of the house when she was alone and coveted these early mornings by herself.

The birds were waking up, and there was dew on the grass. She heard a horse rattling a bucket in the barn.

She slid the big, white, wooden door of the barn open and called out to her horse.

"Good morning, Hope!" she said. There was silence. Hope always nickered at her. Flip stuck his head out of his stall door and whinnied, banging his feed bucket. The other horses peeked out too, curious, blinking in the light. But she didn't see Hope.

"Hope?"

When the mare didn't respond a second time, Tori's stomach dropped. She felt the flow of adrenaline coursing through her as she broke into a run down the barn aisle. What if Hope had colic in the middle of the night and was down? Or worse, *dead?* Phyllis always told her she had to quit coming up with these worst-case scenarios. But she was scared.

In all the years she had had Hope, the horse had never failed to answer her. She came to the stall and looked over Hope's door, afraid she'd see her mare laying on her side, not breathing.

But the stall was empty.

She checked the latch; the stall door swung loosely open. Had she forgotten to latch it last night?

Feeling a little better, she ran down to the end of the barn aisle where the side door had been left open for a cross-breeze. She pushed it further open and looked out. "Hope!" she called. The barn spilled out into a fenced pasture, and she could see in the early dawn light that the pasture was empty. "Hope!"

She jogged the fence line, looking for broken wire where the mare could have slipped through. The fence was intact. She ran back into the barn and looked around. There was no other place the horse could have gone. The other doors were all locked.

She stood there, confused. *Where was her horse?*

She wondered if Hope had somehow gotten over the fence. It wasn't low, but sometimes horses, if frightened, would jump. The fact that Hope was blind made that seem impossible, but she was also a smart horse who knew the boundaries well.

Tori ran toward the house. Inside, not stopping to take her boots off, she ran right up the stairs to her bedroom, pulled open the window, and crawled out. Standing on the widow's walk, she had a complete view of the beach and most of the farm. She didn't see any hoofprints on the sand along the beach, and she couldn't see Hope anywhere near the pastures.

She heard a vehicle pulling onto the gravel driveway out front, the sound of its wheels echoing off the barn to her ears. *William.*

She ran back outside. Now her heart was pounding in her ears and she was breathing fast, her palms sweaty with fear.

William!" she said, running out the back door to his truck, which he had just parked near the barn. "William! Hope is gone!"

"What?" he said, getting out of the truck. She wished he would move faster.

"Hope is *gone!* I've looked everywhere. I think someone took her!"

William looked around. "Are you sure? Maybe you left a gate open?"

"No! I looked everywhere." A sob caught in her throat. "She's gone!"

"Okay," William said. "Let's call the police."

William called 911 on his cell phone, while Tori stood there and listened to the report, unsure of what to do.

"I can get in my car and drive around looking for her," Tori said finally, turning to go.

"No. The police said not to mess with anything so they can look for tire tracks of a big vehicle—one big enough to pull a horse trailer."

Tori began to panic, and took a few slow breaths, trying to calm herself like she did when she was about to enter a show ring. But Hope couldn't see. She'd be so scared in a strange horse trailer without Tori there to tell her it was okay.

"Are you sure she just didn't wander off?" William asked again.

Tori felt a brief prick of doubt. What if Hope *had* wandered off? They'd had horses get out before. But Hope never went far from the barn without Tori. She always stayed within the boundaries she knew.

"I'm pretty sure she didn't," Tori said.

"Start making calls to some of our friends," William said. "See if anyone has spotted her. I'll go look around the farm."

The police arrived within the half hour, which seemed to Tori like an eternity. She had used the time to call everyone she knew in the surrounding area to ask them to keep their eyes open for Hope. She had woken half of them up.

The patrol car stopped in the road and the officers got out. They examined the ground for a few minutes, before walking the long walk up the drive. She went to meet them halfway.

"We found tire marks," said a tall, balding officer, who had been here controlling the crowd on Saturday. "Looks like there might have been a heavy vehicle parked along the side of the road. I imagine he or she would have led the horse out, rather than bring a trailer in."

Tori felt her stomach drop again. It was true. Someone had taken her horse.

"But it's hard to be sure." He pulled out a notepad. The other officer, shorter and stockier, was someone Tori hadn't seen before. He walked around, looking at the ground. "The cars you had in here the other day made a mess of the place."

"Yes, they did," she said. She gave the officers what information she had, and showed them around the barn so they could see Hope hadn't gotten out through any open gates or doors. Then she pulled up a photo of Hope on her phone and texted it to them.

William had fed the horses and was standing next to her now, sucking on a piece of hay.

"Could have been for horsemeat," he said.

Tori shot him a look.

"Doubtful," said the shorter police officer. "They would have taken all of the horses if that was the case."

"Unless they got scared off," said the balding officer.

The conversation was making Tori feel sick. "William, you need to call the meat packing houses." She was relieved to see Phyllis pull in. Her housekeeper got out of her car and walked toward them.

"What's going on?" Phyllis asked.

"Hope is gone!" Tori said, and then felt the tears. She cursed them, because she needed to be strong for Hope, and now here she was getting all hysterical. Phyllis wrapped her stout arms around Tori and held her. "Tell me about it."

She gave Phyllis the quick version.

"What can I do to help?" Phyllis said.

"You go tend to the guests," she told Phyllis. "I need you there. I'm going to drive around."

152

"Any idea who could have stolen her?" the short officer asked.

"No," she said, shaking her head. She wrapped her arms around herself, suddenly feeling cold and shaky. They listened carefully as she told them about the press conference, and who might know Hope.

"Do you have any enemies?" the bald one asked.

"No. Not that I know of."

"What about your clients?"

Tori thought. No, she had good relations with all of the people she had trained horses for.

"No."

When they finished, they promised they'd put out a bulletin and have patrol cars looking.

"Could it be your new boyfriend?" William said quietly.

"What? *Matt?*" Tori said. "No. No way."

"But it was to his advantage to have a mystery horse," he said. "It promoted the story and sold paintings. Now that the horse is revealed, why not have it go missing?"

Tori frowned. "Matt would never hurt me or my horse," she said.

"I'm just throwing out ideas," he said gently.

She knew that it made sense, but she also felt strongly that Matt would never hurt her.

You didn't think Tim would either, a voice inside her said.

She pushed it down. She had to focus on finding her horse. "William, please go talk to the guests after you make calls. See if any of them heard anything last night. Text me if you get any helpful information out of them."

She got in her car and pulled out of the driveway, leaving in a cloud of dust.

She spent two hours driving around, knocking on doors. No one had seen Hope, which meant that she had definitely been taken. She couldn't have gotten that far in a few short hours, especially being blind. And a horse was a big animal, so people would have seen her if she was out.

She was sitting in the driveway of a farmer friend who had just promised her he'd get on his shortwave and was posting the photo of Hope on all her social media when her phone rang. It was Matt.

"Good morning, lovely lady!" he said, his voice groggy with sleep.

"Hope is gone!" Tori said. "Someone took her."

"What do you mean?"

"She's *gone*, Matt!" Tori said. "Someone came and took her in the middle of the night."

"Oh Tori… I'm so sorry! Do you have any leads?" Matt asked.

"No!" Tori said. "Nothing. There looks like there was a trailer out by the end of my driveway, parked in the street. The police think that's what they loaded her."

There was a moment of silence, and Tori felt the anger surging inside of her.

"This is my fault," Matt said softly. "If I wouldn't have revealed her…"

"*Yes!*" Tori said, needing someone to blame. "It *is* your fault! You should have never painted her in the first place. This is your fault, and you need to find her!"

She was angry, and she heard the harshness of her words, but she couldn't stop them. Hope meant the world to her. Before Matt, with Tim, with the uncertainty of her marriage and the grief of Tim's death, and the loneliness and guilt afterward, Hope had kept her going. She had been the rock that Tori leaned on, the "hope" that kept her moving forward. Suddenly, without her horse, she felt vulnerable. Right now, she wanted to run down to the barn, throw her arms around Hope's neck and bury her face in her mane until all the bad stuff faded. Hope would wrap her neck around Tori's body and nuzzle her, comforting her.

"Yes!" she said again. "You need to fix this and fix it now!" She realized then that she was sobbing. She couldn't talk any more.

"Okay," Matt said, not hesitating. "I'm at home. I'll drive down. I'll be there in a few hours."

He hung up. Tori sat there, holding the phone in her hand, and crying.

Chapter Twenty-Two

Matt decided to make some phone calls before he left. He called all the art galleries he had been to in the past month and asked them to send security footage. Then he called Allison, who lived on the other side of town and filled her in. Less than twenty minutes later she was knocking on his front door. She was fully dressed and ready for the day, with two cups of coffee in her hands and her laptop case slung over her shoulder.

"Thanks," Matt said, taking one of the coffees. "I'm getting the security footage from the past several exhibits on our tour. Let's go over them to see if anybody stands out. I think it has to be someone who attended my showings. Someone who has followed the whole mystery, maybe? Some nutcase."

They sat at the little table in the hotel room, the sun slanting in across the room and highlighting the dust motes in the air. Matt sipped his coffee and went over the three films he had received.

"There," he said after the third one. "That guy."

Allison had been watching on her computer. "The guy with the graying hair?"

"Yes." Matt zoomed in closer. The footage was blurry. "Isn't that the reporter who exposed Hope?"

"I think you're right," Allison said. "But why? And why would anyone follow you around the country?"

Matt gave her a wry look. "Gee, thanks."

She smiled a little bit. "You know what I mean."

"I know *exactly* what you mean." Matt zoomed in some more, but the security footage was even grainier. "He was in

New York, in Ohio, and in Traverse City. Look—here in Ohio he's wearing a Tiger's baseball cap. In Traverse City he has one of those man purses with him. The trendy kind. City guy. Maybe a New Yorker? I'll bet that's where we picked him up."

"I didn't see him at the press conference," said Allison.

"Look," Matt said, pointing to the New York video. "He's here at the back of the room in this video, standing next to Emma and Tori. He came in late. The security camera shows him bustling in and standing next to them. He looks flustered."

"Probably because he just drove in New York traffic," said Allison dryly.

"So he got there late but was in time for my talk. Remember, Emma and Tori left early? I wonder if they saw him, or saw which car he came in? I'll ask them."

He snapped a photo of the man and texted it to Tori, then called her.

"Is this the person who took her?" Tori said hopefully. "The photo you sent is blurry."

"I'm not sure. Take a look closely at that man," said Matt. "He's been following me. Do you recognize him?"

There was a moment of silence. Then she said, "Yes! I think he was the reporter I told you about! But I can't be sure from this image, and he was wearing a baseball cap when I saw him at the farm. I see he was standing next to Emma in New York."

"Can you give me Emma's mobile number? I want to ask her as well."

"Sure." Tori hung up and texted him Emma's contact info. He called her.

"Hello?" Emma answered.

"This is Matt Cheval."

"Matt." Her voice was flat and firm. She had apparently heard the news already and wasn't happy with him. "So, you got her horse stolen?"

"I'm going to text you a photo of a man who I think has been following me. He was standing next to you at the showing in New York. Tori thinks he was at the farm too, posing as someone interested in training. Please look at it and tell me if you can remember anything, like what he drove or if he arrived by taxi. He came in late."

"Okay. Go ahead."

Matt sent her the text and waited. Emma finally said, "He smelled like onions! I remember because he was standing next to me and it was making me queasy. But that's all I remember because I was so mad at you at that point. I wasn't really focused on him."

"Onions. You don't remember what he drove? Or if he came by cab?"

"No."

"I think he might be a New Yorker," Matt said.

There was silence as both of them thought. Then Emma said, "I have a lot of connections with the various charities I work with throughout the city. I'll send his photo to every one of them."

"Sounds good," said Matt. "Please keep me posted."

"Will do."

Emma hung up without saying goodbye.

Matt sighed, then looked at Allison. "I guess you need to cancel my plane to LA."

"I'll do that."

"And I guess I should pack my bag."

"Matt," Allison said. He looked over at her. For the first time, he noticed that she looked tired. Behind her reading glasses, there were fine lines around her eyes and dark circles under them. She ran a tight business for him, usually working long before he got up and long after he went to bed. She reached over and gave his hand a squeeze. "I've never seen you look as happy as you have been since you found Tori. I know you love her. This will all work out."

He squeezed her hand in return. "I hope you're right. For Tori's sake, I hope you're right. She needs that horse."

Matt called the main number of the bed and breakfast, hoping Phyllis would answer. He was relieved when he heard her voice and not the answering machine.

"It's Matt," he said. "I just got off the phone with Tori. I was wondering if you could go through the guest books for the past few weeks and see if there are any names that stand out, maybe someone single, or someone who acted strange. There's a man, gray hair, who has been following me."

"I'm on it," Phyllis said. "The police have already asked for the list, but I'll go over it again."

Matt did a lot of praying as he drove.

Please God, let us find Hope alive and unharmed. This is my fault. I never should have gotten involved in Tori's life.

He had been following his heart all these years, unable to give up on a woman who he knew was married. He had never called her again, never tried to make contact, because he knew it was wrong. But, then again, if he had, he would have known she was a widow.

Then maybe things would have been different?

What would have made a difference is if he had just let her go after that weekend. The kiss was wrong. Wanting her was wrong. To be honest, he had tried to forget her. For an entire year he had painted like crazy, painting anything and everything *else*. But he couldn't get her out of his head, or her beautiful horse. So finally, he had put his brush to canvas and his best paintings emerged.

If you could say it in words, there would be no reason to paint. He had that quote by artist Edward Hopper memorized. It was framed and on his desk at home. His feelings about Tori had spilled out onto his canvases. Wrong feelings, about a woman he thought was still married.

He wondered if God was punishing him.

I'm sorry, Lord. I've hurt Tori. I should have stayed out of her life.

He never should have painted Hope. He had made her a star, something to be desired by collectors and art enthusiasts. He and Allison had cultivated the "mystery" behind the paintings and pushed his business and his art into the spotlight at the expense of Tori and Hope. He had used them both.

When he was about halfway there, he called Tori again.

"Anything new?" he asked.

"I looked up restaurants around that area that serve greasy food, and I found a diner close by that offers a steak and onion burger. I called the owner and texted him the photo. I'm waiting to hear back. It's just a wild chance, but maybe this guy ate there before the showing. It was around dinner time."

"Awesome," Matt said.

"Wait! I just got a text! Hang on."

Matt waited, praying, while Tori looked at her text.

"He saw him!" Tori said. "Wow! What are the chances of me finding him through the first restaurant I called!"

Not chance. But God, Matt thought.

"The restaurant owner is calling me. I'll call you back."

About five minutes later, Tori called. "He paid by credit card. I have a name. Robert Walsh. Not the same name he was using when he came to the farm. I'll tell the police. Maybe they can find him."

Matt hung up, pulled over, and did a search on his name. There were a lot of Robert Walsh's in New York. He called Phyllis back to see if she found anything conscious about the guest book.

"Nothing," she said. "We've only had couples come in and none of them looked like the photo you sent me and none with the last name Walsh."

Matt hung up and took a call from Allison.

"Your Twitter feed is exploding," she said. "Lots of tips on the horse. Probably most of them are false, but I'm sending them to the police."

He had finally gained the notoriety he had always wanted, but not in a way he wanted to gain it. And he now had a nutcase fan. He was amazed at how fast they had gotten this far, finding his name. But that was the world of social media. It moved so fast it made his head spin.

By the time he got to the farm it was mid-afternoon, and he was fresh out of ideas.

"Tori's gone," said Phyllis, running out of the house. "She called a trailer rental company in town, Dawson's Trailers. A man with Walsh's name and description rented a horse trailer. She has gone into town to see if anybody else has seen this guy or knows what his plan is."

"I'll find her," Matt said and punched the address of Dawson's Trailers into his navigation system.

He drove too fast into town, and when he got to Dawson's Trailers, he saw Tori's truck parked outside. But she wasn't inside.

"She went looking for anyone else who has seen the man," said an older gentleman, dressed in plaid and sucking on a straw. "I think she went across the street."

Matt hurried out. There was a family restaurant across the street. He trotted over to it.

Tori was inside talking to a waiter. He walked up to her just as she turned to leave.

"Matt!" Tori said, surprised. "The trailer is red and white. The waiter here said he saw it heading west, which would be toward the farm where he picked her up, but then where did he go? This is pointless. I have no idea what to do next!"

"Let's go outside," he said. She followed him out into the parking lot and across the street to their cars. "Okay, so you gave the credit card number to the police, and they're trying to find him, right?" Matt said.

"Yes, but they don't seem too concerned since it's just a horse," she said. "And they told me they can't track him without a warrant. They need permission to track his phone."

Matt sighed, running his hand through his hair.

"This is frustrating."

"Frustrating?" Tori said. "That's *all* you've got to say? My horse is out there—my *blind* horse—probably scared to death. It's more than frustrating! It's terrifying! What if I never see her again?"

Tori was bordering on hysterical.

"Why don't you let me drive you back to the farm," Matt said in a calm voice.

"I'm *not* going back without my horse!" Tori said. "Don't you act all chivalrous *now*. This is *your fault*. If you would never have painted us in the first place…." Tori's eyes narrowed in anger.

Matt's phone rang then. It was Emma.

"His name is Robert Walsh, and he has a mental illness," said Emma. "He was a journalist, until he was fired, and has a restraining order against him from a former girlfriend, so he can be violent when he's off his meds. Also, he has a mother who lives in a rural area not far from there. So you're right, he's a New Yorker, but it sounds like this was a crime of convenience. Send the police to his mother's house. I'll bet that's where he's keeping Hope. I have his mom's name."

Emma texted him the name and address. He showed Tori. She grabbed his phone and forwarded it to hers.

"Let's go," she said.

"You should stay here, and we should call the police," he said.

"There's no time for that." She climbed in her truck and slammed the door. Then, she rolled down the window. "I should have known better than to trust you. Leave me alone. I did just fine before you came into my life. No, actually I did *better*. Now you've ruined everything. I'm going to rescue my horse."

She drove off.

He couldn't let her go alone! Matt jumped in his car and sped after her. He punched the address into his GPS as he drove, then he called the police and gave them the address.

They were on a divided highway, and Tori was speeding. He had to concentrate to keep up with her on the curving road.

Suddenly, he saw a deer up ahead. It jumped out in front of Tori. She swerved too late and hit it. Matt had to slam on the brakes and swerve off the side of the road to avoid hitting the back of her truck.

He stopped about halfway into a ditch. He jumped out and ran to Tori.

Her airbag had gone off. She climbed out.

"You okay?" he asked.

She nodded. They walked around and looked at the deer. It was dead.

"I've got to get to Hope," Tori said.

161

"Get in my car," Matt said. "I'll drive."

She nodded and climbed in the passenger side, as he slid under the wheel. He had to rock it a bit to get it out of the ditch and back up on the road.

"Let's go," he said, hoping the police were on their way.

Tori looked across at him. "You need to fix this," she said. "You need to save my horse. Then I never want to see you again."

The words cut into him, but he nodded. Then he looked forward to the road, and pushed the accelerator. He hoped they were in time.

Chapter Twenty-Three

Tori's heart was pounding. She was both scared and furious. She kept going over in her head when things had gone wrong, and why someone would want her horse. It all came back to Matt. She had been living a perfectly okay life before she ended up at his art show in New York. How could things have gone so bad in such a short time?

Hope would be scared. She was blind and had no idea where she was. Tori wondered if the man who stole her realized her horse couldn't see. Hope would have been easy to steal. She loved people and would go off with anyone. Tori had taught her to trust.

She rubbed the palms of her hands on her jeans. They were sweating.

"You okay?" Matt asked.

"Yes," Tori lied. "Just drive."

When they arrived at the rural address, Matt slowed down and parked just up the road. "Let's take this slow," he said to Tori. "There might be dogs. Or guns."

They walked quietly up the dirt road, keeping to the shoulder. There were large pines lining the road, and the house sat back a little way, half hidden behind overgrown shrubs and bushes. The two-story home had wooden siding, with graying white paint stripped off in huge chunks. It looked old and was in much need of repair.

They stopped at the mailbox and looked up the driveway. There was an old, red barn back behind the house."

"She's probably in the barn, or in a pasture behind the house," Tori said. "He would want to keep her hidden."

Matt nodded. "Try to remain unseen."

They hid behind the trees and worked their way over to some large lilac bushes beside the house. Using them as cover from the house windows, they moved toward the back.

"There!" Tori said, pointing. Hope was grazing peacefully out in the back pasture.

"Stay here," Matt said. "Let's wait for the police."

Suddenly they heard the front door slam. It was Robert Walsh. Or rather, the man who had called himself Brent Simmons at her farm. His eyes were wide and angry.

"That's him," Tori said. "That's the man who came to my farm pretending to want a horse trained for his daughter."

"And the reporter who gave up Hope's identity," Matt said.

"Get off my property!" he shouted. He looked different than the well-dressed "father" who had come to her farm. He was angry, beet red in the face, and dressed in dirty jeans and a work shirt.

"You have my horse!" Tori said.

"And you're trespassing!" Robert said, stomping down the steps of the porch.

"All we want is the horse," Matt said, "and we'll leave."

Robert stepped in front of them, blocking their path. Matt stopped, and tried to go around him, but Robert pushed Matt hard on the chest with both hands. Matt stood his ground.

"We just want the horse back," Matt said.

Robert lunged at Matt, knocking him to the ground. Tori heard Matt gasp, then saw his knee come up and connect Robert in the chest. Robert groaned but didn't move, and punched Matt hard in the face.

Tori saw a garden hose and grabbed it. She swung it and hit Robert across the face with it. It didn't faze him much, but it gave Matt the distraction he needed to get out from under Robert.

Robert ran at Tori, then, but Matt tripped him, and the huge man fell.

"Go!" Matt shouted at her. "Get on Hope and ride out of here!"

Robert was up and running toward Matt. Matt dodged him, then ran toward him again, ramming his head into Robert's stomach.

164

As Robert bent over, Tori hit him again with the hose.

Robert sputtered some cuss words, then suddenly, someone grabbed Tori from behind. She felt her arms pinned against her sides.

"Causing trouble, are ya?" the man said. She had no idea where he had come from. He was huge too, and his arms were covered in tattoos.

She stomped on his foot, and he yelled in pain, but only grabbed her tighter. Matt sprinted toward them, landing a punch in the man's face as Tori ducked.

"Run!" Matt yelled. Tori ran. She headed toward Hope as fast as she could go. She'd jump on the mare, then ride and pull Matt up behind her. Maybe the size of the horse would intimidate the men.

She heard police sirens in the distance.

"Hope!" she yelled, running toward the pasture fence. She had dreams where she ran as hard as she could to get somewhere, but her legs seemed to move in slow motion. This was like that. But then she was there, panting. The gate was just a hotwire, and she unfastened it and threw it aside. She heard the electricity hissing and saw the wire snake along the ground.

"Hope!" she yelled again, and this time her mare picked up her head and whinnied.

Tori reached her and leaped effortlessly up. "Oh girl, it's so good to see you," she said, wrapping her arms around her horse. Hope was muddy, but she seemed fine.

Using knee pressure, she turned the mare, and cued her to go out the gate. Hope, unfamiliar with her surroundings, hesitated, then took a small step, then another, careful of her footing.

"You've got to trust me, girl," Tori said.

Hope took a few more steps, responding to Tori's pressure.

Tori looked at the house, where Matt was tussling with the other man. Robert had regained his stance and was running toward the side of the house. Tori saw a shovel leaning up against it. *Was he going after that?* There was no way Matt could take them both on, especially if Robert used that shovel as a weapon.

"Let's go," Tori said urgently, and squeezed with both legs, trying to move her horse forward faster. Hope's ears flicked, and her muscles quivered, as she picked up on her rider's urgency. Then, she tossed her head and broke into a canter. Moving this fast, there was no way Tori could see the ground for holes, so she prayed and hung on.

She had to get to Matt before Robert did. He was headed toward Matt, shovel raised.

"Matt, behind you!" Tori called out across the lawn as other man punched Matt again. He bent over, but then straightened up and his fist connected with the man's face. He hit him again, then kicked him in the stomach. The man was down.

"Matt, watch out!" Tori screamed, as Hope barreled down on them in a canter.

But it was too late. Robert had the shovel and he swung it hard at Matt's head. Tori heard a sickening thud as it connected. Matt crumpled and went down.

"No!" Tori shouted, and rammed Hope into Robert, knocking him down, just as she heard "Freeze!"

She stopped her horse and saw a policeman pointing his gun at Robert. Two other policemen came around the house. Robert stopped and raised his hands over his head.

"On your knees!" the policeman said.

The other man lay on the grass, unconscious, where Matt had dropped him.

Tori jumped off of Hope and ran toward Matt. He lay unconscious on the grass, large amounts of blood spilling from a gash in his head.

"We need an ambulance!" Tori said. "Somebody, call an ambulance!"

"I'm on it!" one of the officers said. "An ambulance is on the way." The other officer came over and put his hand on Tori's shoulder. "You all right?"

She nodded.

"We need for you to get your horse out of the way so the ambulance can pull in."

Tori glanced at Hope, who was standing in the driveway, frozen, unsure of where to go. She nodded again.

She took one last look at Matt. He was breathing, but very shallowly.

Please God, let him be okay! she prayed, and on shaking legs, she went to get her horse.

Robert's mother apparently wasn't home. Tori hooked the horse trailer up to one of the police SUV's, and loaded Hope into it, while an ambulance took Matt away. As the officer drove her back to her farm, she called Allison and told her which hospital they were taking Matt to.

Allison was still in Traverse City, but said she'd contact his parents right away.

On the way, they passed Tori's truck. There was a police officer putting orange cones around the wreck. His car lights were flashing as they went around him.

"Is that yours?" the officer said.

She nodded.

"Officer Jansen will handle it. You can pick it up tomorrow."

"Thank you," she said. She closed her eyes and leaned her head back against the headrest.

"Are you sure you're okay?" the officer asked her. "You've been through a lot just within the past hour."

"Yes," she said, keeping her eyes closed. But she wasn't sure if she'd ever be okay again. She kept seeing Matt in her mind, and the back of the shovel coming down on his head. *Please God, let him be okay,* she prayed, remembering her harsh words. *I never want to see you again,* she had said.

Now she might *not* ever see him again. Not if he died. There had been so much blood, and his breathing terrifyingly shallow.

"Hurry," she said to the officer.

She called the farm as they drove toward home. William was there to greet her at the barn door. "I'll take care of Hope," he said. "Phyllis is going to drive you to the hospital."

She climbed into Phyllis' car.

"You okay?" Phyllis asked.

She wished people would quit asking her that. Phyllis was staring at her. "What?" she said irritably.

"Your shirt," Phyllis said.

For the first time, Tori noticed the blood staining the front of her t-shirt. "It's Matt's blood," she said, and heard her voice shaking.

"You want to change?"

"No. Just go."

"You can't go like that."

Phyllis was out of the car, keys in hand, before Tori could say anything. In a minute she was back with a fresh shirt. "Put this on," she said. "You'll scare everybody to death at the sight of all that blood."

Tori obediently changed into the fresh shirt while Phyllis drove.

Phyllis broke a few speed limits getting to the hospital— the same hospital where Tim had been taken. She dropped Tori off at the ER entrance.

"I'll go park the car," she said.

The doctors were working on Matt and wouldn't let her see him. A nurse told her that Matt had quit breathing in the ambulance, and they had to intubate him.

Tori sat down in a plastic chair in the hall, her hands clenched together. She remembered being in this hospital when Tim died, sitting in a similar chair, waiting for a doctor to come and tell her the news. Tim had been braindead before he arrived at the hospital, they told her later. He had died immediately.

What if Matt died too?

Tori was so lost in her thoughts that she didn't hear Phyllis come in and sit next to her until the older woman put a hand on her shoulder.

"Let's pray," she said.

Tori listened as Phyllis, in the calm, confident voice she always used, asked God to heal Matt.

"But Lord, it's not what we want, but what is in Your will that matters," said Phyllis, and then said, "Amen."

Tori wasn't sure she was happy with that prayer. She wanted things to happen a certain way, and that way was for Matt to be okay.

She started to say something about that to Phyllis when a couple came into the ER, asking for Matt. They were older, probably in their late fifties or early sixties. The woman was slightly plump and had curls on her head in what looked like a permanent wave. The man was tall and slender, an older version of Matt.

"Those must be Matt's parents," Tori said to Phyllis. "Allison was going to call them."

Tori got up and walked over to them. "Hi," she said. "I'm—" She paused. How should she introduce herself? Friend? Girlfriend? She decided just to go with her name.

The woman said, "Oh, you must be Tori!" and embraced her in a hug before Tori could respond. "How is Matt? I'm Rebecca, his mother."

Tori could tell the woman had been crying.

"He's…he's being worked on," she said. "They had to intubate him. He stopped breathing in the ambulance."

The woman's eyes crinkled and teared up. "Oh no," she said, and her husband reached for her hand.

"We can't see him yet," Tori said.

"Let's go sit down," her husband said. Tori led them over to the plastic chairs.

"He has been moved to the ICU," said the nurse behind the desk. "I'll show you where you can wait more comfortably."

She led them down a little corridor and around a few turns to an empty waiting room with a television. The channel was tuned to a nature show. Turtles were sunning themselves on logs and the sound was off, but the words running across the bottom of the screen were talking about north American wetlands.

"There's coffee and ice water at the back in the vending area," the nurse said, then left them.

Phyllis introduced herself, and Tori found out that Matt's dad was named Charles. Then, Phyllis sat down and motioned for Tori to sit. Matt's parents sat cross from her, and Rebecca produced a tissue from her purse and dabbed at the corners of her eyes.

"So, what happened?" Charles asked.

Tori began to tell them about the events of the past few days. How this one man had come to all three gallery showings, but they didn't notice him at first. And then how he stole Hope and how Matt had helped find and rescue the horse. And how Robert had hit him with a shovel. Tori left out the part that he had struck Matt twice and kicked him after he was unconscious. She wanted to spare them the worst if she could.

"We've heard a lot about you," Rebecca said. "He's so fond of you."

"We knew years ago there had to be somebody special," his dad said, "the way he painted you so much. He'd never tell us though. He'd just say it was a mystery; the same thing he told all his followers."

"And your horse is *so* beautiful. Oh, honey, I'm so glad you got her back," said Rebecca.

Tori's eyes filled with tears. "Me too," she said.

They sat there, waiting. Rebecca started to tell Tori little stories about Matt, about how he had loved drawing from such an early age, and then took up painting later, and how everything in his life was always about art.

"The other boys did sports in high school," she said. "Our Matt loved to ride horses, and he did basketball in middle school and his freshman year of high school. But art was his thing. He has always had such a vision. He can capture amazing things on canvas."

About an hour later, a doctor came out, pulling off his face mask.

"He's stable," he said. "But still unconscious. You can see him, but only for a short time and only two people at a time."

Tori let his parents go first and when they came out, his mom started crying. Charles held her and motioned for Tori to take her turn.

"Do you want me to come?" Phyllis asked.

Tori nodded.

The two women went up the elevator to the ICU, where Matt was. She caught her breath when she saw him. He was still on a machine to help him breathe, and his face was swollen and bruised. His arms, too, had bruises, but it was his head that looked the worst. It was wrapped in bandages and some blood had soaked through them.

Tori slowly approached the side of the bed and took his hand.

"Do you think he can hear me?" she whispered to Phyllis.

"Maybe," Phyllis said.

Tori squeezed his hand. It was warm but limp.

"Matt, it's Tori," she said. "I'm here. Hope is okay. We need for *you* to get better now."

She didn't know what else to say. She was wracked with guilt that this had happened to him.

"Go find my horse," she remembered saying, *"and afterwards I don't ever want to see you again."*

What if those were the last words he ever heard her speak?

"I love you," she said, and felt the tears coming. She shouldn't cry. Not here. She had to be strong. But she couldn't stop the sob that broke from her, and she turned and had to leave the room. Out in the hall, Phyllis put her arm around Tori.

"There's nothing else we can do here. Let's get you home."

Tori shook her head. "I want to stay."

So they went back down to the waiting room to sit with his parents.

"He's had a very traumatic head injury. The doctor said we should know something in the next few hours," Rebecca said. "We should know if he will...make it. They are waiting for the bleeding in his brain to stop."

Tori and Phyllis sat down and waited to see what the next few hours would hold.

Chapter Twenty-Four

Tori stayed at the hospital until early morning, when the doctor said that the bleeding in Matt's brain had stopped, and that the swelling was slowing down. "I think he'll be okay," he said. "We won't know the extent of the damage until he wakes up. We'll try to take him off the ventilator later today."

Meanwhile, there was nothing to do but wait.

"Go home, Tori, and get some rest," Rebecca said. "I'll call you if anything changes. Matt's brother is on his way here. We'll be okay."

After exchanging phone numbers, Tori agreed. She felt she was out of place with this close-knit family, and she wanted to check on Hope.

In the car, Phyllis told her to get some sleep as soon as she checked on Hope.

"What about the you?" Tori said. It was 7:30 a.m. "The guests will be expecting breakfast and you've been up all night too."

"I have some frozen cinnamon rolls I can pop in the oven, and I'll scramble some eggs. It'll be quick and easy. After I serve, I'll get some rest. I promise."

Hope was remarkably okay. She was munching her hay and didn't seem fazed at all about her kidnapping. The police called to say that Robert's motive was money and that he had planned to sell the horse to an art collector. He had already had a buyer.

The other man was a thug he knew from his home back in New York. When they found out that the horse was stabled near Robert's mom's house, they had hatched a plan to steal her. Forcing Matt to reveal her to the public raised her value, and helped him find a buyer.

"Neither of them is very bright, and both have records," said the officer. "And Robert is on some meds for his personality disorder, but apparently he went off of them."

"I see," Tori said. But she was glad to hear that they were taking them back to New York for arraignment, since they both had prior offenses there. She felt better knowing they were far away.

"Now you need to go to bed," said Phyllis. "You'll be no good to Matt when he wakes up if you're ill." She walked upstairs with Tori, pulled the shades, and turned on a fan for white noise. Tori obediently lay down on top of her comforter, insisting she couldn't sleep. But as soon as Phyllis left the room, she was out.

When she awoke, the sun was setting. *Matt!* She sat bolt upright and checked her phone, her heart pounding. She had slept for five hours.

There was a text from his mother, saying he was successfully off the ventilator but not conscious. The doctor didn't want him to have a lot of visitors right now, so it would be best for Tori to stay home until tomorrow morning.

Reluctantly, Tori texted back that she would. Then she got up and showered, and after she was dressed, she went downstairs, knowing that it was nearly dinner time. She smelled Phyllis' chicken pot pie, her favorite comfort food.

She walked through the living room and into the kitchen and was surprised to see Emma sitting at the table.

"Em!" she said.

"I flew here as soon as I could," said Emma, jumping up from her seat. "Phyllis filled me in on everything. I'm so, so sorry about Matt!"

Emma came and put her arms around Tori.

"I'm so glad you're here," Tori said. How often had she and Emma talked each other through hard times?

"You must have been terrified," said Emma, pulling back and taking both of Tori's hands in hers. "Phyllis is making us some tea, and then I want to hear all about it."

"Dinner will be done in thirty minutes," Phyllis said. "I'll set up a table out on the porch for you."

Tori and Emma followed her out to the screened-in porch.

"It's so pretty here," Emma said, walking to the windows and looking out across Lake Michigan. Tori sat at the small table, which seated four. She thought about sitting on the couch or over-stuffed wicker chairs, but dinner would be ready soon.

"You have a puzzle going," Emma said, walking over to the card table that Tori and Phyllis had set up last week. All they had finished was the border and part of a red barn.

"It's a farm scene," said Tori. "We don't have much time to work on them in the summer, so the going is slow."

"I love this room," Emma said, coming to sit at the table across from Tori. "I keep telling Brian that we need a three-seasons room like this one. We could put it in the back, just off of the dining room."

Tori loved it out here too. This was a spot that she and Phyllis kept for themselves, not allowing guests in here. It was a great place to watch sunsets in the evenings or read on rainy days.

Phyllis brought out a tray with a tea service on it and poured each of them a cup. "I'll be back later with your dinner," she said, and closed the curtained French doors, giving them privacy from the rest of the house.

"Phyllis is such a blessing," Tori said. She curled her feet up under her and stared out at the lake.

Emma was sitting across from her, and she could feel her friend's eyes on her.

"Tell me what happened," said Emma. "With this Robert guy."

"Well, it's a good thing you remembered the onion smell," said Tori. "That's how I found his name."

She told Emma how they had tracked down Robert Walsh, and how he had planned to sell Hope for a profit. "But Matt was so badly hurt," Tori said.

"Phyllis told me," said Emma. She sat there quietly for a while, which was unusual for her. She added more hot water to her cup, then stirred some sugar into her tea. "Do you love him?"

174

Tori nodded. "But I blew it. I said some horrible things to him and now I don't even know if he's going to live. I'm a terrible person." She felt her eyes filling with tears, and swallowed, fighting them back.

"Hope is my rock," she said.

"Jesus is supposed to be your rock," Emma said.

Tori nodded. She picked up a napkin and wiped her eyes.

Emma watched her for a few moments. Tori avoided her gaze by staring out at the lake. The wind had picked up and the waves were hitting the beach with big white caps.

"Tori, you were upset when you said those words to Matt," said Emma. "He'll understand that. Does he know that Tim gave you Hope?"

"Yes," said Tori.

"That had to be the worst part. She's your last remaining hold on to Tim. He was so good to you. He gave you so much, and your marriage was…well, we're all still jealous of how good he was to you," she said, laughing a little bit. "My husband gets upset when I compare."

Tori didn't say anything.

"Matt *will* understand. Grief *does* things to a person, and you saw your last connection to Tim disappearing. And I know how much you love Hope just for the horse she is."

Tori looked into her teacup. She had never told Emma about her marriage. Partly because she was embarrassed, but also because she felt the need to protect Tim. He *was* good to her. He gave her things; he bought her a farm, a horse, let her open the bed and breakfast…

Let her.

It seemed like she was always waiting for his permission to do something. To start her bed and breakfast. To pursue her career. She hadn't published her first book until he died, because he didn't want her traveling. He'd miss her, he said. He needed to know she was home, safe.

She had waited to have kids because he wasn't ready. Not that it would be easy to conceive anyway, given the amount of time they spent together.

She had missed many meals with her family because he needed to be home to "rest" after his busy work week.

Her cousin's birthday. Sunday dinners. Her grandparents' anniversary party at a local restaurant. Just little things. But time she'd never get back.

"The Bible says you're supposed to leave your family and become one with me," Tim had said one night in a rare moment of cuddling in bed. "We're together now. I'm supposed to be your focus and you are mine."

And then he had bought her a set of pearl earrings at the end of that week, after he had missed five of the six dinners she had prepared for him.

"Because you're the pearl of my eye," he said when he gave them to her.

"Emma…" she said. Then she felt her heart rate pick up. What was she afraid of?

Emma looked at Tori over the rim of her cup, then set it down. "What's up?" she said, concern in her eyes. They could read each other pretty well after all these years together.

"My marriage wasn't what you think," Tori said. "Tim wasn't that good to me."

Emma set her cup down. "What do you mean?"

Tori began to tell Emma some of the things that had happened. About the dent in the table. About her fractured wrist. The nights and days spent alone. The cruel words he used.

As she talked, Tori felt something inside of her loosening up. Something freeing. The more she said, the more she needed to say. It was like opening a wound and letting out the bad stuff, so it could heal.

When she finished, Emma sat there quietly for a few minutes, thinking. Then she said, "Why didn't you ever tell me?"

Tori shrugged. "I think at first I thought the problems were *my* fault, and that I just needed to figure out marriage. Because it was so subtle. I didn't realize it was a form of emotional abuse. Like you said, he *did* things for me. He gave me a horse."

"So, you were unhappy all those years with him?" Emma asked.

Tori nodded. She remembered the nervous feeling she'd get in her gut when Tim walked into the room. "And unsettled. I knew something was wrong, but I just couldn't figure out what. I was stupid."

"No," Emma said, reaching over and putting a hand on her arm. "Not stupid, Tori. A victim."

"I don't like to think of myself as a victim," said Tori. "Maybe that's why I never told anyone."

"Nobody does," said Emma. "And you're so smart and strong and independent that it must have been a shock to you to realize the man you loved so much wasn't the man you thought he was. You always had everything figured out." Emma took a sip of her tea, and gazed out over the lake. "I remember, in high school, you knew before anyone else what you wanted to do when you grew up. And in elementary school, you always knew what you wanted. What theme for your birthday. What outfit for Christmas. So it had to be hard to suddenly realize you had been deceived and what you thought you wanted, didn't turn out to be...well, *safe*."

Safe. That was it. Tim hadn't been safe to be with. Not emotionally.

"Yes," Tori agreed.

"I wish I had known. Some of the volunteer work I do is with women who are from abusive homes. Most of them are physically abused, not emotionally abused. Actually, at that point, it's both. But some of these women come from good homes, with good careers. They never see it coming. You can't blame yourself. It's not your fault that Tim was a jerk."

Tori nodded.

"Tori, have you talked to anyone?"

"You mean a therapist?"

Emma nodded.

"No. Phyllis gave me a card of a therapist she knows, back after Tim died. I never went. She said it was to cope with losing my husband. But I think Phyllis has always suspected. She practically lived here, after all."

"You should call that therapist."

"Maybe I will," Tori said.

Phyllis came in, then, carrying a tray with their dinner: two plates of steaming chicken pot pie, a roll each, and a side salad.

"Smells amazing," said Emma.

"I'll get you girls a pitcher of water and some glasses, and then I'll leave you be," said Phyllis.

She returned a minute later with the promised items. When she was gone, Tori looked over at Emma.

"I don't want to talk about it anymore," she said.

Emma smiled. "No problem," she said. "I was just about to tell you this funny story from the dinner I hosted last week with Brian's boss. You'll never believe what happened when he popped the cork on the champagne bottle."

Tori dug into her pot pie and listened as her friend shared her stories. She found herself actually laughing. She couldn't wait until Matt got better so she could tell *him*.

Chapter Twenty-Five

Matt's world was dark. He had awoken three days ago to a world devoid of light. Blackness was all he could see.

First, he thought he had a bandage wrapped around his head. It felt full and gauzy. But when he rubbed his eyes, nothing was there.

"Mom?" he called, because he had heard her voice earlier. Or thought he had.

"Matt?" she said. He was laying on a bed, and her voice was coming from beside him. He felt her hand on his arm.

"Where am I?"

"You're in the hospital," his mother said. "You've had an accident, and you have a head injury. But you'll be okay."

"Hey, son!" his dad's voice came from somewhere beside his mom's. "Hit the call button, Rebecca. The nurse wants to know when he's awake.

Matt's hear rate quickened, and his palms started sweating.

"Why is it so dark? Why can't I see?"

"What?" his mother said. "What do you mean?" He felt her squeeze his arm.

The nurse came in. "I'm going to look at your eyes with a very bright light," she said. "Try to keep them open."

He felt the warmth from the light. "I can't see anything," he said. "I can't see the light."

"This is probably from the head trauma," the nurse said. Her voice was soft, young.

"Am I blind?" Matt asked, terrified.

"It's probably only temporary," said the nurse.

That was three days ago. They had run several tests. Apparently, the part of his brain that controlled sight was being affected. His sight could return as the swelling went down, but there was no way to be sure.

"If it returns, it'll most likely be gradual," his doctor said. "Just a soft glow at first, or a flicker."

Matt had spent the next several days fighting through panic. He kept watching for a soft glow, or a flicker. *Any* sign. Now, today, with still no improvement, he felt himself slipping into depression.

"Are you sure you don't want Tori to visit?" his mom asked for the tenth time. She hadn't left his side and was trying to make him feel better, like she had always done when he was a child.

"No," he said again. He didn't want to see anybody. He just wanted to get better.

Whenever he had been feeling down, or stressed, he had turned to art to help him sort through his feelings. He had painted his way out of a bad high school breakup; he had painted when he crashed his first car into the light pole and had to tell his parents; he had painted when he flunked out of physics because he was drawing in his notebook instead of paying attention. Painting had helped him through the grief of his grandmother's death. And it had helped him cope with his impossible love for Tori.

Now, when he really needed to paint, he couldn't. Because he couldn't see.

A fresh wave of panic crept over him, and he sat up in bed. He felt a wave of dizziness, and it took him a moment to reorient himself because he couldn't use a focal point. He just hung on to the sides of the bedrail until it subsided.

He was alone. His parents had gone home to shower and run a few errands.

Carefully, he dangled his legs over the side of the bed.

"Matt?" It was his nurse. He had her voice memorized now. "Hey, hon, you can't get up by yourself."

"I have to use the bathroom," he said.

He waited for her to come to him and let her take hold his arm while he got up. He stepped carefully on the cold tile floor, almost tripping over his IV line.

"Careful," she said.

She led him slowly through the doorway of the bathroom. "Can I have some privacy?" he asked.

"Sure. I'll be right out here," she said and closed the door. He felt his way along the wall until he came to the sink. He turned on the cold water and splashed his face.

This *couldn't* be his life. He had been praying constantly for a miracle. For healing. Begging God to give him his sight back. He longed for the light he loved so much, for the vivid colors of this world. For the feel of his paintbrush in his hand and the miracle of watching a white canvas transform into his creative vision.

He stood there, water running over his hands on the sink, and he cried.

After a week, he was released to a rehabilitation facility.

He had called a neighbor to look after his house. His parents helped him pay his few bills online. Now, he was in a strange new place, with a new nurse, and lots of sounds.

"Mom?" he said. "Can you stay awhile?"

"Of course," she said.

He heard her pull up a chair next to his new bed. They told him he'd be here for up to a week before he went home.

And then what? He couldn't imagine home. How would he cope?

He tried hard to see something during the initial tests at the new center. When asked if he could see any light at all, he wanted to, but he couldn't. The darkness was absolute. For two weeks, he had worked with therapists and neurologists to no avail.

Now, he sat in the ophthalmologist's chair on what was to be his last day at the rehabilitation facility. He had just completed another test, where the neuro-ophthalmologist dilated his eyes and looked into them. He heard the man sigh, put his instruments down, and sit back.

"Am I ever going to get my sight back?" he asked.

"I'm looking at your MRI and CT scans again," said the doctor.

Matt heard him flipping through films.

"Your eyes are healthy," he said. "The part of your brain that controls your sight was injured. You know from what they told you at the hospital, that's the problem."

"I know," Matt said, waiting him to answer the questions

"It won't come all at once, if it comes. My experience with other patients is that it they see a soft glow, sometimes a flicker. And it grows over time. The brain is a tricky thing, and science isn't sure how it works, entirely." The doctor was quiet for a moment. "But we believe that if it was going to heal, it would have started by now. That's not to say you will never get your sight back, but I think you need to be prepared to live without it."

The words hit Matt like a ton of bricks. He wasn't sure what to say, or what to do, because he had held out hope that in just a few days he'd be better.

"I can't live like this," he said.

"Millions of people do," the doctor said.

"But I'm an artist. That's my *job*."

"I know." The doctor's voice was kind. "But your job right now is to figure out how to manage living with blindness."

Matt was released to go home with his parents.

Chapter Twenty-Six

Tori got the phone call from Rebecca while Emma was still there. Matt had woken up, blind.

"Blind?" Tori said. "But...his sight will come back?"

"We're not sure," said Rebecca.

"Can I see him?" The choice of words felt odd. *See* him? She should have said "visit" him.

"No," Rebecca said. "He doesn't want company. He doesn't want to talk to you yet."

Tori swallowed, holding the phone close to her ear. Her eyes met Emma's. "I see," she said.

"He's struggling to cope with a lot right now," said Rebecca. "I think you just need to give him some time."

"Okay."

After she hung up, she cried. Emma held her, then, when the sobs subsided, she made Tori walk to the barn to brush Hope. "Horses heal people," said Emma. "And Hope loves you."

Emma went home the next day, because she had to get back to her work with the charities. She was in charge of a big charity event that was coming up soon. She had stayed nearly a week, and Tori appreciated her willingness to drop everything to help her. Emma's presence was a great distraction from the fact that Matt was hurt and also not willing to see her. Tori tried to keep busy while she gave Matt his space to heal. Every single day she'd text Rebecca and get the same answer. "Not yet."

It was two weeks later when she got a call from Rebecca. "Honey, he told me today that he doesn't want to see you again. I'm so sorry. You seem like a lovely young woman, and

I know he loved you dearly at one point. He probably still does. But right now, he is hurting and wants some space. He asked me to tell you to forget about him."

"*Forget* about him?" Tori felt the words stick in her throat. "I can't just *forget* about him!"

"I think it's for the best right now," Rebecca said.

"No. Let me come. *Please.* I can help him. I know I can. I just need to see him. *Please.*"

There was a long pause. "Okay. Why don't you come up. He was released yesterday to come and live with us. Here is our address." She received the contact on her phone, then heard Rebecca take in a deep breath. "I hope this works because he's going to be really mad at me for inviting you."

Matt usually napped after lunch, so about 2 p.m. would be a great time to visit. They lived about forty-five minutes away, and it was noon. Tori needed to leave in an hour.

She told William and Phyllis that she'd be gone the rest of the day. and then she ran upstairs and took a shower. She blow-dried her hair and walked to her closet. She'd wear the turquoise dress that she looked so good in.

But wait. He couldn't *see* her.

She put it on anyway, and then added a beige cardigan. The weather was cooler, especially in the evenings now that September was here. She put on her matching beige flats.

Then, as an afterthought, she went to her closet and pulled down the woven grass bracelet, and carefully put it in her purse.

She had gotten her truck back, repaired, and she drove it on the two-lane highway up to the town where Matt's parents lived. Their house was a yellow, two-story home in the town, with a small but neat yard. There were planters of yellow fall mums on the porch and a bucket full of purple and yellow pansies. Summer had passed quickly, as it always did in Michigan, and fall was just around the corner.

She knocked softly on the front door.

Rebecca answered. "I'm not sure how this is going to go," she said quietly. She looked tired. "Come in. He's in the kitchen. Why don't you wait in the living room?

"Matt?" Rebecca said, standing at the doorway to the kitchen. "There's someone here to visit. I had to let her in. She drove all this way."

There was a silence. Then Matt said, "Who?"

"Tori."

"Tori, go home!" Matt said loudly from the kitchen.

Rebecca nodded permission, and Tori walked toward the kitchen, stopping at the doorway. Matt was sitting at the small table, wearing sweats and a t-shirt. He had shaved his beard off and looked young and vulnerable.

"I couldn't stay away," Tori said. "Your mom told me to. But I couldn't."

She glanced at Rebecca, who mouthed a silent "thank you."

"I have nothing to say," Matt said. "I'm having a little bit of trouble here, deciding what to do with the rest of my life. That's keeping me plenty busy."

She didn't know how to reply. She had a lot of thoughts that had been running through her mind for the past several weeks, like a therapy dog, or occupational therapy, and how he could use voice texting on his phone. But she knew he didn't want to hear any of that. She wouldn't if she were in his position.

"I love you," Tori said, simply.

"That's not what you said the last time I saw you," he said bitterly. Then he gave a humorous laugh. "The last time I *saw* you. I guess that's quite literal now isn't it?"

"I was upset about Hope."

"Yes, *Hope*," he said. He swiveled in the kitchen chair to face her. His eyes darted around but didn't land on hers. She felt her heart breaking.

"If it wasn't for *Hope*, I wouldn't be in this mess. You and that horse. I should have let it go four years ago when we first met. I never should have gone for that walk with you that day. Heck, I never should have *come* to your bed and breakfast for that artists retreat. You know, I had been invited to a showing in Chicago that weekend? But I thought I needed a break. I felt God calling me to get some rest. To step back for a while. Well, look how *that* turned out!"

Tori swallowed. She didn't know what she had expected, but it wasn't bitterness. Maybe sadness, or even depression. But this bitterness didn't match the Matt she knew.

"I'm sorry," she said.

"Sorry for what? This isn't your fault. I brought it on myself. You were right. I never should have painted you. I'll regret that until the day I die. Go home, Tori. I don't want you in my life anymore. None of this would have happened if I hadn't met you."

The words slammed into her like a physical force. She put her hand on her chest, protecting her heart. Tears stung her eyes, and she couldn't stop them from falling down her cheeks. She brushed at her eyes with the back of her hands.

"Matt…" she said. She needed to touch him, to hold him. She remembered how whole she felt when they were close. She had thought they were meant to be together. *Forever.* But right now, it felt like her soul was being ripped from her body. She went to him and held the bracelet next to his hand, so he could feel it touching his thumb. "I brought you something."

"Go!" he shouted, his voice ringing across the small kitchen. He pointed in the direction of the living room. "Go!"

"Come on," Rebecca said, gently putting a hand on her shoulder. Tori dropped the bracelet on the kitchen table. Rebecca led Tori into the living room and out onto the front porch, closing the door behind them.

Tori wiped the tears from her cheeks with the back of her hand and pulled her sweater tighter around her.

"I'm sorry," Rebecca said. "He's really struggling."

Tori nodded, because she couldn't speak.

"You should go," Rebecca. "If he changes his mind, I'll call you."

Tori nodded again, and let Rebecca give her a stiff hug. Then, she walked down to her car and drove away from the house, and from the man she loved.

Chapter Twenty-Seven

Tori watched the snow fall against the windowsill. Winter had come early in St. Ives and handed them a big snowstorm a week before Thanksgiving. The roads were blocked, and she wasn't going anywhere until the snowplows got out.

William had showed up that morning on his snowmobile and plowed their driveway and fed the horses. Phyllis had spent the night. They had no guests, since most people saved their vacation time and travel for Thanksgiving, next weekend.

It had been more than two months since she had stood in Matt's kitchen and seen him for the last time. She hadn't gotten any phone calls from Rebecca or heard any news. She had called Allison, who explained that Matt had put his tour on hold for an indefinite amount of time and told Allison to look for work elsewhere. Allison said she had a lot to do before she quit. That was in October.

For two weeks, Tori had stayed in her bedroom, coming down for meals in the kitchen and away from the guests. She had only been to the barn twice, when William told her that Hope was getting finicky with her food because she missed Tori.

Usually, the horses brought comfort to Tori, but now even they weren't a comfort. She kept to her room, and William kept the barn running smoothly without her.

Then, after exactly two weeks of moping, Phyllis had come into her room, raised the shades on sunny morning, and declared that it was time to start living again. Tori had moaned and pulled the covers over her head.

"Not anymore, young lady," Phyllis had said, using the firm voice that Tori had heard her use with difficult guests on the phone. "It's time to get to work. This farm needs you. I can't keep doing all the inn work, and William can't handle the horses alone forever. He's old."

"He's not old," Tori mumbled. "He's only sixty-two."

"That's old."

So Tori had pulled on her boots and started training again. Once she got started, the work with the horses was refreshing, and healing. Her world started to right itself.

Robert Walsh and the other man who had stolen Hope and beaten Matt were in jail. William had added security cameras to the farm, and a security system to the house that they turned on at night.

The "mystery" died down, and, in the art world, Matt's blindness made the headlines for about a week. Then they forgot about him. And, thankfully, they forgot about Hope and Tori.

Things started to get back to normal around the farm, but Tori had a deep sadness in her that just wouldn't go away.

"Here," Phyllis said.

Tori took the card and looked at it. It was the same therapist that Phyllis had tried to get her to see after Tim had died.

"I don't need this," Tori said.

"You do," Phyllis said. "You have a lot to recover from, and as important as those horses are to your recovery, they can't talk with you like a human can."

"What do you mean *a lot* to recover from? My heart is broken, that's it. And I feel really bad about what happened to Matt. Guilt. We've discussed this," Tori said impatiently. She glanced at the kitchen clock. She had a horse to train.

Phyllis crossed her arms. "By *a lot* I mean grief and guilt, yes, but I don't think you've ever dealt with the ramifications of your marriage, either."

"What? Tim's death?"

"No. Tim's abuse."

It was the first time Phyllis had ever said the words. Tori stared at her for a moment.

"What do you mean?" she said, pulling out a kitchen chair and sitting.

"Tori, this woman is good. She helped me through some things. Go see her."

Tori swallowed and dropped her gaze to the floor. "Abuse?" she said quietly. She hadn't given any more thought to what that word meant to her. Her mind had been so full of Matt, and his blindness. She had filled the other space with business. Training horses and running the B&B had not given her much time to reflect. Now, or in the past.

"Yes," Phyllis said quietly.

Phyllis had always known when to speak and when Tori needed space. Now, her housekeeper and friend gave her a slight squeeze on the shoulder and then left. "I need to go make beds," she said over her shoulder.

Tori sat alone in kitchen, staring at the name on the card. She thought about what Phyllis had said, about how that one guest's description of emotional abuse had given her the realization that maybe her marriage hadn't been healthy.

And Matt had agreed, and so had Emma when she opened up to her.

What did that mean for *her*? Tim was gone. That was part of another life. Shouldn't she be okay now?

But she knew she wasn't. She got up, walked into the dining room, and ran her finger over the dent in the table. Then, finally remembering something else, she went upstairs to their master bedroom. It was different than the room she used now. Tori had moved soon after Tim's death, and turned this room into a honeymoon suite. The bed was stripped. The guests were either out for the day or hadn't checked in yet. Phyllis was down the hall in another room. She could hear her humming an old hymn.

Tori slid the dresser out a little bit and saw the chunk in the wall. It had been filled and painted over, but the outline of it was still there.

She and Tim had fought about a luncheon he had with a coworker. A paralegal. It was in the law firm's cafeteria, and Tim insisted it was just two friends having lunch. But he and this paralegal had lunched several times a week. Tori first found out when she showed up to surprise Tim one day with a takeout sub order. She missed him, and he had forgotten his lunch, so she thought it would be fun to bring it to him.

"We eat here all the time," the paralegal said. But she seemed nervous, unsure. That night, Tim agreed that he did eat with her often, and when he went to shower, Tori kicked off her heels, changed into her gown, and climbed into bed. His phone was sitting on his nightstand. She grabbed it and looked through it. There were several texts from the paralegal. They were all friendly, non-sexual, but there were *a lot* of them.

"She sees you more than I do," Tori said, waving the phone when Tim climbed into bed.

"Well, I *do* work with her," Tim said. He grabbed his phone back. "Don't ever look at my phone without permission again."

"You don't understand the problem," Tori said. "I *miss* you."

Tim laughed. "I don't understand *you*, Tori. We *live* together. I'm here *right now*."

"But I want…"

"What?" he asked. He fluffed his pillows.

"You!" Tori yelled. "I want *you!*"

"Shhh!" Tim hissed, because the guests were sleeping down the hall.

"Don't you shush me," Tori said. "Are you sleeping with her too?"

Tim jumped out of bed and called her insecure and selfish and a number of other names. Then he grabbed his pillows and said he'd sleep on the porch tonight.

After he left, Tori picked up one of her pumps and threw it hard against the wall.

Tori was still holding the business card with the therapist's name on it. She pulled out her cell phone and dialed the number.

"Hello? New Life Counseling Center."

"I need to make an appointment," she said.

Chapter Twenty-Eight

Matt sat on the edge of his childhood bed, and thought about his art studio back home in his own house. He was thinking it might be nice to go home for a visit. His parents had picked up some of his clothes and handled his bills these past six months while he was living with them. Now, it was April, and he could feel the warm sun coming through the window onto his face.

He longed to sit in his chair and touch his paint brushes, run his hands along a canvas, get his fingers into the paints. He missed their smell, their feel, the excitement of setting a blank canvas up on his easel.

He missed the sound of the waves, which he could hear on certain days when he had his window open. He was, after all, only two streets over from the lake.

Then he thought about Tori's bed and breakfast, and the sound of the lake from her house. From her beach.

Tori. His mind kept going back to her, and he missed her. But he was too ashamed to call her. He had been cruel to her when she came to visit last fall, and he had already messed up her life enough by painting her and the horse.

Well, she'd never have to worry about him painting her again.

He sighed. Self-pity wouldn't get him anywhere his therapist had said that morning during their session. It was time to start living again.

Matt had taken some small steps. He agreed to let his parents apply for a therapy dog for him. He wouldn't hear back for a few weeks yet. He went to see a therapist once a week to talk about his "feelings." And he had started some art therapy, where he was making textiles. He didn't really enjoy gluing the small square tiles onto a larger tile. To compensate for the blindness, they lined bowls of tiles up in an order so he could remember which colors were in each bowl. Then, as he glued, he was supposed to be forming a pattern in his mind's eye.

Whatever that was.

He could see that it gave him something to do, but it didn't compare to the creations he used to make.

His hands were dry, and he opened his nightstand drawer, looking for the hand cream his mom had bought. He could swear she had put it in here yesterday. As he rooted around, his hand felt something else, something dry and stiff. It was the grass bracelet he had made Tori.

He remembered her giving it to him the day of her visit. But he had thrown it on the floor. Apparently, his mom had saved it.

He ran his fingers along the braided grass. The bracelet was tiny, because Tori had small wrists. He thought about that day so long ago when they sat on the dune, as friends, and he had made it for her. She laughed and slipped it on her wrist. She had worn it for the rest of the day.

And kept it all these years.

"I could never forget about you," she had said to him last summer, when she pulled it out of that box in her closet.

He sighed and laid back on his bed. If only he could forget about *her.* Then, maybe the pain wouldn't be so bad.

His mom had quit asking him to contact Tori after Tori's visit last fall when he had chased her out of the kitchen. His parents had settled into a kind of routine with him. His mom, who ran a small online business selling antiques, took him to all of his doctor's appointments. His dad still worked, but he was handling Matt's affairs in the evenings, helping him pay bills and make sure his paintings were all brought home and stored. Right now, the paintings were in his house, stored in his studio with sheets over them, a security system keeping them safe.

Allison had been great about canceling gallery showings and making sure his paintings were moved correctly, unharmed. He had been short with her several times, but if he had hurt her, she never showed it. Gradually, he was accepting the blindness, and last week he had called her to cancel his job for the calendar next year, and the few paintings for the big box stores.

She was reluctant.

"You could still heal," Allison reminded him. "That's what the doctors said. They said sometimes it can take up to a year."

"But there should be some improvement by now," Matt said. "It's not going to happen."

That's what he had started telling people, and himself. *It's not going to happen.* But secretly, he held on to the hope that it would.

"Okay," said Allison. Her voice broke a little bit. "So, I guess there's nothing left for me to do?"

"I guess not."

"Well." she said. He heard her sigh and could imagine her squaring her shoulders and putting her chin up. "I guess this is goodbye."

"Yes," he said. They had talked about it for a few weeks. He had no need for her anymore. His dad could handle any sales of the remaining paintings. Allison was good at her job and should find work elsewhere. "Goodbye, and thank you for everything. You've been awesome."

After she hung up, he fingered the grass bracelet again. He longed to call Tori, but he knew it would be wrong. He had disrupted her life once and paid a dear price for it. He couldn't disrupt her again. What would he ask of her? To love him in his current condition? He didn't want to burden her, or anyone. It was hard letting his parents take care of him.

The grass bracelet felt dry and brittle between his fingers. He tried to remember what color it was. He thought it had turned brownish gray as the grass dried. But maybe there was some green still in it.

He'd never know.

He squeezed it in frustration, and felt it break. He gasped, and reached for the broken part, feeling along the floor until his fingers encountered it.

"Oh Tori," he said, pressing the grass up against his lips. "I'm so, so sorry. For everything."

Chapter Twenty-Nine

Tori had just finished showing a new client what she had taught his horse. The young chestnut mare was gentle and kind, and Tori had enjoyed working with her. When her owner climbed up on her and rode her through her paces, he was pleased.

"This is incredible!" he said, laughing as he turned her into the center of the ring, asked her to halt, and then backed her up a few steps. "I love this!" His wife, who was standing next to Tori and watching, clapped her hands.

New to horses and farming, he and his wife had bought a place in the country to raise their kids. This mare's loving attitude and pretty blaze down her face had captured their hearts a few month ago when they attended an auction looking for farm equipment. But they had had no idea how to train her to ride. That's when they hired Tori.

"She's really a sweet horse," Tori said. "You shouldn't have any problems with her. But if you do, give me a call."

She helped them load the mare into the trailer and watched as they drove down the drive and pulled onto the road.

Job well done, she told herself.

She turned back to the barn and decided to take Hope for a ride down the beach. She grabbed the mare's bridle off the hook in the tack room and went out to the pasture to get her.

"Hope!" she called. The mare lifted her head, her white mane blowing back in the wind. She whinnied.

"Come here!"

Hope tossed her head and turned to walk toward Tori. Sometimes, Tori missed how Hope had ran to her full speed when she was younger and still able to see. Now, she always had to carefully pick her way toward Tori.

"Come on, girl," Tori said. She tried to talk to her mare a lot, using her voice as a grounding point so Hope would know where she was.

She slipped the bridle on and climbed aboard. Today was warm and sunny. Because it was late April, it would be cold at the beach, but she wanted to ride there. She was glad she had a sweatshirt and jacket on.

Riding bareback, they made their way down the path in the dune that led down to the beach. The wind was cold and the waves lapped up against Hope's legs as they walked north. Gulls cried overhead, and Tori saw a freighter far out on the Lake, probably heading to Chicago, or maybe north to one of the steel mills.

She closed her eyes for a moment, feeling the muscles of the horse under her and laid her hands on Hope's neck for warmth. She took in a deep breath, and then another, relaxing the way her therapist had taught her.

Therapy had been a good idea.

"Why are you here?" her therapist had said on their first visit. There was a photo on her desk of her riding a pretty bay mare.

"Is that your horse?" Tori said, dodging the question.

"Yes," she said. Her therapist's name was Della, and she told Tori about the mare. She'd had her for twelve years and used to show other horses when she was younger.

Della was a petite woman in her fifties. Tori learned over the weeks that Della had been married twice, once to an abusive man, and the second time to a loving, Christian man. They had two college-aged children. And most importantly, she had horses, so she spoke the same language as Tori.

Tori liked her immediately.

"Why are you here?" Della asked again.

Tori was nervous. She took a deep breath and looked around the room. "I'm not sure," she said quietly.

Della looked at Tori's file, which were papers that Tori had filled out in the waiting room. "You're widowed." Dell said. "Almost five years ago. Tell me about him."

Tori started with the usual story, about how Tim had bought her a horse farm and a horse, and how he had given

196

her anything she wanted. She mentioned Phyllis ("That's how I found you") and how busy she was training horses; she mentioned that she didn't really have time to be here.

"Why do you think your friend Phyllis wanted you to come today?" Della said.

Tori shrugged. Then she said, "She thinks my deceased husband was abusive."

Della raised an eyebrow. "Was he?"

Tori looked at her hands. They were bare. She had taken the wedding ring off about a year after they married, because it was dangerous to wear rings when handling horses. If one got caught, she could lose her finger, or worse.

But she had never put it back on. Not even when she went out for the evening.

"Yes," she said quietly. And slowly, she began to share her story.

Over the winter, Della had helped Tori see her marriage for what it was. Tim wasn't perfect; no one was. The way he treated Tori was wrong, but human. He was reacting to a rough childhood, an over-loaded schedule, and the need to prove himself to everyone. Underneath his criticism and anger, he was a scared little boy with self-esteem issues. The only way he could feel in control was to make sure Tori was smaller than he was. So, he started breaking her down.

"We are all victims of victims," Della said.

Tori thought about that, and about what she knew of Tim's parents. They rarely visited them, and he had hardly ever called them. "I'm too busy," was his excuse. She really didn't know much about his childhood, but looking back, she realized it was a subject he carefully avoided.

And it had hurt them both.

"I should have left him," Tori said one sunny afternoon. Della was wearing a horse-print shirt, and Tori kept looking at the different horses on the material.

"Probably," said Della. "But to be fair, I think you wanted to fight for your marriage. You're not a quitter, and I can see why you hung in there."

A few weeks into therapy she had mentioned Matt. That had been a whole other issue to work through. Della made her see that Matt's accident was circumstance and not her fault.

Hope stumbled, bring Tori out of her thoughts. She patted the mare reassuringly on her shoulder.

She had been having dreams about Matt a lot lately. He was on her mind. She had tried to forget about him, but she couldn't. She wanted to call him, but he had forbidden her to. The few times she texted Rebecca, she had gotten short texts: "He's doing okay," or "Still blind."

After a few months, Tori stopped texting.

Overall, her world was going well. The new book came out to five-star reviews, and she had been touring a few weekends every month. Every now and then, someone would mention her or Hope in connection with the paintings, but not often. They were more interested in her work with horses.

The bed and breakfast was booked through the summer, and over the winter they had hosted a few murder-mystery weekends to get through the cold months. Each had filled up quickly. For the most part, she was happy. Happier than she had ever been, because she had finally faced her past.

But she missed Matt.

She had come to realize that her happiness didn't depend on Matt, or Tim, or anybody else. Her happiness was her own to cultivate. And she did that at Hopeful Farm. She truly loved where she lived and what she did, and, right now, that was enough. It had to be.

Hope found a patch of grass on the beach and stopped to graze. Tori slid off and stretched. They were far enough up the beach that she could see the statue of St. Ives in the distance. She watched the sun sparkle off the ripples in the waves and thought about Matt, who might never see that again. Light. His glorious light.

She bent down and picked up a handful of sand.

"Hope, I used to love to come to the beach and build sandcastles when I was a kid," said Tori. The sand was set, and easily formed a ball in her hands. She tossed it out into the water where it made a splash. St. Ives stared at her from afar.

Then, she had an idea.

"Hope!" she said, excited. "I've thought of something to help Matt!"

She climbed on her horse and asked her to canter. They raced down the beach and back home.

She knew he wouldn't speak to her or see her. Writing a letter was out of the question because he wouldn't be able to read it. So, she recorded her message and downloaded it onto a flash drive.

Her voice was shaking, and she had to redo it a few times, but, finally, she got it the way she wanted it. Then, she went outside and picked three strands of dune grass. She braided them together to form a bracelet that she thought would fit his wrist. She addressed an envelope and mailed it to his mom.

Please God, let him listen to it, she said.

If he contacted her, that would be great. And if he didn't, she'd be okay with that, too. This wasn't about her anymore. It was about him. She had moved on and healed, and she could only hope that he would do the same.

Chapter Thirty

Matt was sitting in his bedroom at his computer, trying to get a listening device to work so he could have his computer read his social media posts to him, and he could post by talking into a mic. But every time he opened the software's microphone, it faltered out. Something was wrong and he couldn't see to fix it.

He was near tears. He had never been a crier, but the challenges with his blindness were too much. More so, he missed art. He missed *painting*.

"Read," he commanded again, and his computer beeped; then, silence. He could imagine the little ball spinning as it tried to "think."

He sighed and pushed his chair back. He turned so the warm sun came in on his face. What was he going to do with the rest of his life?

There was a gentle knock on his bedroom door.

"Can I come in?"

It was his mother.

"Sure," he said, hoping the emotion didn't show on his face. His parents were broken-hearted about his condition. They tried to remain cheery, but he could tell from their voices that there was a sadness about them. His mother kept trying to do little things to make it up to him, like cooking his favorite foods. His father tried to find new ways to interact with him, and just the other day had asked him if he wanted to go for a walk. Matt's dad didn't usually like walks.

"Um…so I got something in the mail today," his mom said. She was trying to sound cherry again, but he heard the hesitation in her voice.

"Yes?" he said, swiveling his chair around in her direction.

"It's from Tori."

Tori? He imagined a card with horses on it, or a letter that his mother would have to read to him. That might be humiliating. He felt pathetic.

"I can't read a letter," he said gruffly.

"It's not a letter," his mom said. "It's a flash drive. And there's something else in the envelope. Why don't I put the flash drive in, and we can see what's on it?"

What could she have sent him? Matt wondered if it was photos of the paintings.

"The envelope was addressed to you?" he asked.

"Yes," Rebecca said. "And inside was a sticky note that said, 'Please give these to Matt.'"

"What else did she send you?"

He heard his mom open the envelope. "It's a bracelet woven out of grass," she said.

"A bracelet made out of grass?" he repeated, swallowing hard and hoping his mom didn't notice how much that shook him up. If she did, she didn't say anything.

"Here, let me put this in." His mom came over to stand by him, and he heard her put the flash drive into the computer.

"It's an audio file," she said. She took his hand and moved it to the "ENTER" button. Her hand was warm and soft, and she smelled lightly of lotion. "I'll leave so you can listen to it alone."

She laid the envelope down, so it was touching his other hand. "The bracelet is inside," she said, then gave him a soft squeeze on the shoulder. He heard her leave and shut the door.

An audio file? What would Tori send him *that* for?

His finger hovered over the ENTER button. He was afraid to push it. It was probably a "goodbye" letter from her. He knew Tori liked closure, and he hadn't ever given her that. He had just chased her off.

He felt his hand shaking.

Matt, don't be a wimp, he said to himself. If his brother were here, he'd say, "Just click on it, moron!"

Matt took another deep breath, then clicked.

Dear Matt, I hope this finds you well. You have no reason to want to hear from me, but please, listen to all of this before you turn it off.

Tori's voice was soft and light in tone, like she was calling an old friend with good news.

I've been working on myself a lot over the winter. Phyllis gave me the name of a good therapist. I know you're probably up to your ears in therapy and don't ever want to speak to another one, but I needed to speak with this woman. During my sessions, I dealt with a lot of the issues that I had with my marriage, and I realized that I was a victim as well as a perpetrator. I should have left him, but I didn't. I tried to make it work. This was brave but unnecessary and ended up hurting me more in the end.

I have missed you terribly, but I needed this time to work on myself, to figure out the person I was before I talked to you again. I was afraid when you came into my life, afraid of being hurt, and afraid of not being in control. Some bad things happened to me, not really bad things, but things that made me question what a healthy relationship was. I'm nowhere near figuring out these things, but I feel stronger and better about myself now.

But here's what I wanted to share with you:

I was riding Hope the other day, and I realized something. Hope does many of the things that a sighted horse does. She eats, she works, she goes out to pasture, she plays. But she also RUNS. She never, ever runs by herself, because she could fall. But when I am with her, she feels she can run along the beach without fear, because I am her eyes.

Secondly, my mom wrote a verse inside my bible and I re-read it every now and then to remind myself of it. It's Jeremiah 29:11: "For I know the plans I have for you," declares the Lord, "plans to prosper you and not harm you, plans to give you hope and a future."

God has a plan for you, Matt. A plan to give you a hope and a future. Remember that anything is possible with God on your side.

Remember that beautiful grass bracelet you wove for me the first time we met? The one I kept all those years? Separately, those blades of grass are weak, and if I tied one around my wrist, it might break. But when they are braided together, they become stronger. We are like that. You and me and God. Alone, you and I are weaker, and can only accomplish some things. But together, with God as the third strand strengthening us, we become stronger. We can hold up against much more.

I know you probably hate me, but I felt a connection with you the first time we met. As I said, I feel like a stronger, more complete person now that I've worked through some things. But when you are with me, everything I am is brighter. Stronger. It's like the light you used to paint. The love I feel when I'm with you shines off of me. It enhances the person I already am and those around me. And with God by our side, I feel that together we can accomplish anything.

If you never want to speak to me again, I understand. And I will be okay. But if you can find it in your heart to forgive me for the things I said, and maybe to ever love me again, I am here for you. Waiting.

I had a vision on the beach, and I imagined you doing your art again and going to gallery showings and being able to live a normal life. Maybe in a different way than before. But the gift that you were given is still there. I am certain of that.

You're an amazing, wonderful man. I hope you realize it.

Love,
Tori

The audio ended, and Matt sat back in his chair. He realized he had tears in his eyes, and he roughly wiped them away with the back of his hand. Then he felt for the envelope and took out the bracelet. He held it gently in his hand, then brought it to his lips. It smelled faintly of dried grass and of her lavender scent.

"Please, God, help me see the way," he prayed.

Suddenly, all of the anger and fear that had consumed him for the past seven months faded. He felt a peace come over him, like he hadn't felt before. Maybe he had been praying the wrong prayer all of these months. Maybe "heal me" wasn't the only payer he should be praying. Maybe God had a bigger, better plan.

"Not my will, but yours," Matt said. It was a difficult prayer to pray, and he felt his stomach tighten for a moment into a knot. But he prayed the words again, knowing that God loved him more than anything.

"I surrender," he said. In the quiet of the room, he felt the tension melt out of his body, and he was left feeling like he had been running a marathon. Weak, exhausted, but somehow, *finished*. He didn't need to run anymore.

He got out of the chair and went over to his bed. Still clutching the braided grass bracelet, he curled up and fell into a deep, peaceful sleep.

Chapter Thirty-One

After she mailed the package, Tori was filled with a desire to learn about the blind. She called her next client and told him that she needed a week off before she started his horse. Then, she took her laptop and went out to the screened-in porch. The sun shone in, offering warmth even on a chilly April morning.

She started researching art therapy for the blind. Filled with a strong desire to know more, even if Matt never spoke to her again, she read articles and took notes. By the end of the week, she had filled an entire notebook with knowledge and information.

It was noon on Friday, and she had just finished helping Phyllis clear away lunch dishes.

"I'm going to go ride Hope," Tori said.

"How's the research going?" Phyllis asked, buttering a piece of leftover sandwich bread.

"I'm finished," Tori said. "I know everything I need to know. I don't know what I'm going to do with all of this knowledge about the blind and art therapy, but I felt compelled to learn."

She laughed. She was happy. No matter what the future held, she would be okay. She knew that now.

She had mailed Matt the bracelet and flash drive last weekend. He should have gotten it on Monday or Tuesday. She hadn't heard from him. Maybe she never would, but she *had* to send him the message. She still held out hope that someday he would want to speak to her again. She had needed time to work on herself. She knew he needed that to. They had to figure out how to become individuals before they could ever become a couple.

Tori went out to the barn and put the bridle on her horse. She climbed on and headed down the dune toward the lake. The sun was warm on her shoulders, and the sweater she had on buffered her from the wind. It was a beautiful day. Hope tossed her head and pricked her ears toward the water. She pranced a little bit, asking to run. Tori turned her into the surf, and when the water was hitting her feet, they turned north and ran along the water's edge. She laughed as her horse galloped through the surf, splashing. Gulls chattered, crying out in annoyance. The wind caused her eyes to tear, and she felt alive and full of spirit.

After they had run about a mile or two up the beach, she asked Hope to slow down. The mare was breathing hard, but still full of energy. Hope shook her head, asking to run more.

"Let's take a little break," Tori said, patting her neck. Up ahead was the state park, so she turned Hope around, and they headed toward home at a walk.

Hope's feet made a steady four-beat splash through the shallow waves. The ebb and flow of the tide washed away her horse-shoe prints behind her. The hoofprints from their run up the beach were already gone, leaving a long stretch of unmarked, white sand in front of them.

The sunlight sparkled off the water, and Tori wished she had worn her sunglasses. The water was pretty, catching the light in prisms that seemed to dance along the surface.

Hope's ears pricked forward, and Tori looked ahead to see what bird or fish had caught the attention of her mare. But it wasn't an animal walking toward them. A person was walking slowly up the beach, but all Tori could make out was a dark figure and no face. She wondered if it was Phyllis, come to get her for something, but the person seemed too big, and Phyllis would have called.

She raised her hand to shield the sun from her eyes and get a better look. The figure was walking with a stick. As the distance closed between them, she realized it was a cane. A white cane with a red tip, and the person holding it was gently tapping the ground in front of him.

It was Matt.

Her heart leapt in her chest. *Matt!* He was making his way up the beach slowly, feeling his way with a red-tipped, white cane.

She glanced up toward the house and could see Phyllis watching him from the widow's walk. She waved her hand up over her head until Phyllis finally saw her and waved back. Her housekeeper had been watching Matt, making sure he was okay. But now that she knew Tori had seen him, Phyllis went back inside.

Matt! Tori was so happy to see him! She asked Hope to gallop and the mare took off, happy to run again. When they got closer, about thirty feet away from him, she pulled her down to a walk.

"Matt!" she yelled.

He raised his hand up and waved.

She trotted Hope closer, and when she reached him, she stopped and hopped off.

"Hey," she said.

Matt stopped and stood facing her. He was wearing dark sunglasses and he was clean-shaven. He looked good. He had gained back some of the weight he had lost the last time she saw him. She searched his face and could faintly see his eyes through his sunglasses. They didn't directly meet hers.

"Hey," he said, and smiled. It was a crooked smile, a half smile, uncertain. But he was here.

"I've missed you!" she said.

"I got your flash drive. And the bracelet."

She wanted to touch him, to throw her arms around him, but she wasn't sure why he was here. She squinted up at him but couldn't read his face behind the sunglasses and in this bright light.

"I missed you too," he said. "I'm sorry I never contacted you. I was working things out."

"Me too," she said. Hope had moved closer to them and playfully bumped Matt with her nose. The movement startled him, but then he laughed and put his hand out toward her, finding her forehead and rubbing her around the ears.

"She missed you too," Tori said. "Do you want to keep walking?"

He nodded. The wind had died down, and it was warmer and quiet on the beach, or, as quiet as Lake Michigan could get on a sunny, calm afternoon. She turned and they headed back up the beach toward the state park.

They made small talk for a while. He told her about a new computer program he was working with that would allow him to read and write through dictation. She told him about her book tour.

"You look good," Tori said.

"You smell good," Matt said. They both laughed.

She couldn't imagine how hard it must be for him to have lost the sense that he relied on so much. His sight was everything to him. She knew that.

"I'm so sorry," she said. "I didn't mean the things I said."

"It's okay," Matt said. "We've both said and done things we regret."

They walked on in silence for a few minutes. Finally, Matt spoke again.

"I've been thinking about what you said." He tapped at a rock that was in his way and stepped around it. "About the three strands. And I agree. If you can forgive me, I'd like to start spending time with you again. I think we're better together."

Tori stopped. "I think so, too," she said.

Matt turned toward her.

"Can...can I hug you?" Tori asked.

"I'd like that," Matt said, his voice barely above a whisper.

She stepped forward and wrapped her arms around him, pulling him close her. She smelled his aftershave, and felt his heart beating against her chest. He put his arms around her and held her close. Tori closed her eyes and listened to the sounds around them. She felt Matt's warmth against her body. This where she belonged.

Then, he bent his head and pressed his lips against hers. She raised her hand to his head, and ran her fingers through the soft, curling hair hanging down the back of his neck.

"I like your hair a little longer like this," she said.

"I'm glad," he said. "It makes me look more artsy, don't ya think?"

She laughed and pulled him in for another kiss. She felt his hands moving up, reaching for her hair. He ran his fingers through it and the kiss deepened.

Hope bumped them both with her nose.

"Somebody's jealous!" Matt said, laughing. It was good to see him more upbeat. The bitterness she had encountered last time seemed to be gone.

"Can I show you something?" Tori asked. She had waited for this moment, dreamed about it, planned it out for months.

"Sure," he said. "Although I'm not sure "show" is the correct word now."

"I'm sorry," she said, then realized he was teasing. She laughed, then grabbed his hand. She pulled him away from the water's edge, a little way up the beach, until she found the kind of sand she was looking for.

"Here," she said. "Sit down."

"Here?" he said, rubbing his bare foot in the sand. "It's a bit damp."

"It needs to be," Tori said. She kneeled in the damp sand. Matt shrugged and did the same. Then, she scooted around so she was behind him.

"What are we doing?" he asked, confused.

Tori took his hands in hers and pushed them down into the sand. "Scoop," she said.

Matt did as he was told, until a small puddle began to fill the hole they had dug out. Then, Tori took the wet sand and piled it up. She took Matt's hands. Holding them inside of hers, she helped him to smooth the sides, using the water in the hole to pack it.

"Are we building a sandcastle?" he asked.

She nodded, then spoke for his benefit. "Yes."

Using just their hands, she helped him mold and form the sand into a roughly castle-shaped mound.

"Now it needs windows and a mote," she said.

"Where should we put the windows?" he asked.

"You decide. You're the artist."

Matt felt the castle and began to dig out little windows with his fingers. Then, he made turrets and a moat.

After that was finished, he started forming a dragon with his hands, first shaping the tail, then the body and head. It was about the size of the castle.

"One hot fiery breath and the entire castle will be gone!" Tori said.

"If you're going to build a dragon, it's gotta be worthy of its calling," Matt said.

He was lost in his work, adding water and sand accordingly until the sand was solid and holding together well. Then, he used his fingers to shape scales, eyes, and an open mouth with teeth.

"Wow," Tori said, and meant it. Matt had just transformed sand into a detailed fairytale scene, all through the use of his hands. She looked up at his face, and it was peaceful, smiling even, as he worked. He was having fun.

He gave the dragon a final pat. "All done," Matt said. "I think."

"That's pretty incredible."

Tori's jeans were damp from where she had been sitting on the ground, and she was getting cold. Hope had wandered closer to the dune to eat grass. Matt sat back on his heels, as if to admire his work. His shoulder was touching hers. He looked toward her.

"Thank you," he said.

Their hands were covered with sand, but Tori reached up to touch his face. He took her hand in his, the loose sand falling from them, and leaned into her, kissing her again.

"Never leave me," he said.

"Never," she whispered back, and taking his hands in hers, rose up on her knees to kiss him again. She felt his hand go to the small of her back, pressing her closer, and realized her knee had just sunk into the back of the dragon.

"Your sculpture!" she said.

"Forget about it. I can make more."

He said it with such confidence, that she knew he would be okay.

Thank you, Lord, she thought. She had no idea what was next, but she knew that wherever this new path took Matt, he was going to be incredible.

Chapter Thirty-Two

Matt sat at the kitchen table that night, listening to Tori's excited voice as she poured through a notebook of ideas.

"I did all of this research, and it's just amazing," Tori said.

Apparently, art therapy for the blind was a thing. But, instead of *taking* art therapy classes, Tori wanted Matt to *teach* them.

"I know I'm hitting you with all of this too fast," she said. "But I'm just so excited! You can tell me any time to stop."

"Keep going," Matt said. "This is interesting."

Being with her had lifted his spirits considerably. Her enthusiasm was contagious, and he felt himself beginning to believe that sculpture art and teaching might be possible for him.

Phyllis brought them some cherry scones and warm herbal tea. She was always feeding him.

"I love you, Phyllis," he said as she sat the warm plate of scones down in front of him.

"Hey!" said Tori. "I thought you loved *me!*"

"I love you both!" Matt said, "and sometimes, Phyllis just a little bit more because there's food involved."

They all laughed. He felt good. He had called his parents earlier from the guest room Phyllis offered him to let them know the taxi had brought him here safely. He excitedly told them how happy he was and all about the sandcastle and dragon. He thought his mom started crying, but when he mentioned it, she said she was peeling onions.

"I have one more thing," Tori said. "I was saving it as a surprise."

She took his hand and led him downstairs. He had never been in the basement. It wasn't stuffy, or musty, but felt airy, and smelled of clean sheets.

"This is the laundry room," said Tori. "But right through here I made you an art studio."

"A what?"

"Yes. It's simple, but you have a window. William helped me bring a table down here. And along these walls," she took his hand and touched some packages wrapped in a film of some sort, "are clay and tools. I found the name of a sculptor who can come and tell you how to use them."

She had gone the extra mile. He was amazed at how hard she had worked to set up a world so perfect for him.

"Tori?" he asked. "What if I hadn't come?"

"Oh, I knew you'd come." He heard the smile in her voice. "And if you didn't, then I could boast of a sculpting studio for guests."

She unwrapped a slab of clay and led him over to the table. "Sit down. Let's see what you can do with your hands."

It turned out that Matt was pretty good at sculpting. In May, he called Allison and asked if she could contact the art galleries and see if he could still hold his showings for this year. He'd talk about the "Woman and the Horse" series (Tori's idea) and show off his other art. Now, he had a whole new line of sculptures to include.

Within a week, he had showings booked for every weekend throughout the fall and winter, and he had already given two interviews about his sculptures.

But his favorite sculpture was the one of Hope. He had been staying at the bed and breakfast now, in the guest room, and he came down to the art studio late at night when Tori was asleep in her room. He had worked hard on the sculpture of the mare. She stood tall, her head lifted high, her nostrils flaring, as if she smelled something on the wind. He took careful time to make sure her mane and tail flowed out behind her. As his fingers worked, he could feel what his eyes couldn't see. And he was pleased.

It was going to be Tori's wedding present.

Chapter Thirty-Three

They got married in the back yard on a warm June evening at the top of the hill overlooking Lake Michigan. The air was scented with lavender from the surrounding fields, and Tori held a mixed bouquet of lavender, sunflowers, and baby's breath that Phyllis had picked. Matt was dressed in khaki pants and a light blue button-down shirt, open at the collar. It showed off his blue eyes.

Tori rode in on Hope, then dismounted at the beginning of the grassy aisle. Hope bowed, then William (who agreed to trade in his jeans and wear a suit for the occasion) took her aside, so Tori's dad could walk Tori down the aisle. She was dressed in white, wearing a sleeveless dress that came down almost to her ankles with a delicate lace edge. Her neckline held a small amount of lace too, adding just enough femininity to give it charm. Her hair was loose, and a circlet of wildflowers crowned her head.

The music played softly, and Matt turned toward her. She walked down the aisle for the benefit of others, but her eyes were only on Matt's. When she got to him, she handed her bouquet to Emma, and took his hands in hers. He squeezed them, then ran his hands up her arms, to her face. He felt her cheeks, her hair, and traced his finger softly across her lips, then her lace neckline.

"Nice," he said softly, raising an eyebrow.

She laughed. "You look amazing as well," she said.

She had told him all about her dress before the wedding, describing it and the flowers in detail. He had helped with most of the wedding preparations, so he had a pretty good idea of what everything looked like.

"Hope is here," said Tori. "She bowed at the aisle when I entered, like I trained her to do. William is holding her."

"I heard you got William to wear a suit?" Matt said.

She laughed again. "Yes. Now that's a sight I wish you could see!"

They said their vows to each other there on the lawn under the beautiful Michigan sky with the Great Lake as their background. Their vows were short and sweet. The minister read the passage in first Corinthians about love, and Emma, Tori's maid of honor, wiped tears from her eyes. Phyllis sang "Amazing Grace." Then, they were proclaimed man and wife, and kissed.

William led Hope up the aisleway then, along with a mounting block, which he had painted white for the occasion. He set it down and gave Tori a hand up onto her horse's bare back. Emma arranged the wedding gown so it hung just right off of the horse.

"Beautiful," Emma said.

Then, Matt hopped up behind Tori, putting his arms around his wife's waist.

Tori turned Hope, and they walked through the lavender-lined archway and down the sloped path of the dune, toward Lake Michigan.

"We're riding off into the sunset," she whispered to Matt.

"I can feel its warmth on my face," he said.

Hope picked her way carefully down the dune, trusting Tori to steer her clear of the rocks and ledges. Tori breathed in the fresh lake air and felt the arms of her husband around her and her horse underneath her.

"Life is good," she said.

"It is," said Matt. "Sometimes, I think I see things more clearly now than I ever have before. I really appreciate the little things. And life is beautiful."

"It sure is."

And together, with their horse, they rode off into the sunset.

Matt leaned his head against his wife's back. The dress was cut low, and her skin was warm against his cheek. He kept his eyes closed, feeling the soft sway of the horse underneath him. He heard the voices of the wedding guests in the distance, laughing, talking. He heard a few glasses clink.

"I love you," he said. He couldn't seem to say it enough. She was everything to him. "You are my sunshine."

"And you are mine," Tori said.

She stopped Hope at the bottom of the sand dune, just out of the water. "Here we are. Another beautiful Lake Michigan sunset. You want me to describe it to you?"

"Yes," Matt said.

He listened to the sound of her voice as she talked about the golds, reds, and purples that caressed the water's surface as the globe slowly sank.

"Are we going to see the green halo tonight?" he asked.

"Maybe," she said. "Can you feel the warmth?"

It would only be a matter of minutes before the sun was gone and the coolness of the evening set in with the darkness. He lifted his head to face the sun and capture the last rays of warmth. But he didn't need *that* to stay warm. He had Tori now.

And he had so much more.

The pottery studio that Tori created for him was large enough to expand into a teaching classroom, and he already had three students. He had met with the first one last week. The teenage boy, who had lost his sight through an accident several months ago, was sullen when he first sat down with Matt. But, by the end of their session, after he had sculpted a flower for his girlfriend, Matt heard excitement and a new hope in his voice. The satisfaction Matt felt at reaching this kid lingered for several days. He was making a difference.

He leaned his forehead against Tori's back and breathed in her scent.

"They're going to want to cut the cake," Tori said. "Let's gallop Hope back to the barn. Hang on!"

He thought of the blind horse, trusting Tori to run through the darkness. He had Tori to trust, too, to help lead him through life. But even better, the Master he trusted offered him a future full of hope.

Through the darkness, he had found the light once again.

The End

Read more books in the "Horses and Hearts Inspirational Romance" series. In *Healing Faith*, Rachel Walker volunteers as a therapist at Three Hearts Ranch, an equine-assisted therapy center, a place she herself comes to feel whole. But when Afghanistan war veteran Chris Adler comes to the ranch for treatment with his PTSD, he turns her world upside down.

Turn the page to start reading...

Healing Faith

Chapter One

Rachel Walker pulled her car into the long, winding drive of Three Hearts Ranch and headed back toward the big, brown barn and indoor riding arena. There were several cars in the dusty lot near the barn, which she knew belonged to the farm's volunteers and clients. She turned in and shut off her car. Sighing, she tried to shake the off the workday fatigue. Three Hearts was her safe place. The place she came to feel whole.

Her phone vibrated, and she looked at it. It was an incoming call from her mom.

"Not *now!*" she said.

She'd ignore it. But she hesitated for a moment, her finger hovering over the button. What if was something important? But it was probably just her mother calling again to tell her how disappointed she was.

Rachel sent the call to voicemail. Then, she turned her phone off all together. She didn't want any disturbances while she was here.

Rachel had started volunteering at Three Hearts Ranch two years ago, a few months after her divorce. She needed something to do, some reason to go on with her days, and her therapist had suggested this.

Three Hearts was an equine-assisted therapy facility. Rachel had always loved horses, and here, she could use her career skills as a child psychologist to work with the kids who came for equine-assisted therapy. When she left, she felt renewed. It was incredible to see the emotional bond that formed between rider and horse, and how the riding itself helped clients heal both physically and emotionally.

She locked her car and headed for the barn, her honey-colored hair bouncing in its ponytail as she walked.

"Rachel!" It was Kim, the farm's owner. "I'm so glad you're early. I want to talk with you for a moment."

"Sure," Rachel walked over to meet her. Kim was dressed in dirty jeans and had the sleeves of her white t-shirt rolled up to reveal her farmer's tan. She was about five-foot-six, with short-cropped brown hair that had streaks of gray running through it. "I need you someplace else today. We have enough volunteers with the kids, but we have a new adult coming in that I think you'd be perfect for. I'm short on therapists. Don couldn't make it in today."

Rachel preferred to work with the children, not the adults. Kim knew this.

"Since he's new, just concentrate on getting him near a horse. Should be simple." She nodded for Rachel to follow her into the barn. "I don't think he knows anything about horses."

Rachel gave an inward sigh. Kim never *asked*. She *told*. Kim had a way of coming up with ideas and making others think they were theirs. Rachel *had* worked with adults on a few other occasions before. She preferred the kids, but she supposed it was okay to change it up for just this one day. Only she'd miss working with Dixie, her favorite client. The ten-year old was a charmer.

As if reading her mind, Kim said, "Dixie's not coming in today. Stomach bug. So you won't miss her lesson."

"Um…" Rachel trotted to keep up with Kim, a strong woman in her fifties. Kim had seen enough pain in her life to put them all to shame. Rachel had no right to complain about a lesson change. "Okay. What do I need to know?"

"He's a war veteran. Afghanistan. His therapist sent him here to work on anxiety. PTSD. He came by yesterday and filled out the paperwork, so he's all set on that. Just get his hands on a horse. Brushing. Rubbing. You know the drill. Teach him to tack up the horsebeast. Maybe get him on."

Rachel nodded. "What's his name?

"Christopher." Kim stopped to put a bucket of water in Rissa's stall. She was one of their best therapy horses. Kim glanced at her watch. "He'll be here in about ten minutes." She looked at Rachel and smiled. Kim's smile could sell cars. "Thank you. You're a dear."

Before Rachel could answer her, Kim left, hurrying on to do other chores. Rachel walked over to look at the chalkboard that hung on the wall in the aisleway near the feed room. She saw that Dixie's name had a line drawn through it. Jennifer, the physical therapist, would now be using the indoor arena with two other kids during that time. Today, in the 5 p.m. lesson slot for the outdoor arena, the name "Chris" was written down with her name beside it. He had a one-hour slot. Angel's name was written next to it. She'd be their horse for today.

Rachel had seen equine-assisted therapy do amazing things. It was used regularly with teens and younger kids to combat anxiety issues. She had heard about it being used for veterans with PTSD before, and she figured it would be a good shot for Christopher if that's what he was here for.

Equine-assisted therapy was a great strengthening tool for physical therapy patients., It was helpful for people with closed-head injuries, and it even worked miracles with kids on the spectrum. Over the two years Rachel had volunteered at Three Hearts, she was starting to believe that equine-assisted therapy could help with *most* things.

The therapy was doing more than she did in the clinic, anyway. Watching those kids come in dealing with such traumatic things in their lives was tough…divorce, death of parents, bullying, drugs, abuse…

She stopped her train of thought there before it went to the client she had failed. But it was too late. The girl's face formed in her memory. Small, thin, dark hair with curls, dark circles under her eyes. So small and curled in upon herself, it was like she was trying to disappear. And she had been.

If only Rachel had seen it.

Rachel was past the point where the lump formed in her throat. Now, on her good days, she could push the girl's face away, bury it deep down, and get on with her life. Maybe if she helped just one more kid it would make up for how she had failed that girl.

A loud whinny pulled her out of her thoughts. It was Max, the red chestnut gelding next to Angel's stall. Rachel stopped to rub his face. Usually someone would have brought Angel in by now to get her ready, but her stall was empty.

Rachel sighed, trying not to let this new frustration fuel the anxiety she already felt because of work and her mom's call. She grabbed Angel's lead rope and went outside to the pasture in the back where her horse would be. Looking out over the grassy field, she saw Angel in the far back.

"Angel!" she called. The bay mare looked up, a bite of grass hanging from her mouth. "Come here, girl!"

The horse looked at her, then put her head back down and continued to graze.

Rachel knew Christopher would be here soon. She didn't really have the time to walk out after her.

"Angel!" she called again. But this time, she dug her fingers into the front pocket of her blue jeans and pulled out a plastic baggie containing a handful of baby carrots. Angel watched her intently, then, as if they had all the time in the world, she slowly started walking toward her. But so did Tommy, Bell, and Tudor.

Rachel counted her carrots. Five carrots. Four horses. Enough.

She fed the horses their treats, then rubbed Angel's neck and put her halter on. "It's your turn to work today, girl," she said. She led the mare through the gate and brought her into the barn, where she put her in cross ties.

"Hello."

She jumped at the voice, and turned around, figuring it was Christopher here for his lesson. What she *didn't* expect was Chris *Adler.* They had graduated from the same high school. She hadn't seen him since then, but the thick, sand-colored hair, the green eyes, were the same.

Her stomach did something funny and took her mind back to the one night that had changed her life. The night she had lost everything.

She stood there a moment, her mouth open. Then she abruptly shut it. She hated him. Could this day get any worse?

"Chris," she said curtly.

"Rachel." His tone was softer than hers had been.

He looked different. The last time she had seen him, he was leaning against the wall outside their high school after graduation, tipping back a cold one. He had said something to her then, something she'd never forget.

The two of them stared at each other for a moment and neither spoke. Then he cleared his throat. "I didn't know you worked here."

"I *volunteer* here," she corrected. She crossed her arms over her chest and frowned.

"Oh." The cockiness she remembered was gone. In its place was a bit of uncertainty. His eyes couldn't seem to find a place to rest. They skittered back and forth between her, the horse, the brushes, and back to her. He seemed fragile somehow. Not like the over-confident guy she remembered.

"Why are *you* here?" she asked.

He met her eyes. He was still as handsome as she remembered. Tall, nearly six-foot, with sandy brown hair with a lock that fell over his green eyes. He was better built than when he was younger. More solid. Manlier. Arm muscles strained the sleeves of the dark blue t-shirt he was wearing. She imagined there was a six-pack under there somewhere. He obviously *lived* in the gym. She tore her eyes away from his torso and back to his face.

"I'm here for…" he jerked a thumb toward the horse. "Some lady named Kim told me to come back here. That there was a woman who would give me a…therapy session."

He shrugged, like he didn't believe that he was here. He seemed uncomfortable. Even a little embarrassed.

"Give me a minute," Rachel said. She left him standing there alone with the horse, which was against barn rules, and went to find Kim. The barn was built with the indoor arena in the middle, and two aisles on either side where the horses were kept.

Kim was in the aisle on the other side of the barn. Rachel navigated around the arena to avoid interrupting the lesson going on. She found Kim breaking apart a hay bale for feeding.

"Kim," Rachel said. She kept her voice to a whisper. "I can't work with him."

"Who?"

"Chris. Christopher. That man you assigned me to."

"Why not?"

Rachel stalled. "Because…" She didn't want to go into the long story of their history. Of what he was like in high school. Of how he had ruined her life.

"I knew him once. Before. I don't like him."

Kim stopped working and put her gloved hands on her hips. She studied Rachel for a minute, the fine wrinkles around her eyes crinkling in thought. "Hmmmm," she said after a while. "When is the last time you saw him?"

Rachel had to think. She was 30 now. She had been…18.

"Twelve years ago," she said, a bit sheepishly.

Kim snorted. "People change. He needs help, and I don't have anyone else who can work with him. I thought you'd be perfect with your background in psychology. Besides, his insurance is paying for this, and we could use the money because of last month's vet bills."

"But.."

Kim held up a finger and Rachel hushed. This woman had a way with that.

"Just for today," Kim said. "Put on your professional face and get him through the hour."

Rachel started to protest again but then thought better of it. In her line of work, she had met with plenty of parents she disliked, especially after she saw what a mess some of them had made of their kids. She was professional with *them*. She could get through this, too. The last thing she wanted was for Christopher Adler to think that she couldn't handle him.

"Okay," she said.

"Good. Now go. Time is money."

Rachel walked back across the indoor arena to where Angel was tied. Chris hadn't moved toward the horse. Instead, he had taken a few steps away and was leaning against the wall, his hands in the front pockets of his jeans. He was talking quietly to the horse. He didn't see Rachel, and she hung back, just out of sight.

"I don't know how you're going to be of help," he said to Angel. His voice was kind. "I've had six doctors, art therapy, and an odd assortment of pills that were all supposed to fix me. Now they've sent me to *you?* I guess they've gotten desperate." The mare was watching him lazily, her ears pricked toward his voice.

The Chris that Rachel used to know would never have talked to an animal. He was "above" that. He had always been so full of himself.

She cleared her throat. Chris jumped and stood up, pulling his hands out of his pockets.

"So, let's get started," Rachel said, not meeting his eyes. She picked up a brush. "Your first job is to brush the horse."

"You want me to *work?*" Chis said.

So. Still the cocky guy she remembered after all.

"It's not *working*, it's *therapy*," she said in the patient therapist voice she saved for the unruliest kids.

"I mean...I guess I thought you'd get the horse ready, and I'd ride or something."

Ignoring his words, she took the soft brush and started at the horse's shoulder, brushing down with the grain of the hair. Angel stood quietly, enjoying it. Rachel brushed one stroke, then followed it down with her other hand. Brush, rub. Brush, rub. "It's a rhythm. Plus the contact with the horse is soothing." She looked over her shoulder at him and offered the brush.

He stuffed his hands in his pockets. "Do you even know why I'm here?"

He was clearly as uncomfortable with her as she was with him.

"Yes. Kim said for anxiety. We treat that all the time."

Chris snorted. "I saw that you guys do a lot of work with kids here. This is a little bit more than a teen with test anxiety."

Rachel rounded on him. *The nerve!* "You think that's what these kids are here for? *Test anxiety?*" It was a sore spot with her, adults downplaying what some of these kids were feeling and going through. She realized her voice was too harsh the minute she heard it.

Chris flinched from her anger and immediately back peddled. "No. I'm sorry. Look, I know you don't like me. I don't blame you. But I'm different now."

It was Rachel's turn to snort. "A zebra doesn't change his stripes."

"Well, this one has." Chris reached for the brush. "Let me try."

Rachel handed him the brush, and he stepped closer to Angel's shoulder.

"What do I do? Just brush?"

Rachel pushed her feelings below the surface. She was good at that. She'd pretend he was just one of her teens, and she would work with him with that mindset. She reached out and took his hand, placing it palm-open on Angel's shoulder.

"Feel her," she said quietly.

Chris laughed a little. "*Feel* her? What do you mean? Like... she's soft...dusty."

"No. Like this." Rachel pushed down on his hand with her own palm, pressing his against the horse. "Close your eyes."

"This is stupid."

"Do you want to get better or not?" She heard the impatience in her voice.

He sighed, but closed his eyes. They stood there, his hand on the horse's shoulder, her hand over his. She realized then how strong and warm his hand was, and how good he smelled. He wore a different aftershave than he had in high school. Fruitier. She felt her stomach flutter slightly, but she pushed that feeling down too. She couldn't let his sexiness distract her. Not again.

"Do you feel her?" she asked.

She closed her eyes, too. Through his hand she could feel the beating of the horse's heart, the pulse in her skin, the pulse of life. Warmth. Strength.

She took Chris's hand and rubbed down with the horse's hair, gently. Then she lifted it up again, and rubbed it back down Angel's shoulder.

"Now do that and on every other stroke use the brush."

227

Chris did as he was told. One. Two. Three strokes, then he quit. "This is stupid. How is a stupid horse going to help me heal? I'm supposed to pet her and feel better?"

Rachel bit her tongue and held back an angry retort.

"No," she said quietly. "It's about *focus*. Focus on what you're doing. On where you are *now*. On the warmth and strength of the animal. You have anxiety, so clearly you are a control freak." *Wrong words, Rachel. You're going to make him defensive. You'd never talk to one of your teens like that.* "I'm sorry. What I meant to say—"

"No. You're right," Chris said. "I'm a control freak."

She turned to look up at him. His green eyes met hers. He gave her a sideways smile, the smile that had won so many hearts in high school. The smile that had won hers.

"Well, we've made progress," she said. "We have agreed on *something*." She returned his smile, but it didn't reach her eyes. "Horses are big animals. Too big for us to physically control. But Angel here will listen to your commands. She'll *let* you control her, because you will build a bond of trust with her. And that bond starts with brushing."

Chris didn't say anything. He just nodded. Then, he put the brush back on the horse and started again.

"Keep with the grain of her hair," she said. "You can brush her entire body. She likes it."

Rachel watched him brush for about five minutes. His hands shook a little, and he seemed nervous. It occurred to the psychologist part of her brain that he was calling this "stupid" because he was scared. Rachel might hate him, but she should at least treat him with the respect she would any other client. She was supposed to be *helping* him, after all. She would try harder.

When he came to the withers at the base of Angel's mane, the mare curled her lip up in pleasure. Rachel laughed. "See? You're making a friend!"

"Is this all we do?"

"Nope. I think we'll tack her up so you can ride her."

Rachel went to get the saddle, looking at her watch. Only thirty-five more minutes to go, and then she'd be free of Chris forever.

To continue reading *Healing Faith: A Horses and Hearts Inspirational Romance*, visit PamelaGossiaux.com!

Other Books by Pamela Gossiaux

Meet Amy Summers, a big-hearted heroine whose simple life gets turned upside down when she finds a winning lottery ticket worth millions...but should she cash it?

Amy Summers has it all: the world's best job, an awesome boyfriend, and a happily-ever-after in sight. Then, in one very bad day that involves burnt toast and a police arrest, she loses everything – except for a winning lottery ticket her ex left behind.

Afraid to cash it, she decides to give up men and become a Bohemian novelist. She takes her laptop to Starbucks and literally bumps into caffeine-free, easy-going Josh Gray, a life coach and very handsome man. (Not that she's noticing.) When he offers to help Amy get back on her feet, she decides to hire him.

Her heart is telling her that he's the man for her, but Josh is big on honesty and Amy has a huge secret that could push him away if he ever finds out.

"Richly meaningful while wildly entertaining, GOOD ENOUGH is a major new book by an exceptionally talented author."
– Grady Harp, Amazon Hall of Fame Top 100 Reviewer

"This story is such a fun read, it is impossible once you have opened it not to be thoroughly captivated by Amy's escapades."
– Susan Keefe, *Midwest Book Review*

"GOOD ENOUGH touches a nerve every woman faces. Are we ever going to be good enough? Gossiaux has written a funny, revenge romance that will have you cheering on the heroine, Amy, until the very end."
—Diana Lesire Brandmeyer, author of CBA Best Seller *Mind of Her Own*

Available at PamelaGossiaux.com

Read the first three books in the bestselling
Russo Romantic Mystery Series

A charming, Shakespeare-quoting cat burglar.
A beautiful and savvy librarian.
An irresistible mystery.

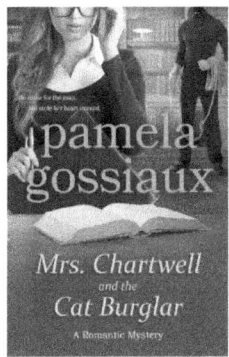  

What reviewers are saying about Mrs. Chartwell:

"I highly recommend it!"
Susan Keefe, **Midwest Book Review**

⭐⭐⭐⭐⭐

"This heartwarming tale is impossible to put down!"
John J. Kelly, **Detroit Free Press**

⭐⭐⭐⭐⭐

Cozy, inspirational, romantic mysteries!

Available at PamelaGossiaux.com or anywhere books are sold.

About the Author

Pamela Gossiaux is the international bestselling author of the *Russo Romantic Mystery* series, the romantic comedy *Good Enough*, and the inspirational books *Why Is There a Lemon in My Fruit Salad?* and *A Kid at Heart*. She is also a keynote speaker, freelance writer, and teaches writing workshops. She lives and writes at her horse farm in Michigan, where she resides with her family and three cats. Visit her website at PamelaGossiaux.com. Follow her on Instagram, Facebook, Twitter, and BookBub.

www.ingramcontent.com/pod-product-compliance
Lightning Source LLC
Chambersburg PA
CBHW071519110726
47908CB00003B/893